You'll Be In My Heart

by
Darrel Huisinga

authorHOUSE

AuthorHouse™
1663 Liberty Drive, Suite 200
Bloomington, IN 47403
www.authorhouse.com
Phone: 1-800-839-8640

© 2007 Darrel Huisinga. All rights reserved.

No part of this book may be reproduced, stored in a retrieval system, or transmitted by any means without the written permission of the author.

First published by AuthorHouse 9/7/2007

ISBN: 978-1-4343-3250-9 (sc)

Printed in the United States of America
Bloomington, Indiana

This book is printed on acid-free paper.

Chapter 1
The Dreams

Do you remember your dreams? Most people remember some of theirs. My wife Peggy does. On rare occasion she awakes angry at me because of something mean I'd done to her in a dream. Try defending yourself from that scenario. Then she smiles and says she loves me anyway.

I rarely remembered a dream. Even when I had it was a small piece of one. Therefore what happened last night took me by total surprise. I discovered what it was like to have a dream so real, graphic, and eerie that I awoke in the proverbial cold sweat. Shaken, bewildered and helpless were attributes I had rarely encountered.

I remembered a bright light that engulfed me in bed. It picked me up and held me motionless. I could see Peggy still sleeping. How could she not wake up from the intensity of the light? Why couldn't I move? How could I protect my family? Then a strong voice told of a dire situation, spoke of someone being the key and finally asked me a question. Why would I be asked such a question? How could I answer such a question? Then the voice demanded that I answer the question in the very near future.

The next thing I remembered was waking up drenched in sweat. Peggy took one look at me and asked if I was sick. I told her no but uneasiness prevailed. "Babe, did you hear or see anything last night?" I asked.

"No," she answered. "What happened?"

Now I fumbled for an appropriate answer. I prided myself on being a man's man who would not reiterate such a story that made me appear weak or crazy. I responded, "I thought I heard something, but it must have been nothing." It was one of those answers that were a borderline lie. A white lie. One of those things people did that I detested.

Peggy nodded her head as if she was satisfied with the answer, but she knew me a 1,000 times better than anyone else. She knew my appearance and response were so unlike me that the story didn't really end there. I knew she was giving me a free walk away from the moment. Thankfully!

All day I thought about the episode. Being the extremely logical one, I concluded the whole thing was a reaction to the chili I had eaten the night before.

I approached bed that night with a high degree of confidence of a better night's sleep. That shouldn't be too hard as I felt exhausted after last night's escapade. Still, I admit I looked for bed bugs that may bite and an additional glance into the closet to make sure the boogeyman wasn't there. Peggy was already asleep and I had hopes of getting there quickly. An hour or so of tossing and turning did the trick.

Again the bright light engulfed me, lifted me up and held me powerless! The same voice from last night told a dire story involving evil and ended with a ridiculous question! Again the voice demanded an answer soon! A list? A list of what I needed to complete my mission? I tried to ask questions but I couldn't speak. I tried to wake Peggy up but I was helpless. I….faded…. away into unconsciousness.

I again awake in a heavy sweat. This time Peggy insists on knowing what is wrong. She insists on taking me to the doctor. However, she knows that unless I have lost a limb I will not go. I tell her, "I just had a weird dream."

"What was it", she asks.

"I'd rather not talk about it," I replied. My usual bluntness opposed to any form of lie was something she understood coming from me. "However, I'll tell you one thing baby. I am done with chili before bedtime."

The dream questions dominated my thoughts all day long. They consumed me. I answered the first question in my mind only to change it time and again. Finally, I achieved peace with my answer. Then I moved on to the list question. I decided an impossible mission required an impossible list of powers. "OK voice, I am ready for you now," I thought to myself.

Peggy had trouble sleeping that night. I knew she was keeping an eye on me as she was worried. True love did that and true love was something we had. To be honest, I was glad she was awake. I really needed to sleep but was fearful of it for the first time in my life. Finally we went to sleep and morning came without any intervention during the night. I admit I was very relieved, yet, something seemed amiss. It felt like someone had been there but left no evidence of it. I started hearing the theme from "The Twilight Zone" in my head.

Chapter 2
Trust

Trust and love are the strongest of the positive emotions. Love is the more glamorous of the two. It is written far more about in verse and song. It is what the "good" in us strives to give and receive. Love can be fickle. It can be gained and lost and gained again. Love can be short term as is often the case, but it is richly rewarding even in bits of time.

Long-term love is more rare. Total long-term love is the most rare. It is earned through the accumulation of countless deeds, touches, trusts, smiles, kindnesses, devotions, and honesties that create a total entwinement of two hearts. It is rare to find in today's world and a blessing to those of us who have found it.

As strong and cherished as love is, I believe trust is a more difficult attribute to obtain. Love endures without total trust. Love doesn't allow a person to take a leap of faith to totally trust a loved one, if doing so intrudes upon life's logics and prejudices. Therefore, love can be exclusive of total trust. However, total trust has to have total love as an ingredient. It is simply not possible to trust or act upon the wishes of another person in totality without the power of love's enhancement.

Trust is more difficult to obtain than love because it has far more barriers to overcome. Adults find it nearly impossible to give total trust because the first time it is violated, it immediately becomes less than 100%. Violations can be real or perceived. Perceived violations include challenges to beliefs and logics that individuals hold as solemn truths. One thing is for sure. Once total trust is lost it is nearly impossible to get back, and what adult has not been disappointed in some manner by everyone they have loved?

Oh, but a child, a precious child will naturally love and trust those that give love and kindness to them. They totally trust their father to catch them when he throws them in the air and laugh from the belly when they do. They totally trust their mother to love, protect and heal them. Yes, they totally trust loved ones until those loved ones show distrust towards them, lie or act unkindly. As acts cannot be undone, total trust is probably lost forever.

Chapter 3
The Family

My name is Darrel and I've had a good life. I grew up on a farm with loving parents. Dad was convinced that hard work and discipline would make a boy into a man, keep him out of trouble and teach appreciation for things achieved. I had more nasty jobs than I care to remember. That was why I valued every job I had ever seen since I left the farm. Everyone's job seemed more important than most of the jobs I ever had. Although I never agreed back then, Dad was right that hard work made me stronger in the long run.

My Mom is a great person. She truly loves other people. I believe she knows everybody in the county and stops to talk to anyone she meets on the street. It makes it a tad difficult to make progress sometimes. However, I don't know a single person that dislikes my mother. Mom was always pretty religious and hauled me off to church when I was growing up until I rebelled in my teens.

I grew up strong, athletic and motivated. I was blessed with a good mind. I fought my bad attributes of impatience, intolerance of people doing stupid things, bluntness and lack of desire to follow the crowd. After many years in business, I took a sabbatical from work.

My pet peeves list includes greedy people, liars, loafers, lawyers and psychologists. We, the baby boomer generation did a grave disservice to future generations in a few areas. Most of us worked very hard to get somewhere and we developed a common fault of wanting to make it easier on our children than it was for ourselves. Maybe that was admirable, but it led to a declining discipline across the nation. When our little Jane and Johnny misbehaved, we became the generation to blame those we used to revere. Suddenly teachers, principals, neighbors and police officers were blamed for our children's shortcomings, rather than us siding with them when our children were the problem. Then our generation spawned an avalanche of lawyers that I believe became our plague. We turned more lawyers out of our schools than we needed for legitimate work. So naturally, the legal profession expanded their field into chasing ambulances. They also entered and soon dominated the political arena and got too many of us fools to vote them into office. Their next step was to create laws so complicated and convoluted that it took (guess what) lawyers to interpret them across the land. Therefore we became a nation of the lawyers, by the lawyers and for the lawyers. To top everything off, we then acclaimed psychologists as the authority on how we raised and disciplined (or not) our children. Is there any wonder why evil in the hearts of man has become so prevalent?

To put it simply, Peggy is the love of my life. We met in high school. I was a junior and she was a sophomore when I asked her to the football Homecoming Dance for an outstanding reason. That reason was my previous girlfriend did not like her. OK, so I was immature, but fate could also be very kind. It sure was to us. Those next two years were the best of my life. We learned about love and life together. The following year I went out of town to college and suffered through the college freshman blues. We were engaged that next summer and married during the Christmas holidays. The next two years were the toughest. We worked countless hours to put me through college, had a baby and graduated early out of necessity. When asked how we made it through those years my answer was quick. It was because of Peggy. She refused to let us fail in times when failure was only one give up away.

She has become the finest person I know. She is so nice it's sometimes bizarre, such as sending someone a thank you note because they sent her one. She gives endlessly of her time to causes such as the Girl Scouts. She is quite religious but has never brought it to our personal relationship. Now after 35 years of marriage, she is still my one and only, my best friend, my hero and the wind beneath my wings.

Peggy grew up a Navy brat. She was the middle child of five sisters living with her mom and dad in a trailer and then a small house. Her dad Andy retired from the Navy after twenty years service at the ripe old age of 35. He was one of the original deep-sea divers in the Sea Lab program. He allowed himself to be a guinea pig for tests to chart safety standards for scuba divers. Andy became a union millwright the rest of his career with a twinge of a militant. Others assumed we rubbed each other wrong as I was running a business at the time. However, I learned the value of the workingman a long time ago on the farm. I watched and respected him display the grace and value of the workingman. To this day I cannot remember one time that Andy raised his voice or displayed anger towards me, although I gave him many reasons to do so.

Andy wouldn't talk to merely hear himself speak. He spoke with purpose. I remember four specific times he had something to say to Peggy and I. The first two were at our wedding. He and I were alone in a room at the church waiting for it to start. He called me over to a window and said, "I don't see any bars on it so you can still escape." Then at the reception he told Peggy, "You're our daughter and you will always be welcomed back at our house, as long as you bring your husband." The third was that first summer of marriage when I was working multiple jobs like a dog to provide for the coming baby and us. It was late on a terribly hot day and I looked like death warmed over. He said, "Darrel, as bad as these hot days were, the cold ones were worse. If I had your brain I'd probably go back to college." Until then I was seriously questioning if I would go back to school. His few words and their timing were the perfect jolt I needed to send us back.

The fourth time he spoke with purpose to me was the last time I saw him alive. We went to their house to visit. He waited until we were alone in the kitchen. Andy had never been a sentimental man. That night he told me how proud he was of me for where I had gone in my career. How proud he was of me for taking great care of my family. How proud of the man I had become. I didn't know what to say. As I got up to leave he grabbed my arm with affection, clinging to me for the first time ever. I heard every word that he spoke. However, as adults are prone to do, I did not hear what he was saying. I told Peggy in the car about the conversation and that I was worried about him. She said he was just getting more affectionate as he aged. Two weeks later he died. What he said to me that night was, "Darrel, I'm dying. I need you to watch over my family." I don't know if there's an afterlife. If there is and you are listening Andy, I promise that I have tried. How did I feel about Andy? He, my dad and one boss I had were the only three great men I had known.

Peggy's mom Rose was the most religious person I knew. As I was not, she prayed for my soul constantly but rarely made religion an issue. She was alone with five daughters in a trailer when Andy went out to sea, but certainly had them disciplined. Her life always appeared tough to me but she described it as being totally blessed. She passed that attitude along to Peggy. Four years after Andy's death she was diagnosed with cancer. We moved her in with us for several months in St. Louis so we could take her to a big city hospital. We took turns taking her for chemotherapy and radiation treatments. I felt it was necessary to get her out of the house at times and took her to the zoo and Botanical Gardens. I put her in a wheelchair and pushed her up and down the hills. "Honey," as she always called me, "I hate that you have to push me up these hills."

I said, "Don't worry Mom, if you don't behave I'll let you go down the hills on your own." She laughed even through her pain. She fought the good fight but died too soon thereafter. Andy and Rose treated me like the son they never had. I swear they treated me better than their own daughters. Andy and Rose gave me a lot during their lives. Without a doubt, the best thing was Peggy.

Our son Rich was a wildfire as a kid. If something could be moved, kicked or thrown, he was all over it. On the small side growing up, he was quick and athletic. As with most boys, he would test the limits of his freedom. As with most dads, I wish I'd had a mulligan to some of my responses to those challenges. Through high school it was evident he was smart but not driven by school. He did well at college and went into the business world where he has excelled.

Now a tall man's man, he has a wide range of interests and is meticulous in everything he does with talents that didn't come from me. Those are talents that have eluded most of my generation - computers, electronics and handy work. The truth is, he now takes better care of Peggy and I than we do of him. He has a great work ethic and caring nature. I cannot wait for him to be a father. He is so more ready for it than I was when he was young.

Denise is our daughter-in-law. I hate that in-law tag. Whether it follows daughter, son, mother or father, it seems to label a person as if they are second rate. There is nothing second rate about Denise. So forgive me world when I think of her and call her my daughter. She is such a quality person and has brought a new flair for different things to our stagnant choices. Denise is very bright, hard working and is an affectionate young woman. Her mom did a great job raising her. My son made the best decision of his life by bringing her into our family. She will be a great mother.

Chapter 4
Politics

The dream questions still haunted me. They challenged my thinking of problems and solutions. They inferred the status quo had to be broken. They specified evil had to be addressed. If evil and status quo were a combined problem, then politics had to be involved.

I follow politics closely. I'm not driven by passion for any individual or party and certainly have no interest to become a politician. I follow politics because I am mesmerized and fearful of the total ineptness, corruptness, greed and power-crazed attributes of our elected officials in Washington. What wonderful choices we have in the current and seemingly permanent two-party system! Trial lawyers and Hollywood morals dominate one party. They promise everything to everyone and deliver on nothing. They want to assure every criminal is treated kindly. Their rhetoric promotes class, race and religious warfare. And why not? If they never met a lawsuit they didn't like nor an ambulance not worth chasing, then continuing the lawyers' annuity fund on the backs of the public is a natural.

Then there is the other fine party with the motto straight from the movie Wall Street. "Greed is good." So if greed is good, more greed must be better. Don't be concerned if those individuals and companies you pander to are destroying the ozone layer and poisoning our one and only Earth because they'll have enough money to buy another one. Besides, however inept they may govern, everything will be fine as long as they wave flags and quote scriptures. If even that doesn't work, then they'll blow up everybody who doesn't agree with them.

Choosing between the two parties makes me want to puke! In my opinion, I have seen us elect presidents that were a bootlegger's son with low morals, a power-crazed one with low morals, one that professed he "was not a crook", one with high morals but ineptitude to govern, an actor who ended the cold war by making the other side outspend their economy, one whose lips read different than they spoke, one who was morally broken who epitomized the legal doctrine of blaming all others for your mistakes, and finally one who is clueless. The common thread to all these fine men is their strong leaning to the radical wing of their parties. You know, the wings that have all the money. They have no chance to get their own party's nomination if they don't pander to the radical wing. Sure, in the national election they move to the middle. Somehow the middle is forgotten when those elected repay those whose money put them in office. Now, on the brink of electing our next president, our quality of choice is again the same. It is sad that only the names change.

The only thing the two parties readily agree on is that two parties is the perfect number. That protects their power base. They know House of Representative members are re-elected over 90% of the time. They know we will foolishly send our gallant representative back regardless of performance or our disenchantment with that body as a whole. How can we break this pattern?

I can think of two ways. Neither is very likely to happen. The first is for the midstream politicians, as few as they may be, to bolt their party and create a new middle ground party. It would take at least one strong member of each party to have any chance. However, as the effort most likely would be political suicide, I doubt if two with such conviction exist. There are only a few senators I like and respect. Senators Joe Lieberman and John McCain are on that short list. What would the public reaction be if those two decided to run on the same ticket, each blasting the radical powers of their previous party? What if the two ran a campaign without declaring which was running for president and the other for vice-president? Those positions would be decided by a flip of the coin just before they had to declare. Accepting a coin flip would prove they were dedicated to the idea that change had to happen to end the further slide of the country towards the powers of evil. Either way the coin flipped would be preferable to the status quo. What would you do as a voter if presented with that choice?

The second way is much more radical. It starts with the premise that our form of government is broken beyond repair. We currently elect 535 representatives and senators of which the vast majority act like they were elected king or queen. Kings and queens do not take orders from others.

Gridlock is the status quo. Modifying pieces of legislation or tax codes is the most they can ever accomplish. The result is modifying an already nonfunctional law into something worse. Our form of government has been around over 230 years. What besides the wheel and fire are still effective after 230 years? I am convinced we would be better off with an elected president, dictator, king or whatever we call them with significant power. It takes real power to drastically change things. I don't believe the power to drastically change things exists in our political system. The power given to our elected officials in Washington, D.C. can only prevent the opposing party from instituting drastic necessary change. However, if the "One" elected person has such power then they would be held 100% responsible for their actions. The one assurance that system would require is shorter terms and absolute prohibition of re-election. Goodbye House and Senate. Replace the Supreme Court by law with persons from nine different professions to assure no profession has the undue influence that the legal profession has today.

Regardless of the fear of change, this system would be much more effective and cost conscious than our current system of committee and pork barrel spending. What are the chances of such radical changes? Zero, unless something forced change upon us. Unless the dreams foretold the future.

Chapter 5
Religion

The dream questions targeted evil and status quo. As I equate politics synonymous with evil and status quo, they are the bull's eye of the target. I believe religious intolerance would be a second bull's eye. I grew up amidst religious people in my family. My three best friends and I were an inseparable foursome through high school. We were comprised of a devout Baptist, Catholic, follower of the Christian Church and myself, however I may be defined. Funny how there was never a religious problem amongst us. Most of my good friends since high school have been religious. In my opinion, as a whole, religious people are more moral and good than those who are not.

However, from my perspective there is way too much evil and greed within the borders of religion. There is more fanaticism in religion around the world than in any other field. Virtually all religions preach love towards their fellow man. However, the fanatics in religion, and they exist abundantly in every faith, really mean within their own religion. Why is it that the fanatics tend to be leaders of their faith?

I think God has been confused by man's honor of him. Religion has been a direct or indirect cause of most wars in human history and in every war God has been called on to help both sides. It seems like God would be shooting at himself. Today, some religious fanatics glorify God's name by recruiting children as suicide bombers and murdering thousands of innocent people. I wonder how God feels about that? Still, they are not to be outdone by the Christian leader calling for the assassination of foreign leaders and vilifying all who differ with his views. I wonder how God feels about that? Furthermore, I wonder what made God a him. I believe if the female was the gender in power throughout history then God would be referred to as her.

I wonder how God feels about the ever-growing intolerance of one faith for another? Or race? Or nationality? Am I to believe that God instilled different beliefs, pigments and lines in the sand to create chaos? Evil would have to be involved in such a plan and that doesn't appear God-like to me. 90% of humans choose their religion based on their parents' religion or place of birth. If the religious fanatics believe damnation awaits those who differ in faith, then a baby born elsewhere is likely destined for Hell at birth. I wonder how God feels about that?

I believe everyone is entitled to his or her own peaceful, religious faith. I believe that every faith has been altered and influenced from whatever the true story of God really is by man's egotism, greed and thirst for power over others throughout history. Yet, I am completely tolerant of everybody's faith. I wonder how much tolerance all those different faiths have for me?

I was brought up in the Christian faith. The problem I had was finding so much of it implausible. One was the contention that God created man in his own image. If God was the creator of all things then that would include himself. Why would he choose to look like something as comical as man? Who would really want unattractive extremities such as noses, ears and feet? Why would they design male reproductive organs on the outside, so vulnerable? Was it possible God liked this look or was it man's ego that determined God to be humanlike? I believe it was more likely the solar system was created in God's image.

I have trouble with the concept of hell. All my life, people of authority would say you will go to hell for this infraction or that infraction. Is that true or simply threats to keep a child in line? I have trouble believing the most evil person in the world can escape hell by repenting in the last moments. Meanwhile the best person on earth is doomed for being a nonbeliever.

I have trouble picturing Noah building the huge boat required to house all the animals, collecting all species near and far, and having them march in one by one like an army in harmony. I have often wondered how Moses would be looked at today coming down from a mountain after days alone with the written message of God in his hands. If such a story is told today, will people believe the story?

Yet religion is based on faith. Faith alone allows miracles of the Bible to be held as truths. However, man wrote the Bible and every other religion's Bible. With man's history of egotism, embellishment, selfishness and thirst for power, I don't have the faith that allows for total belief in his religious documents. My faith is further strained when considering those documents were generated centuries ago when so few had access to the pen. Is there no wonder friends have labeled me atheist or heathen?

Regardless of my religious doubts, I'll confess to something that even my family doesn't know about my faith. I totally believe in God. Everything has to have a beginning. Even the "Big Boom" theorists cannot explain where the ingredients to "boom" came from. Something had to create them and something had to create them and so on back to the beginning. So whether it is "boom" or creation, the responsible party has to be "The First" and to me that is God.

Man cannot comprehend the sheer size of the universe. Man talks about the known universe, but how do we know if the total universe is a thousand or a billion times larger? Is it so abstract that it's like infinity or does it eventually roll around to itself? Can it be that God is the border to the actual universe and therefore we are inside God?

The God I believe in is a good, no great, God. I believe the wrath and vengeance of God on an individual basis is a creation of man for man's use against fellow man. I don't believe those in the land of religious fanaticism when they play "my God is better than your God". I don't believe God would take an interest in each individual's every action as that would grossly overstate our importance compared to the well- being of the universe. I believe God created a climate on earth as on a billion other planets to foster life with the opportunity to coexist with the universe. I believe if man's evils turn Earth into a poison to the universe, then God will become more interested in us. If that happens I believe we can all worry about the wrath of God!

The dreams spoke of great peril to the earth. Is it the Armageddon spoken of in the Bible or possibly the result of the great evil in religion?

Chapter 6
Haylie

Rich and Denise tried to get pregnant for years without success. Then they tried in-vitro for a couple more years. Poor Denise got more shots than a lifetime should allow. Still the results were a few days of hope followed by disappointment. I admit I was selfishly disappointed for Peggy and I. We wanted a grandchild so much, but our hearts grieved more for the kids. It didn't seem fair. How could there be so many babies conceived unwanted when the two most ready to be parents were without? The kids handled it well as they did with most things, but still the hole in their and our lives continued. Peggy accepted the situation with the "if it's meant to be it will be" faith. I wish I was that good of a person.

The kids opted for the adoption route. They aligned with two agencies, created their own web site to open discussions with expectant mothers and waited for the best. A few months passed with nary a contact. Faith was getting even smaller in my corner. Then again, maybe there really was a power-to-be that decided to give my faith and trust a much-needed wake up call.

We were out of town in January when we got a call from Rich. They had received a contact that went very well. No item in the conversation raised any antennas of concern by either party. Rich cautioned about premature hopes and we all guarded against undue expectations. Then February brought more conversations, more optimism, pledges to take care of all expenses and an oral commitment that the kids were the selected parents to be. The due date was less than two months away. Everyone was brimming with excitement, but with excitement came the first fear I had with the process. What if the rug got pulled out from under us? That my friends was another character fault I had. How many faults could one man possess?

Things continued to progress smoothly. The kids made plans to immediately travel the 500 miles to the birth site, selected the many baby items they would need and reluctantly agreed to a baby shower. Now that really made me nervous. I think the kids were too. Why jinx what was going great? We were so close. My character fault of expecting the worst rather than trusting fate was in overdrive.

My trust got the wake-up call it so sorely needed. It came from Rich early, early on an April morning. The birth mother was in labor and they were sailing down the highway. Peggy and I forgot about sleep and prepared ourselves for a potentially long day. But wake up trust! Barely thirty minutes passed when call number two from Rich came through. "Hello grandpa," were my son's words. Granddaughter and mother were doing great! We got the birth statistics and anxiously waited for a call later that day. It was funny how tears could come from happiness as well as sadness. That was the moment when I decided to make two changes in my life. The first was to trust in fate rather than fight her! The second was a vow to trust this child in addition to loving her!

The rest of that day I reminisced about my life. Too many times I had done things for which I wasn't proud. I could honestly say nothing major, but bad things just the same. Then I thought about many things I had done pretty well and felt good at help that I had given others. There were even thoughts about the few things I had done great. Nothing in my past compared to my giant promotion to GRANDPA! I swore to my little granddaughter that I would hit the "good" column with her so many times and shut out the "bad". Of course, little ornery things wouldn't fit either column.

The call that night brought all good news because fate was my new friend. They received temporary custody of the baby and had her in their possession. "Dad," Rich said, "she is perfectly formed with no delivery problem. I think you're going to love her. We named her Haylie."

"Rich," I said, "I am already way past going to love her." I spent the rest of the night trying to convince grandma that we should not pack the car and hit the road. The baby needed to get out of the hospital and the kids needed time to bond with her. The kids would be spending up to three weeks in that state while the initial adoption paperwork was processed. Though never in agreement, grandma cooled her jets until the fifth day.

The days passed slowly and the news continued to be great (atta girl fate). Haylie was healthy, they left the hospital, moved into a quiet, nice facility and had the paperwork proceeding nicely. Oh and yes, Peggy and I hit the highway. It was the first long trip we ever made that she didn't require a lot of pit stops. I kept asking her if we should stop every ten miles and finally was told, "Listen grandpa, just drive." When we got to the motel I told Peggy we probably should check in.

Her response came directly from the Darrel School of Bluntness. "You check in grandpa, I'm going for the baby." Reluctantly (yeah right), I agreed seeing the baby was a higher priority than check in.

The kids opened the door and I didn't know what was bigger, their smiles or the bags under their eyes from being newborn parents. We gave kisses and hugs and congratulations to them before …please…get out of my way. Grandma beat me to Haylie but it was a close race. She was so small, so helpless, so beautiful and so OURS! Hours later (OK seconds later), grandma gave her to me. The first thing I told her was, "My little darling, you and grandpa are going to have a lot of fun." The rest of the day passed quickly, containing a lot of ogling and goo gooing - from grandma of course.

That night I was giving her a bottle. I sang the first song to her out of a thousand to come. I had written the song in anticipation of her birth. It was a simple song of hope, fear, love and trust. I hoped that someday she would sing it with me. The song was "You'll Be In My Heart."

The first time that I saw your face…the sun began to shine
The first time that we touched I knew…my life was not just mine

You'll never have to wonder if… my love will ever end
I promise that til' my last breath…on me you can depend

The power of your precious love…you gave me from the start
The power of your trust has put…a spark into my heart……

So whether you're beside me
Or whether we're apart
You'll…Be…In…My…Heart……

As our love grew and you did too…we walked life hand in hand
No limit to what you can do…and now I understand

*I will never have to wonder…the times I'm down and out
You'll always be right there for me…my one thing without doubt*

*A day with you, a touch or two…gives power not explained
The beauty of your love and trust…has opened up my brain……*

*So whether you're beside me
Or whether we're apart
You'll…Be…In…My…Heart……*

*And I know I've always wondered…of powers there may be
That gave us life and challenges…and brought you here to me*

*I now believe in miracles…I see one in your face
An angel who has touched my life…the world's a better place*

*No power can exist on earth…to take away your smile
You give me strength to rise back up…and walk that one last mile……*

*So whether you're beside me
Or whether we're apart
You'll…Be…In…My…Heart……*

*I walk through life in search of truth…and answers are too few
The one thing I will guarantee…I'd give my life for you*

*If I had to unlock the world…then you would be my key
A walkin' talkin' miracle…but who else would believe*

*You heal my wounds with just a touch…and fill my loving cup
Your precious love lights up my life…and how it lifts me up……*

*So whether you're beside me
Or whether we're apart
You'll…Be…In…My…Heart……
Yes You'll…Be…In…My…Heart…………*

There was no way possible to know how important this song would become!

Chapter 7
Music

Music had always been an important part of my life. It was my escape from the farm when I was a boy. Every night I had the transistor radio next to my ear picking up WLS in Chicago, so far away. I'd listen to the rock n' roll of the 60's for hours.

I still listen to songs every day. I have a wide range of music I enjoy. Peggy says I have very eclectic musical taste. Where else but on my I-pod will you hear songs back to back such as Joe Dowell's "Wooden Heart", George Strait's "Best Day of my Life", Andrew Lloyd Webber's "Music of the Night", Smokey Robinson's "I Second that Emotion", "If I Only Had a Brain" from the Wizard of Oz, The Beatles "Magical Mystery Tour", and the children's song "Knapsack on my Back"?

Who else wants such a collection? I am often asked that question. That is what's good about personal taste. Each of us can enjoy our diverse tastes. For me, if a song has good music, great words and can be sung along with, it has quality. If the song uses loud instruments or bass to drown out the singing, has filthy, disgusting words or promotes unhealthy culture and illegal activities such as drugs and violence, I have no use for it.

I am deeply drawn to great lyrics. I have incorporated them in my life forever. I particularly like great words in love and inspirational songs that bring a tear to my eye or make me want to go out and give everything I have to an effort or cause. There are a thousand such songs I love. I'll share a few of my favorites from each group.

Love Songs

When You Say Nothing At All by Alison Krauss
>The song says words aren't really necessary when two people are truly intertwined. How many among us are lucky enough to hear another who isn't speaking?

You Light Up My Life by Debbie Boone
>Have you ever been desperately lonely? Then someone enters your life and turns it completely around. This song tells that new person how important they are. Do I forget to tell my special person how important they are to me?

I Second That Emotion by Smokey Robinson
>The song speaks of the trepidation of entering a new love for fear of being cast aside later. Yet, the singer holds out hope that it may be a lifetime love that he is very interested in pursuing. How often do we fail to pursue a dream because of our fear of failing?

You Baby by The Turtles
>This is one of the simplest songs I love. I can relate when the song says another has total belief in the singer despite the crazy things they do, say or dream. In my case, she sleeps next to me each night. How lucky and powerful can one be if several people totally believed in them?

Wind Beneath My Wings by Bette Midler and Lou Rawls
>The song speaks of a hero. I think it's sad when famous athletes, actors, celebrities and, even more sad, politicians are heroes to some. Like the song, my hero is the best person I know. Yes, she too sleeps next to me.

Inspirational Songs

The River by Garth Brooks
>This wonderful song is a classic about chasing our dreams. It tells the listener it's impossible to take your life as far as you can or want if you never start. It foretells that bumps and bruises will litter our path when we're running after something of value and we just may

get a helping hand along the way. Will I fear the failure or will I chase my dreams?

Run for the Roses by Dan Fogelberg
This song says that circumstance will bring opportunity to our lives. When it happens, that is exactly the moment we have to seize our goals. If we're not willing to give it all to achieve our goals, then we're merely returning to the barn of losers. Do I become an old nag full of excuses or do I run like a thoroughbred?

I Hope You Dance by Lee Ann Womack
This is my favorite song. It tells me I am truly unimportant to Earth and I am. It tells me everything in life is precious and it is. It tells me we have a choice on how we live our lives. Do I live mine by going for the gusto or do I sit on the sideline as the music plays?

I have used lyrics from these songs and others in pep talks to children, employees, spouse and self. I've sung them unabashedly at Karaoke. I used them in my retirement speech. I've used them endlessly in my life's joys and endeavors to remind me that passion in feelings and effort are how I'll be judged.

One of my major disappointments is that I never learned how to read music or play a musical instrument. I always wanted to learn. However, the most pressing priority of the day always pushed it back. Maybe there still is time.

One of my major life's accomplishments was to write and record two songs. I came up with the melodies in my head and the words came easy. I was put in touch with a young man in the music business with the equipment, computers and knowledge to help me finish the product. One song was made for my Dad and featured his contributions to my life's accomplishments. I swear he played the song for every friend he knew or might meet. It felt so good to me that my effort made him so happy.

The other song was made for Peggy and about her effect on my life. It capped off the best day of my life excluding the birth of children. I wrote the song to celebrate our 10,000th married day. If that sounds bizarre, it was. No one else ever heard of such a thing either. Those things only happened to us who had crazy thoughts sometimes. It was a daylong event showering her with cards, lyrics and gifts. She was beside herself trying to figure out what was going on. It culminated at dinner that night with the kids and great friends participating. She started crying halfway through the day when someone made the next gift and presentation. By the time she was finally told the purpose of the day, had fixed her makeup a dozen times and was presented the song, she was a wreck. She was so happy and so discombobulated at the same time. She first heard the song in the car on the way home. She was at a loss for words when we got home. Finally, she said, "I didn't know that I was loved that much."

Somehow I knew music would become very important to Haylie. I sang to her every time I saw her. I put up a swing in our basement and would put her to sleep by swinging and singing to her. She would stare at me until the cobwebs filled her head. As she grew she was most attracted to various toys that made music. As she approached one year old she knew exactly where to push each such toy to make it play. Then as it neared the end of its little ditty, she would reach to push it again before it stopped. Throughout the song she sat on the floor and rocked back and forth while the music played.

Little Haylie was about to take a giant step forward in the music arena!

Chapter 8
Joys of a Grandpa

All grandparents know about these joys. No, I don't mean the ones where everyone claims to have the cutest, smartest, fastest and all-around best grandchild. Nor when the newborn smiles at you and you know it is only gas. I am talking about the many little things, and an occasional large one, that brings a smile or fills your heart with gratification. Things that create a lasting bond between you and that precious little one.

The initial adoption paperwork continued to go smoothly. The kids brought Haylie home sooner than expected and started showing her off properly. Rich and Denise were really good about sharing her. They seemed to know when grandma and grandpa needed a fix. Maybe my hints that I hadn't seen her since yesterday helped. It made it easier being grandpa because the kids were better persons than me.

The first few months brought the usual joys of simply watching Haylie sleep, feeding her and listening to others (not me of course) make baby talk. Babies matured slowly so joys were sought out such as finding a way to hold her that she liked that was different than anyone else. I learned she was more attentive to a whistle or singing than she was to talk.

Then came the day after a few months when she first smiled at me and I knew it was not a reaction to an internal function. I knew because she repeated it. Just to make sure, I made her repeat it a hundred times. That was the day my heart truly melted. I was positive on that day her love and trust for me were 100%. I intended to keep it at that level.

Every time I first saw Haylie, I would get close to her face and announce loud and long - "Its GRANNNNDPA"! Around the six-month mark my joy came when I would make that same announcement out of her sight to find her looking around for me. That same age brought some serious games of peek-a-boo. She laughed out loud so hard and I started to do the same. It was the hardest and longest I had laughed in years. She cracked me up.

Shortly thereafter she started sitting up which brought a whole new arena of adventures. This was a time of pushing music buttons, taking walks and being super attentive to the surroundings. This was also a time of smearing grandma's meticulously clean windows and mirrors by exploring them with her touch. She was particularly entertaining with mirrors as she loved seeing herself in them. She loved it so much she gave the baby in the mirror some big, old wet kisses. There were kisses and handprints on all the glass in the house. Funny how grandma thought they were cute enough to keep for days. Funny how grandma thought similar spots I made on the glass needed to be wiped off at once.

Do I ever remember the day I was holding her when a stranger decided to take her from me? Haylie showed them by burying herself in my chest. There was no way they were adequate to replace grandpa! At nine months she was learning how to make noises. They were all strange sounds to nearly everyone, but not to grandpa because I made them right back. She started to crawl and loved to walk assisted by holding someone's hand for stability. Ah, mobility! It was a curse to others but not to super grandpa as it allowed for more things to look at and get into. Was there any greater joy than the day she first waved goodbye or the day I blew a large bubblegum bubble that she popped all over my face? Even though Denise had her on a strict sugar free diet that I adhered to, it was a God given grandpa's right to slip her a piece of chocolate on rare occasion.

Yes there were setbacks to this sea of joy. There were messy diapers, crying, sicknesses, attitudes, occasionally a need for constant attention, a stiff back from bending over and holding her hand when she was learning to walk and the countless little things she wanted that made an old man feel really tired. So how did I really feel about these potential offsets to the joy she brought?

I loved changing her messy diapers because she would laugh when I told her to put her butt in the air. I loved it when she peed on me when I was changing her because it saved me one more exasperating time of figuring out which buttons go together on her outfit. I loved when she was congested and sneezed, blowing snot out of both nostrils down to her cheek. That only meant she could breathe better and grandpa was gentle in wiping her sore nose. I loved it when she gave me the flu as it felt like

I was taking away some of her misery. Besides, how else could a little girl help grandpa lose so much weight so fast? Crying just meant she needed something and I needed to learn how to understand what. An occasional attitude was an opportunity to show discipline can come from grandpa without violating love or trust. Wanting my attention was only what I wanted to give her. As for my physical duress, she was merely reinforcing the fact grandpa should be in better shape.

Now as Haylie approaches one year old, she has started to walk on her own. Total happiness comes when your grandchild first walks straight to you with her arms wide open because she truly loves you. That's love. That's trust. That's my girl. That is the night of the first dream!

As she slept peacefully in my arms tonight, I thought it was impossible for me to love a child more. I had been wrong so many times in my life. I know I would be wrong many more times in the future. However, thinking I could not love her more was the most wrong I had ever been!

Chapter 9
The Birthday Light

Haylie turned one year old today. Until today, this story of love and trust was probably common to those who had been similarly blessed. However, that changed today. Any first birthday guaranteed it to be a special day. Looking back on that eventful night made me realize it was also Earth's new birthday. Nothing was ever going to be common again. What happened that night became the catalyst for when love and trust would stand up and be counted and when evil would be held accountable.

It was a sunny, warm April day. We joined family and friends at the kids' house for the birthday party. Haylie was on the smallish side as was proved out in her one year height, weight and even hair length measurements. Haylie had yet to say real words but recognized a bunch of them. She was bright and cute, even to those not named grandpa.

The party was typical in the fact that there were too many gifts. There was an abundance of adults trying to hold, play with and get Haylie's attention. As I had been fortunate to have steady access to her, I allowed the others to have their day. Of course there was a big cake and the obligatory birthday girl diving into it. A few hours later as night was approaching, only the immediate family remained. At last grandpa got to hold the birthday girl. It had been a spectacular day. Everything was about to change.

Being a beautiful April night, we all went out into the backyard. It was one of those rare nights that was crystal clear. The full, bright moon gleamed overhead and billions of stars shone. Everyone admired the brilliant sky. I wandered to the back of the yard with Haylie in my arms. What happened next was hard to explain. A point in the sky got very bright and began to move like a shooting star. The trouble was the shooting star was headed straight for us.

A narrow tunnel of light came dead at Haylie and me. It engulfed us before we could move. Then we couldn't move at all. It lifted us slightly off the ground. I could see outside the tunnel but nobody seemed concerned by it. I tried to shout but was unable to speak. I looked at Haylie who appeared both bewildered and curious. Though eerily familiar to my dreams, there was no voice.

Then a second colored light started flowing within the tunnel. I could see it approach me. I could feel it enter my head and flow throughout my body. There was no pain. Instead, there was a tingling sensation and a sense of warmth. It flowed through me head to toe and started to flow out of my arms towards Haylie. There was nothing I could do to protect her. Just as it reached my fingertips, it paused and lightened in intensity. Then it flowed through Haylie in the same manner and disappeared. We were lowered slowly to the ground and the tunnel of light was gone. We could move again.

I began yelling, "Haylie, are you alright! Are you alright?"

What happened next went far past strange. I could hear Haylie's voice but her mouth wasn't moving. "Light. Grandpa. Light. Where. Mommy. Light. Daddy. Light. Sky. Moon. Light. Grandpa." Everyone was running towards us.

Rich	What's wrong?
Darrel	What was that?
Rich	What was what?
Darrel	That light that surrounded us!
Rich	What light?
Darrel	What do you mean what light? It grabbed us! It lifted us up! It went through us! It was right there in front of you!
Peggy	Honey slow down. You're scaring us and it's not funny.
Darrel	You didn't see the light either?
Peggy	No. There was no light.

Darrel   Denise. Did you see the light?

Denise   No.

How could this be? They were looking at us the entire time. It was impossible to miss. Could I be losing my mind? Totally bewildered I looked at Haylie who was calmly taking it all in.

Darrel   Oh, my little darling, did you see the light?

Haylie   Yes Grandpa.

Now everyone was in shock. Haylie had never spoken a real word until then and she almost started speaking with a sentence. Certainly she spoke with full understanding and purpose. Everyone started asking her questions but she merely stared back. Amidst the entire ruckus I noticed something else highly unusual. There was a glow around each person in my family. Denise's was distinct but not overbearing. Rich's glow was 15% stronger than Denise's. Peggy's was 15% higher than that of Rich. With Haylie in my arms, our glow was 100 times more than that of Peggy. I put Haylie down and her glow reduced drastically but was still at least ten times stronger than Peggy's and equaled my own. When Denise picked her up, their combined glow was roughly half of what Haylie's was alone. What was this? I somehow had so much new knowledge in my head that wasn't there a few minutes ago, but I didn't understand the glow at all. In the midst of total confusion we all went into the house.

I sat by myself in the living room as the family tried to comprehend why Haylie started talking so directly and not to look at me like I had grown a second head. My head was being inundated with new information. Somehow I immediately knew this new knowledge was factual. However, for every one piece of new information I received I had five new questions with nowhere to go for answers. Was insanity setting in? Finally, Rich came and sat beside me.

Rich   Dad, what was that all about?

Darrel   Son, I really don't know but I know we're all in trouble.

Rich   How do you know that?

Darrel   I don't know that either. I just do. I'm scared.

Rich   Dad, I haven't seen you scared of anything in my life.

Darrel   Son, take a good look because I'm scared to death. Rich, I have to write something down. Please get a pen, paper and an envelope.

I scribbled a few things down as the whispers kept coming from the other room. I continued to hear Haylie's voice blurting out words in random, still without moving her lips. I asked everybody to come to me as I had some things to say. I sealed the paper in the envelope, wrote Denise's name on it and gave it to her. "Honey," I tell her, "I want you to keep this sealed in your purse. Keep it in your possession at all times until I ask you to open it. Will you do that for me with no questions asked?" She nodded yes.

" Some very bizarre things have happened here tonight and I don't have a clue as to why," I said. "Things I cannot explain, at least not yet. Somehow I know that even if I can explain, the adults in this room will never believe me. So please don't ask me questions at this time. Please hear me out. As sure as I stand here, I know eight things I didn't ten minutes ago that I have to tell you. I beg you to try to hear what I say and not just the words I speak.

1. Haylie and I were changed tonight.
2. Haylie is going to start growing rapidly.
3. Haylie is going to start learning very rapidly.
4. Haylie is the key to something very important, though I don't know what it is.
5. I have been given a mission, though I don't know from whom.
6. Your trust in me will fade and that will be catastrophic.
7. We are all in terrible danger, though I don't know from what.
8. The dreams I had a few days ago…they weren't dreams."

The family started firing questions but I raised my hand in a stop position. "I can't answer anything more right now. If I do, you will think I am even crazier than you do right now. Still, if I am correct on what happens next, I want you all to be witnesses."

Darrel	Haylie, come to grandpa. (She came to me and took my hand.)
	Haylie, do you see the glow around everybody?
Haylie	Yes Grandpa.
Darrel	Haylie, do you know what a promise is?
Haylie	Yes Grandpa. It is a solemn vow given to another assuring you will, or will not do something.
Darrel	Haylie, do you know what love is?
Haylie	Yes Grandpa. It is an intense affection for another person.
Darrel	Haylie, do you know what trust is?
Haylie	Yes Grandpa. It is confidence in the integrity, ability, character and truth of another.
Darrel	Haylie, I so solemnly swear I will love you 100% and trust you 100% the rest of my life.
Haylie	Grandpa, I so solemnly swear I will love you 100% and trust you 100% the rest of my life.

It was amazing how total silence could be deafening. No one could now deny something had happened. No one wanted to be the next to speak. Peggy and I got our things and headed to the car. "Happy birthday Darling," I said, "I sure hope you have a lot more." Not a word was spoken on the drive home. As we walked into the house I put my arms around Peggy and said, "Baby, I can read your mind. Do you really wish that I had lied?"

She jumped back in disbelief with "how" written all over her face and walked away.

Chapter 10
What is happening to me?

What adult hadn't lost a night's sleep to a thought they couldn't get out of their head? Now try sleeping with a thousand such thoughts and a hundred new ones that came every hour. Morning gratefully had Peggy going to Girl Scout council for the day. In fact she was planning to be there all week. I was grateful as I couldn't face any more questions yet. Morning also brought a wealth of new knowledge. My perception and reasoning powers had risen to astronomical heights. I searched deeply for the answers to last night's many questions.

What was the source of the light and what was it? Was the source God, an alien, an unknown force of nature that connected with me like a magnet, something shot from a man-made object such as a plane or satellite, or merely my imagination? I didn't know. The only one that could be ruled out was the last. Something happened that gave Haylie immediate power to understand and talk to me and gave me pieces of knowledge not previously possessed. It had to be some force of energy that flowed through us. It had to be in response to the dream questions and answers as the same method of contact was used. The tunnel had to create a stealth vision from the outside while so vivid inside.

Haylie positively started understanding what I said. I knew the energy force changed us physically and intertwined our brains to the same wavelength. I knew because even after putting her down, I could understand her baby noises just as she understood my words. I could sense her presence and anticipate her next move. I could read her mind, although the mind of a one-year-old was active, erratic and maddening to understand. Why the intensity of the light changed before it entered Haylie was still a mystery to me.

However, I now knew exactly why there was a strange glow around my family members. It went back to the second dream. The voice asked me to list ten powers I would need to complete my mission. My first power requested was the ability to identify and measure the level of trust towards me from another. The power to see the intensity of the glow around each person was that newfound ability. Why the intensity of Haylie's glow would change from 100 times Peggy's while in my arms to 10 times when she stood alone to 5 times in Denise's arms was still a mystery.

The dire situation the dreams spoke of was still beyond my ability to accept. Though some answers were falling into place, I had no clue as to the why. Why, why, why, why, why kept pounding in my brain and their answers stayed so elusive.

The fifth power I requested was the ability to learn and teach at the fastest possible rate. As knowledge continued to flow in my head at an amazing pace, I decided to invest the day in that pursuit. I started by reading every reference book we owned. My retention level was absolutely 100%. I could read as fast, no faster, than I could turn the pages. However, with the massive amount of information, this method was not near fast enough. I fired up our computer and impatiently waited for connections. I called up more reference books only to find I could read and retain information far faster than I could scroll down and load other sources. This too was wasting my precious time.

To learn faster, I had to break through the barriers of traditional learning methods. In short, I had to find a new way to learn. Therefore, I had to know everything about the human brain. Downloading truckloads of data, definitions, pictures, surgeries and test documentations on the brain was a start. Then I moved into all data related to nerve interaction with other nerves and the brain. During this process, the next leap of my development occurred. I felt the actual sensation of the brain working, which sent millions of impulses in a split second. I felt the transfer of impulses from one nerve to another. I knew the pattern was very strategic. The impulses flowed with a purpose, devoid of randomness. The brain sent so much data to the body with every heartbeat and with no direct input from the person. If I now could feel the transference of impulses between my nerves was it possible for me to alter their normal flow? This had to be tested.

I held my two index fingertips one inch from the other. I concentrated on directing nerves in my right fingertip to jump to those in my left. Immediately, a white light jumped between the two and remained constant until I commanded it to stop by thought alone. I had no idea what the white light was but it was really cool! Next, I held my finger straight up and commanded the light to be emitted into space. Again, the white light jumped forth to the ceiling. Super cool! I was so excited I jumped up and hit my knee on the desk. Pain and anger overrode my previous giddiness. The white light turned black, intensified and burnt a hole in the ceiling. Not cool! It was time to back down until I understood this better.

Prior to today, I was a computer and electronic idiot. I decided that ended now. One hour after researching, reading and retaining the software and hardware details of my computer, I decided to take the internet into my own hands. Off to the stores I went. I came home with a computer cable for insertion into the USB port and a finger monitor for pulse detection from the health store. I wired the two together, placed my finger into the monitor and plugged the cable into the port. Lo and behold, I made the computer work by transferring my impulse commands by thought alone.

The next order of business was to install my own software. This allowed priority access into the internet, thereby bypassing all the garbage to go online or any unwanted spam or attachments from any site. Now that improvement was amazing. The speed was incredibly faster. Priority access put my request for sites ahead of all others out there surfing. It was nearly instantaneous. The use of impulses not only allowed me to request data at the speed of thought, but also allowed me to receive and process data just as fast. It was almost learning by osmosis. I no longer needed print on the screen so I eliminated the print and the time delay for the computer to do that task. It was as if the computer and internet had become an extension of my brain.

The day flew by with my engrossment in the new learning skills. It hit me that in addition to no sleep last night, I had not eaten a thing all day. This also coincided with Peggy getting home from council.

Darrel	How was your day?
Peggy	Fine. And yours?
Darrel	Interesting but good.

Peggy	How so?
Darrel	I decided to learn about computers.
Peggy	That's nice.

It was a nice cool atmosphere, but preferable to questions I'd rather not answer. She walked into the computer room.

Peggy	What happened to the ceiling?
Darrel	(I had forgotten) I had a little accident. Anger took momentary control of a situation. I'll fix it tomorrow.
Peggy	Got impatient with the computer again, did you?
Darrel	Something like that.

We fished out leftovers for dinner and ate in quiet. As usual, during the rare spats we have ever had, we gave each other some space. Things were mellowing out until my next bizarre behavior. Just as the clock chimed seven o'clock, I suddenly dove from my chair, extended my arms as if catching something, felt an invisible power surge from my hands and landed on my belly on the floor.

Peggy	I can't wait to hear this explanation.
Darrel	I don't know. I just felt something falling.
Peggy	You are starting to test my faith.
Darrel	Baby, it may be tested, but don't lose the battle.

I was certainly ready for a good night's sleep. Even as new thoughts continued to surge into my head, exhaustion brought sleep. I was excited about what tomorrow might bring.

The next morning, Peggy was off to council again and I went back to the computer. I was disappointed that no new answers had come to me about the birthday party questions. Still, I knew that Haylie was chosen by me to answer the first dream question and that she was to be given the power to learn anything that could be taught. Tomorrow, I was babysitting Haylie all day. That always warmed my heart. That gave me today to learn all I could.

The second power I had asked to receive was the power to heal another, equivalent to the level of trust that person had in me. With that in mind, I decided to concentrate my learning efforts on understanding the complete physiology of the human organism. By morning's end I had learned on a cellular, DNA and chromosomal level, every function and fault of every component that made up the human body. Like yesterday, I could feel the sensation within me of each organ, bone, muscle, etc as I was learning. However, today I also felt something not described in any medical publication. I could feel a force flowing inside me that created a symbiotic relationship between all parts of my body. I named it the "life force". I realized it was a force that maintained the internal balance necessary for continuation of life. I could only surmise that if the life force went out, so did the life of its organism. Additionally, if I could heal those who trust, my life force had to be the unknown source. As I was confident I trusted myself totally, it was time for a new test.

This time I made sure my thoughts were on the pure, good emotion of healing as I sure didn't want anger to emit the black light again. My thoughts ordered my life force to join with the impulse light to be emitted from my right finger. The white light came forth again, but in a softer and more controllable intensity. With some trepidation I aimed the light towards the scar on my left wrist I had worn for the past 30 years. As the light went down the scar it was healed immediately with no pain or negative sensation. I now knew the white light was a healing light. I had asked for the power to heal, but this was the power of physics. It had only been the lack of knowledge that had prevented man from achieving this healing power. By lunchtime, I knew more about the human organism and healing it than anyone on earth.

That afternoon, I took on the entire body of physics. Volumes upon volumes of data on physics and chemistry were brought forth and learned. It became frustrating when contradictions between advanced theories existed. I had to do more mental testing to determine which theory was correct, if either. The field of physics was based predominantly on the known universe, and usually, the written version was factual. However, the doctrine of physics had not progressed into the abstract of the universe such as I had just discovered with the existence of the life force. The life force working in conjunction with a transporter impulse produced a physics of healing outside the organism. It begged the question of how much other abstract was out there that could be identified and molded into practical use?

The search for knowledge had become an obsession. By late afternoon I was exhausted but happy with my progress for the day. I finished patching the ceiling just as Peggy got home. After the usual "How was your day" we went for a walk. Things were fine between us as I had not done anything weird in front of her for two days now (other than the ceiling and diving on the floor, of course). We were exchanging a light banter but my thoughts kept darting elsewhere.

Darrel	Yes, I remember I have Haylie tomorrow. (Why did I see the sunlight refracting off certain clouds and not others?) Yes, I am feeling well. How about you? (That tree limb was arced at a perfect 45-degree angle, which gave it a great balance between holding its weight and wind resistance.) What is that you said? (That individual grass blade was arced to the setting sun and spread out to best collect the morning dew.) Oh, absolutely!

It was 48 hours after we left the birthday party when I started getting sick. Just as I had felt the impulses and detail workings of my body parts yesterday, I could feel something oozing through my system. The trouble was it was reacting like nothing I had just studied and I had just studied everything ever to be documented. I vomited for the first time in 45 years. Peggy was concerned I might give the flu to the baby, but I assured her it wasn't the flu. It must have been something I ate. She said if need be, she could stay home tomorrow and baby-sit. I knew I had to assure myself that Haylie was all right.

I was sick all night. I tried my new-found healing ability but it couldn't faze what was ailing me. In the morning, Peggy asked me how I felt. Though I rarely tell a lie, I tried my best, "Pretty well," I said.

"Yeah right," was her response. She left me in bed and waited for Rich to bring Haylie over.

Rich	(Sticking his head around the bedroom door) Mom says you're dying?
Darrel	She exaggerates. I just need to see the little one.
Rich	You're not going to make her sick are you?
Darrel	She will never be healthier than when she is with me. Trust me son.

In came Haylie. "GRANNNNDPA," she called to me, "I can tell you don't feel well." She shut the door and I lifted her onto the bed. The glow I noticed when I held her the other night was again dynamic. I decided to try something.

Darrel	Haylie, do you trust me?
Haylie	You know I do Grandpa.
Darrel	I have some things to show and teach you. Don't be frightened darling.
Haylie	OK Grandpa.

The softest of light came from each of my hands. I placed my hands on each side of Haylie's face. The light came back out of Haylie's hands ten times stronger than it had entered her head. She placed her hands on my heart as if she had a specific purpose. Instantly my sickness disappeared. Instantly she knew I felt better. I had to understand what just happened. We went out to Rich and Peggy and their whispering stopped.

Rich	Dad, I was just telling Mom about the strangest thing that happened two nights ago. Denise and I took Haylie to the playground. She fell off the slide. We thought she really got hurt. But when we picked her up, she didn't have a mark on her and wasn't even crying.
Haylie	Grandpa caught me.
Darrel	Wow, that was lucky.

Peggy	(looking at me) Yeah, it happened around seven o'clock.
Haylie	Grandpa caught me.
Darrel	Babe, I thought you were going to council.
Peggy	I thought I should stay here if you were sick.
Darrel	Don't be silly. I feel great now. The bad food of last night must have left my system. Besides, Haylie and I are going to have a lot of fun today.

Peggy and Rich left and a phenomenal day began. Haylie and I headed for the computer. I concluded Haylie couldn't produce the healing light because she didn't know about it. I concluded correctly that she had absorbed the healing light and conducted it back to me. Why it intensified in the process remained unknown. If she could absorb the light, then could she absorb knowledge as I did?

I put her on my lap and inserted her finger into the monitor. She thought that was funny. Nothing happened. Dumb I thought to myself. Even if she could communicate with the computer as I did, she wouldn't know how to start. I lifted her onto my shoulders and put her hands on the sides of my head. I placed my finger in the monitor and she nearly fell off in shock. I didn't need a mirror to see her wild-eyed expression for I could now sense what she was feeling and anticipating. She was learning at the speed I could teach as per my dream request.

In one hour she was the smartest child on earth. At the end of the morning she could have graduated from college. Her thirst for knowledge was as great as mine had been, but I felt her growing weary. This was the perfect reminder that she was a one-year-old and her learning had to be balanced with fun. We ate lunch and went for a walk. However, the walk also turned more educational than fun. When we returned home it was time for swinging, singing and a nap. The swinging was normal, but when I started singing to her this time, she started singing back. How could she do that? She couldn't possibly remember the words from before, could she? I convinced her to take a nap while I thought about this new mystery.

That was the point I made a few good decisions. First off, I decided to never again think or start a sentence to her with the word "How". In this context, how expressed disbelief which inferred distrust. Trust was what I so solemnly swore to give her and was stressed as critical in the first dream. Second, I swore to open my mind to all possibilities and avoid all inhibiting parameters. After all, how many times must a man be slapped in the face to realize that what he thought were limits were only his own limitations? Third, even though I believed and trusted going forward, I knew no one besides Haylie and me would be able to understand. Therefore, for the time being I would not show any new powers to anyone except Haylie until the day I was forced to do so.

Haylie was still sleeping, but I could feel her presence and read her thoughts if I tried. If her thoughts were erratic the other night, her dreams after she received a billion new pieces of information were chaotic. When she awoke, she climbed on my lap until she was ready to go again. I asked what she would like to do and she said, "Sing." Interesting!

I asked, "Do you want to sing for fun or learn how to sing well?" Yes, it was a loaded question and it got the desired answer.

We first determined that she too could feel her individual body parts functioning if desired. She had just learned that morning what all of them were. She experimented with her stomach muscles, esophagus, larynx and vocal cords. We watched medical videos of each of them working to produce different sounds. Then we sent her to music school on-line to learn breathing techniques, voice reflection, mouth positions etc. She listened to my I-pod for styles she liked. She asked who were my favorite female singers. I suggested she listen to Karen Carpenter, Marilyn McCoo and Vanessa Williams. We then brought them up in concert on-line and studied their singing styles, although there was little footage of the late Karen Carpenter. Then my little angel combined all these mental building blocks of singing into a voice from heaven. She talked like a one-year-old but sang with the combined strength and melodic voices of my three favorites.

At this point, I couldn't help myself. We left a note saying we would be back soon in case we weren't and headed for a local self-recording studio. Haylie continued to act like she could not understand others, all the while understanding everything I said. I hired a young man to create the music. There for the first time, Haylie and Grandpa sang and recorded a song with video. I guess there was little surprise it was *"You'll Be In My Heart"*. Though admittedly biased, I thought it was awesome. Well, at least her part was awesome. We started for home with several copies of the recorded song and the karaoke music.

I still couldn't understand her total communication ability with me but not with others. However, I was developing a theory to be tested. I made a quick stop at a medical research lab where a friend of mine worked, picked up a few microscope slides and asked if I could have access to some equipment tomorrow. He told me that was no problem and he'd see me tomorrow. Back in the car I told Haylie I wanted to test our blood. I told her I would use the healing light so she wouldn't feel a thing. She said, "OK Grandpa." With the healing light aimed, a pin prick, a drop of blood and instantaneous healing thereof, she felt no pain and I had a job tomorrow.

By the time we got home, both Peggy and Denise were there. "Where have you two been?" they asked in unison.

"We went for a walk and sang some songs," I replied. Again, I was border-lining the truth, but it was the truth just as well. Haylie, always happy to see mommy and grandma gave them some much wanted and needed hugs and sloppy kisses. They asked her questions only to get the usual blank look back or baby grunts. However, as they carried her towards me it became Grandpa this and Grandpa that. I felt the chill surface once again. "Haylie," I said, "you have worn me out all day and I need some rest." I moved further away from her. Peggy and Denise talked for awhile and played with Haylie until it was time for goodbyes. Denise brought Haylie to me.

Darrel   Bye bye Darling.

Haylie   Bye bye Grandpa.

The chill resurfaced. I had to find a solution for this problem. God love Peggy as she again did not press the issue although she obviously was filled with questions. I responded by asking her question after question about her day, accomplishments, help from others at council, her sisters' health, the CD she was listening to and …. well, you get my diversion.

The next day I was relieved to see only my friend at the medical lab. He asked if I needed any help. I told him I had done a little studying on the equipment and could probably handle it myself. My goal was simple; I wanted to break Haylie's and my own blood down to their chromosomal level. I put a sample of Haylie's blood into the machine and another below the microscope. I could not see anything out of the ordinary. I was relieved about that fact. The printout from the chromosome mapping also proved nothing was awry.

Next, I needed a drop of my blood. A quick pin prick and … what … was that? Blood was normally red when exposed to air. It could be bluish when carrying a high level of carbon dioxide. Mine was a bright green! I had to admit that panic set in. Somehow I knew I had been altered by the energy light. I wasn't quite ready for this much proof. It took nearly 30 minutes for me to regain my composure and get on with my analysis. I again put a sample into the machine and another under the microscope. For the most part, it looked normal. However, it contained a pigmentation which had a minute organism in it that I could see invading surrounding cells. White corpuscles were engaging the predator but were easily defeated. Nothing in all the data I had researched had ever documented such an invader to the body. I now knew why I had been sick. I now knew I would get sick again. I didn't know how Haylie gave me relief from the sickness. Death seemed far away as you live your life. Suddenly I knew it wasn't that far away.

I awaited the machine results in stunned silence. Finally, the results came and with them the answers to some haunting questions. Other than gender, Haylie and my chromosomes were exactly the same, right down to the chromo mere that formed them. In other words, we were the same person other than gender. The energy light had entwined the two of us. She could understand me because she was me. As long as she was physically close enough to me our brains functioned together. That was why she could understand me and not others. That was why she felt my presence and knew I didn't feel well yesterday. That was why I expected her to someday read my mind. Those were the three things I could do with her immediately. That was when the greatest fear of my life hit me. If she was mirroring my newfound abilities then was the pigmentation organism next for her? For the first time since I was a kid, I prayed. I could only hope that the difference in the intensity of the energy light that went through us would spare her from my fate.

At the bottom of the machine printout was an exception report containing one line: Blood sample contains a specimen with no known chemical makeup. I could only think with contempt, not from this world anyway!

I brooded about my pending mortality for quite awhile until my advanced brain started fighting back. If the purpose of the energy light was to kill me, then why didn't it? Obviously it could have done so easily. It had to go back to the first dream. It spoke of impending doom not just for me but for everybody. I had chosen Haylie as the key and the power to gain all knowledge would be a weapon. That power had already been received. My job had to be transferring all knowledge I could to her. Suddenly my death seemed insignificant.

Chapter 11
The Rift Develops

The rest of that day and the next I dove into learning. I thought finding a cure for the organism in me would be a good beginning. However, with no place to start because it wasn't definable, logic dictated it would take too long if ever to find a cure. Therefore, any time spent in that direction would be selfish. Next, I considered learning all about man's weaponry in case the doom came from an assault. I concluded that man's weaponry was meant to kill fellow man. I couldn't imagine it would be effective given the power that had touched me. Therefore, I concentrated on a massive range of knowledge from weather to defense shields. At the end of the day, I had to be the smartest person on earth and the smartest person on earth did not have a clue what he was looking for.

48 hours after last seeing Haylie, I got sick again. Was this the end already? I didn't think so because I still felt a strong life force inside. Tomorrow was Saturday and we were to go to the park with the kids and Haylie. Hopefully, she could give me relief again. Peggy was threatening to call 911 but I asked her to give me another day to recover. At noon on Saturday, Peggy drove us to the park as I was too weak to drive. Her intention, which I could sense was to enlist Rich and Denise in an effort to get me to go to the hospital.

I was sitting in the sun when they arrived. As the adults contrived their strategy, Haylie ran straight for me with her strong glow abounding. The glow again intensified ten times when she touched me. I kept Haylie between me and the others to block the healing light from their view. Haylie again absorbed, strengthened and fed the energy back to my heart. Instant relief! Taking the assault to the military strategy being planned against me, I jumped up, declared I felt great and suggested we all go for a walk. Reluctantly, they gave agreement and we set off on the nature trail. Immediately Haylie started talking to me. Then it was a steady stream of "Grandpa this and Grandpa that and Grandpa why and Grandpa teach me and on and on."

I finally picked her up and whispered to her, "No more questions until we are alone."

"OK Grandpa," she replied.

From out of nowhere sprang four large, vicious dogs only 20 yards in front of us. Then they started charging us. "Get everyone out of here," I yelled at Rich. He already had Haylie in his arms and was backpedaling. I stepped towards the dogs and instinct took over. Fear and anger instinctively emitted power from my hands. It laid out a shield in front of us as the lead dog arrived. "Yes," I thought, "a shield just like the 10th power requested on my list." The shield must have been invisible as the lead dog ran right into it, which knocked it backwards with a painful yelp. The other dogs stopped, sensed danger and high-tailed away. The lead dog was in bad pain. I decided to help it with the healing light. It worked immediately. I petted the dog and sent it on its way just as Rich made it back from getting the others to safety.

Rich   Are you alright?

Darrel   I'm fine.

Rich   How did you stop them?

Darrel   They weren't as bad as their bark. After the first one got smacked in the nose, the others high-tailed away.

We went back and joined the family.

Haylie   Grandpa stopped the puppies.

Things settled down quickly as we got back to the cars. Now I prepared for the onslaught of questions I could feel were coming.

Denise   Dad, Peggy said you have been really sick. You should have it checked out.

Darrel	Don't worry honey. I'm positive it will be short term (like death).
Rich	Wouldn't hurt to get a check up would it?
Darrel	I already had my blood tested two days ago. No doctor saw a problem with it.
Denise	I have to be honest about one thing. I find it spooky that Haylie talks to you and no one else. Ever since her birthday, the only word that comes out is "grandpa".
Darrel	I am positive she is on the verge of talking to everyone. We just have a lot of fun when we're together. I'm sure that is an influence.
Denise	I just don't think it's healthy for her to be connected that strongly at her age.
Darrel	Darling, please don't go there. I promise that her health is assured with me. I also promise she will communicate with all of you very soon. You'll see.
Peggy	Too many strange things are going on. You have been sick as a dog twice and feel great as soon as you see Haylie. Haylie talks like she is 15 around you. I know you're forever on the computer instead of being active, as you are normally. No one can forget your strange ravings at the party. And I've witnessed a couple of weird things since then. Talk to me!
Darrel	What can I say? Haylie does make me feel good. Exactly how, I haven't totally figured out. I know you didn't believe me at the party. Repeating myself would create more disbelief. Disbelief and other negative feelings towards me increases the sickness. I know nothing can be gained by me undergoing tests by a doctor. I can see your trust level in me is already fading as I predicted. 99.99 % of the love I have for things on earth is near me now. Time will bring me some answers to the "why's" I have now. I know I need your trust now more than ever.
Peggy	Can you understand why our trust in you has been challenged?

Darrel   Yes, I can. But sweetheart, that is why they call it trust. And that is what I need. How about we enjoy the rest of the day without more questions?

That was what we did to the best of our ability at the time.

That night I kept thinking about something I had said. I blurted something out naturally, only to find it had a lot of meaning later. I said, "Disbelief and negative feelings increase my sickness." It was an off the cuff avoidance answer. The opposite in Haylie seemed to give me relief. Haylie gave me total love and trust. Her trust glow was ten times anyone else when she was untouched, 100 times when I touched her and less than ten when another held her. There had to be an arithmetic answer. No other adult at the stores had a glow. If Peggy's glow, being the strongest of our adult family was equivalent to one, then the kids were less than one. Haylie's glow would be a ten as would mine. Touching had to be a multiple factor of the two. That was why Haylie and I went to 100. If Haylie's glow went down when touching grandma, then grandma would have to be less than one, albeit close, as Haylie stayed close to ten when they touched.

Why was there no individual glow from a point just less than one through ten? There had to be a block at the point of one. Maybe it was like centrifugal force around a circle. It took a force of one to make a complete lap. If a trust level was less than one, that point was the block in the circle they couldn't get past. Therefore, even at 99% trust, they couldn't make the full loop and continue. However, at 100% trust there was no block on the circle to stop the movement. The force kept increasing to a maximum value of ten. It must also be that if a person's trust level was below a minimum, then I couldn't see a glow as it had no positive value to me.

That had to be the answer to Haylie reducing my sickness when I couldn't do it alone. The power of the organism in me must be so great that my power of ten couldn't effect it. The exponential power with Haylie of ten squared, or 100, was enough to ease the pain. It obviously could not kill the organism as it resurfaced, but relief (apparently 48 hours) would give me more time and energy to teach Haylie. Then again, if a third person reached 100% trust combined with Haylie and I to take the power level to ten cubed, or 1,000, could that kill the organism? Maybe, but how could an adult trust 100%? Regardless, I had removed one big "Why" off the list.

Sunday started with much more hope after last night's revelation. I also knew I had to do something to avoid or at least delay the coming family rift over access to Haylie. That started with Peggy. I asked if she wanted to go to a movie as she always did. "You could pick which one," I told her. She was instantly happier. We had our best day since the party. We saw a good movie and topped it off with dinner at a restaurant. I missed enjoying time with her this last week and was afraid nothing could prevent some tough times ahead. I desperately needed a break away from my mission.

Haylie was the key to the mission. Somehow, I needed to get her in a position of notoriety so people could come to know of her and her talents. Throughout every decade, it seemed TV had a show to find amateur entertainers and gave them a chance to become a star. The current rendition was "You Are -The Star". I decided to send the video recording Haylie and I made to them with the hope of becoming contestants on their upcoming show. I suspected the talent level between contestants would be nearly equal. I also knew ratings would be important. I just couldn't imagine a top performing voice in a one-year-old package wouldn't peak their interest. I wrote a narrative of our story to set a seed and waited to see what would happen.

Monday came and I was approaching the 48 hour window. I called Rich at work to see if I could pick Haylie up. He was hesitant. I felt the coming rift getting closer. I told him I wanted to see her for a couple of hours and would have her at their house when Denise got home from work. He relented, but I felt telling Denise was the reason he hesitated. I couldn't blame her, for if our roles were reversed I'd feel the same doubts that she did. I picked Haylie up at the nursery around 2:00 with my trusty monitor in hand. I knew I had her for about four hours. I received my health fix and we got started.

This session was a little different. I needed to find a way to get her to communicate with the rest of the family better. However, getting information into her brain was easy while getting it out proved difficult. It just would not flow out to someone else. I finally gave up and went old style. We began with the ABC's and moved to phonics and grammar. Though she was faster than any child alive in its grasp, forming words with her mouth was a motor skill problem. Furthermore, this exercise in learning was not fun for a one-year-old. Still, when Denise arrived, Haylie was short on talk but long on delivery.

Haylie	(running to Mommy) Hi Mommy!
Denise	(with a big smile) Hi sweetheart. Have you and grandpa had fun?
Haylie	(right on cue) I love you Mommy. You look so pretty.

Like I said, it was short on talk but should get me a full day with Haylie in a couple of days. I kissed them both goodbye. Just as we practiced, Haylie simply said, "Bye Bye."

The plan worked well for a week. I got her all to myself for the day on Wednesday as Peggy was again volunteering. She was extremely eager to learn again. If anything, she was even better this time as she already knew what to expect. At day's end she also knew everything about physics and chemistry. During the fun times we scheduled, I managed to discuss what I had learned about the life force, energy lights and the power of the trust glow. She was inquisitive on how to make the energy light, but we just couldn't get her to emit it. I knew it wasn't a physical problem because I learned that the power to emit the light was merely physics. The symmetry required between her life force and impulses could not be reached. As there was no written knowledge, pictures or movies on the matter, it was difficult for her to grasp. Yet, like everything I told her it was automatic for her to trust.

Grandma came home for some one-on-one time. Haylie tried to leave grandpa out of her vocabulary. Although she was very smart, she was only one-year-old and would slip up when she got excited. Still, grandma had a ball hearing, "Hi Grandma." Rich picked her up and all was well.

Denise dropped Haylie off the next day to run some errands. Peggy went with her. Haylie and I were on the computer. Mathematics were a snap for her to learn. I found anything finite and factual were easy transitions to the brain. We were so engrossed that we didn't hear the girls get home.

Peggy	What are you doing up there? (As they came in the room from behind us.)
Darrel	(While smoothly removing the monitor) Going for a horseback ride. (I stood straight up and took off with her.)

It was a short visit. I got my Haylie health fix and no one could challenge her in math games.

Saturday we asked the kids to join us for a bike ride. It had been the previous fall since the last one. They had a pull trailer for Haylie that attached to Rich's bike. It was a great day and Haylie was attentive as usual. She again slipped up by talking to me in sentences. That was somewhat offset by her talking to everyone else more. She was progressing with language well, but it still was an open sore. I was set for two more healthy days and received approval for Peggy and I to take her to the zoo on Monday.

Haylie loved animals and was excited. Unfortunately, when she was excited she loved to talk to me. Grandma saw and heard so much adult conversation from Haylie she became concerned once more. The questions started. The answers were not satisfactory. I felt the fear develop. I was at a loss to put the fear to rest. Both Rich and Denise stopped by after work and got a renewal of "Grandpa this and Grandpa that". Peggy felt obligated to tell part of the zoo escapade. I knew what was coming. The kids said Haylie needed a break away from grandpa. I told them I would pay a price if that happened. I wish I had told them the absolute truth.

By Wednesday night I was sick. Thursday morning I was death warmed over. I told Peggy I needed to see Haylie. She said that was the one thing I couldn't do. Then I did one of the worst things I had ever done. I straight out lied to Peggy. I told her I was going to the store for some medicine. She said she'd get it for me, but I said I wanted to get out of the house. Anyone could guess what I did next. I went to the nursery and got my health fix from Haylie. Peggy knew it as soon as I got home feeling better. Rich and Denise knew it when the person in charge at the nursery mentioned she had seen me that day. They were as angry as they could be. I knew they had the right to be. Rich called to tell me how disappointed he was in me. That hurt a lot. Then he gave me my new restricted schedule with Haylie. I told him that the schedule would literally kill me. He said I should go to the hospital in that case.

Like clockwork, the sickness struck Saturday morning. By evening, Peggy was out of sympathy if I wouldn't go get help. I told her I guess I would be dying in my bed. Sunday morning came and things were worse. Peggy went to church. By the time she returned, I was gasping for air and near convulsions. Peggy called Rich and pleaded for him, Denise and Haylie to come quickly.

Chapter 12
Family Confrontation

Peggy met the kids at the door. "Get in there quickly," she screamed. Everyone moved swiftly to the bedroom. Rich came to the bed and could instantly see I was in trouble.

Rich	Dad, we're getting you to the hospital now!
Darrel	No son. I need Haylie.
Rich	You're going if I have to carry you!
Darrel	It will kill me. I need Haylie.
Peggy	Rich, for God's sake. I have seen it. Let him have her.
Haylie	Daddy. Grandpa needs me.
Rich	OK, you have five minutes.

Haylie sat on my stomach with her hands over my heart. I told my family I was cold and pulled the covers over the two of us. I was so weak I could barely emit the energy light. What little energy I did emit was magnified and given back to me. There was no instantaneous healing. I surmised it was my initial lack of power. However, I did feel a little stronger. The next emission of energy light was stronger and I felt even better when it was returned from Haylie. It took six times, but I was feeling well once more. The adults saw the favorable results and shook their heads in disbelief.

I told them I knew we needed to talk, but I needed to rest for awhile. When Haylie took her nap, I'd be as forthright as I dared. They all ate lunch while I rested. Haylie took a nap on a blanket on the floor of our bedroom. I told them I'd be out in 30 minutes. Behind the closed bedroom door, I knew I had to tell them more of the story. I knew there was no way they could believe, which would put me back on the path of sickness much earlier. Haylie was sleeping in the midst of her erratic dreams. I wondered, "Little darling, what can grandpa do?" Trapped between the proverbial rock and hard place, I went to my family in the living room.

Darrel	I know you have a lot of questions. Far more questions than I have answers. For I have been searching for answers since her birthday, three weeks ago today. What answers I have you will not and cannot believe. Your disbelief is a factor in my sickness and you cannot believe that either. Everything went back to the energy light at the party that you could not see and therefore cannot believe. Yet, you have seen changes in Haylie and me that you cannot explain. It all makes for quite a paradox. What do you want to know?
Peggy	How does Haylie take you from near death to well so quickly?
Darrel	I never get to "well" status. The sickness remains. She gives me relief from the sickness but it's only temporary. Somehow the birthday light that you don't believe happened, gave Haylie and me the ability to learn at incredible speed. I discovered inside all of us is a "life force" not previously known to man. The life force is an energy that creates harmony between all the body's components. It has a natural lifetime. When it runs out from natural causes, so does the life-form it is within. It is the overall director of the body's healing agents. I have found it can be emitted from the body and used to heal outside. That force combined with the power of total trust is how Haylie makes me feel better. Unfortunately, the sickness is more powerful than our healing ability. I can see the total disbelief on your faces.
Rich	Dad, that is real hard to believe.

Darrel	If the situation was reversed, I'd be saying the same thing. But since her party, I swear I have only told one lie. That was to Peggy when I told her I was going to the store when I knew I was going to see Haylie without permission. I'm sorry I lied baby. That will not happen again. I'm sorry for the consequences of seeing Haylie without permission but not for doing so. I swear to all of you, on my love for all of you, I have not lied about anything else. And the truth is I'll die in a few days without access to Haylie.
Rich	Dad, stop saying that. The whole thing is preposterous.
Darrel	Preposterous, I agree. But tell me Rich, how do you explain what you just saw with your own eyes?
Rich	I can't. But maybe an expert can.
Darrel	If I go to the hospital, I'll never leave alive.
Denise	Darrel, why does Haylie communicate with you far better than us?
Darrel	It is physiological. The birthday light changed the makeup of our bodies. Our chemical makeup is now the same. When she is near enough to me, she is directly linked with my brain.
Rich	OK, I've heard enough.
Darrel	No you haven't son! The trouble is, like all adults, you hear the words but don't hear what is being said. You usually accept what you can see. But if it is outside your stream of logic or belief, you cannot trust the possibility of a different fact. You have seen so many changes these past three weeks that you have accepted because they suited your desires. I foretold them, but you didn't hear what I was saying. Lets count them off: 1. I told you at the party that Haylie was going to grow rapidly. If instead I had said that in three weeks she would grow three inches, her hair would grow three inches and she would gain eight pounds, then you would not have believed me. But she has. Check it out. Her unusual growth is believed because you saw it and you wanted her to grow.

2. I told you at the party that Haylie was going to start learning rapidly. Again you believed because you wanted and expected her to learn. But if I had told you she would become the second smartest person on earth, then you would have thought I was crazy. But I assure you she is now that smart. The changes made her into a learning machine. And learn she has. She is talking much better to you than three weeks should ever allow you to expect. That is part of her learning. But it is much easier to get knowledge into her than back out.

3. I told you the first time you saw me sick that Haylie would be alright. In fact I told you that she would never be healthier than when she was with me. Haylie has had a runny nose since birth. But it stopped that day. She lost her ear infection that day. How much coincidence do you believe in?

4. I told you I needed Haylie. How much more proof do you need than you saw today, before you can hear what is being truly said? How can I tell you something when you cannot or will not hear what I say?

5. I told you I can sense Haylie's presence and she can mine. I haven't told you I can read her mind. Yet, I know when things are about to happen.

Peggy	This is all beyond us. Can you show us proof that we can understand?
Darrel	I'll give you a list of her talents you cannot fathom:

-She knows everything about the physical sciences and mathematics. Do you believe? No!

-She can sing incredibly well. Do you believe? No!

-She sings adult songs, not children's. Do you believe? No!

-She sings as well as any music star. Do you believe? No!

-I made a video recording of a song we sang. Do you believe? No!

-I sent the recording to that TV show "You Are-The Star". Do you believe? No!

-They sent a letter back saying if we could prove her age and the recording was real, they would put us in the upcoming show. Do you believe? No!

Rich	Dad, I don't know what to think. I believe that you believe what you're saying. But how can anyone else? I am afraid…
Darrel	Afraid? So, that is the new element. Yes, I can sense it now. You are fearful of Haylie being with me now. Hear what I say family. Haylie is never safer than when she is with me! There are forces in play you cannot comprehend. You want to restrict me from seeing her. That will kill me - literally. But it also stops the learning process so vital to her being the key.
Rich	What key? Show us something.
Darrel	Alright I will. But you have to agree to give me access to her if I can break down some of your walls of disbelief.
Rich	If you can show enough, then we will consider it.
Darrel	Fine. I told you I can feel her presence and anticipate her thoughts and actions. I am going to tell you what and exactly when she will do some things. No one can believe in so much coincidence to not challenge their disbeliefs.

I know that Haylie just woke up. She will lay there for awhile until she's ready to move. She will open the door and I will tell you exactly when. She will come out and sit between her mommy and daddy as she is still tired and that is where she feels the safest. She will lean against Denise and I will tell you exactly when. A few seconds later she will lean against Rich and I will tell you when. A few seconds later she will get up and come to me and I will tell you when. She will ask me if we can sing our song because she loves music and wants to sing for all of you. The rest is up to you. Is that good enough to discount coincidence?

Rich	This I've got to see.
Darrel	Well get ready because the door opens -- Now.
	(Haylie opened the door.)
	Coincidence, I'm sure!
	(Haylie climbed up on the couch between Rich and Denise.)
	More coincidence. You got to love it. Now.
	(Haylie leaned against her mommy.)
	Coincidence is on a roll ! Now!
	(Haylie leaned against Rich.)
	How much coincidence can you all stand? Now!
	(Haylie got up and came to me.)
Haylie	Grandpa, may we sing our song?

Once again, the silence was deafening. There were no questions forthcoming. There were stunned looks on all faces. I admit I was enjoying the moment.

Darrel	Honey I would love to sing with you, but I don't think anyone else believes you can sing.
Haylie	(She went to Rich.) Daddy, do you believe I can sing a big girl song?
Rich	(hesitating) Haylie, you're just a little girl and that takes time. (No one else spoke and sadness came across Haylie's face.)
Darrel	That was a terrible answer. But it was no worse than the rest of you supporting it with your silence. The most important thing to me and to the world is that Haylie trusts me 100%. She also trusted you 100% - until now. Your disbelief in her has lowered her trust level in you! Tell me, how do you get something back that is lost, like trust? It is nearly impossible!

Peggy	Haylie, I would love to hear you sing your song. The others agree.
Darrel	Now that is a great answer! (I put the karaoke version of the song in the machine and returned.) What you're about to hear is something you can't believe beforehand. If you cannot challenge your disbeliefs and give me what I need after this, there is nothing else I can do to convince you. That means doom for all. You have to decide. (The music started to play from *"You'll Be In My Heart"*.)
Darrel	*The first time that I saw your face…the sun began to shine*
Darrel	*The first time that we touched I knew…my life was not just mine*
Haylie	*You'll never have to wonder if… my love will ever end*

(Haylie sang strong as the others' mouths dropped open)

Haylie	*I promise that til' my last breath…on me you can depend*
Haylie	*The power of your precious love…you gave me from the start*
Haylie	*The power of your trust has put…a spark into my heart……*

(Her voice strengthened into the first dramatic line of the song. Mouths hit the floor. Grandpa was proud.)

Both	*So whether you're beside me*
Both	*Or whether we're apart*
Haylie	*You'll…Be…In…My…Heart……*
Darrel	*As our love grew and you did too…we walked life hand in hand*
Darrel	*No limit to what you can do…and now I understand*

Haylie	*I will never have to wonder…the times I'm down and out*
Haylie	*You'll always be right there with me…my one thing without doubt*
Haylie	*A day with you, a touch or two…gives power not explained*
Haylie	*The beauty of your love and trust…has opened up my brain……*
Both	*So whether you're beside me*
Both	*Or whether we're apart*
Haylie	*You'll…Be…In…My…Heart……*
Darrel	*And I know I've always wondered…of powers there may be*
Darrel	*That gave us life and challenges…and brought you here to me*
Haylie	*I now believe in miracles…I see one in your face*
Haylie	*An angel who has touched my life…the world's a better place*
Haylie	*No power can exist on earth…to take away your smile*
Haylie	*You give me strength to rise back up…and walk that one last mile……*
Both	*So whether you're beside me*
Both	*Or whether we're apart*
Haylie	*You'll…Be…In…My…Heart……*

(I picked Haylie up. My pride in her brought tears. Everyone else sat in stunned silence.)

Darrel	*I walk through life in search of truth…and answers are too few*
Darrel	*The one thing I will guarantee…I'd give my life for you*
Haylie	*If I had to unlock the world…then you would be my key*
Haylie	*A walkin' talkin' miracle…but who else would believe*

Haylie	*You heal my wounds with just a touch…and fill my loving cup*
Haylie	*Your precious love lights up my life…and how it lifts me up……*
Both	*So whether you're beside me*
Both	*Or whether we're apart*
Haylie	*You'll…Be…In…My…Heart……*
Haylie	*Yes You'll…Be…In…My…Heart…………*

Tears rolled down my chest as Haylie finished the song as well as any singer could have done. She put both hands to my face and brushed the tears away.

Darrel	(I turned to the family while breaking down.) Now put that in your untrusting and disbelieving hearts and ask yourself whether I deserve more of Haylie's time or not!
Haylie	Grandpa, may I go on the walk with you?
Darrel	(I ripped Haylie's hands from my face.) No. You just scared grandpa to death. You stay here and play with grandma. (I turned to the family.) How can I ever keep it from her now? Denise, now is the time for you to open the envelope and read what I wrote. And by the way, you can all read the letter from the TV show. (I took it from my pocket and gave it to Rich.) I have to get out of here for awhile. (I went for a walk.)

The family stayed behind and tried to comprehend what just happened. Silence was prevalent except for Haylie playing and humming the song.

Peggy	I don't know what to think. This is all amazing. I think it's time we challenge ourselves.
Rich	There has to be more than what is being said.
Peggy	Yes, but would we really listen? It's obvious to me that we haven't been listening so far.
Denise	I don't know what to say. I am angry, happy, excited, scared and all at the same time.

Peggy	As for me it's simple. I am going to stand solidly with the man I love. And certainly more solidly than I've stood lately.
Haylie	Where's Grandpa?
Rich	Dad certainly has proved a point. The story is so bizarre, but so too are the parts he proved.
Denise	Peggy, what about the sickness?
Haylie	Where's Grandpa?
Peggy	I have never seen a man as sick as him this morning. This is the fourth time I have seen a remarkable recovery around Haylie. He would have to be bound and gagged to be taken to a hospital. I know he knows more about the sickness than he's saying. I think he is protecting us from something.
Denise	Do you think he believes all he has said?
Peggy	Without a doubt. What scares me is that I'm starting to believe it all too. I promise you one thing though, even if what he believes is wrong, he will never tell us a lie going forward.
Haylie	Where's Grandpa?

Two hours passed. The family was still trying to sort out what happened and what would come next. Rich read the TV letter requesting the act of Haylie and Grandpa come to New York for confirmation and inclusion in the show. Denise opened the envelope and read it to everyone. "In the next three weeks, Haylie will grow three inches, her hair will grow three inches and she will gain eight pounds." The facts were confirmed when they weighed and measured her. All the while, Haylie was asking, "Where's Grandpa?" and getting panicky. She went to grandma.

Haylie	Where's Grandpa?
Peggy	He went for a walk. But he has been gone for awhile.
Haylie	(grabbing daddy's hands) Where's Grandpa?
Rich	Grandpa will be back soon.

Haylie	(starting to scream) Grandpa needs me now! Grandpa needs me now!
Peggy	Rich, maybe you should go find him?
Rich	OK, but I don't know where to look.
Haylie	Grandpa needs me now!
Peggy	Take Haylie. I think she knows.

As soon as they left the house, Haylie pointed up a hill through a fence to a baseball field. There they saw me lying on a bench in convulsions. Rich put Haylie down, ran to me and stopped me from falling off. Haylie got to us as fast as she could run, climbed onto my stomach and put her hands over my heart. The healing process began in front of Rich. It took three more times of the process for me to get up and start walking. Rich held on to me the entire time without saying a word. We walked back home.

A new round of questions were about to begin. This time I welcomed them. I asked Rich and Denise if it was alright for Haylie to go play with the young girl next door. They said yes, as did our neighbor. I told her it would only be for half an hour. Haylie left and I said, "Now we can talk."

Peggy	You got sick again, didn't you?
Darrel	Yes.
Peggy	Why so soon this time?
Darrel	I think it's because I allowed myself to get angry. Anger has already proved to be unpredictable. That, and the negative emotions have a way of inciting the sickness. Rich, why don't you tell everyone what you saw?
Rich	I am not sure.
Darrel	What's the matter Rich? Are you afraid they will look at you like you have two heads? You know, the same way you all look at me. Tell them what you saw!
Rich	I…saw…a light emit from your hand. It went into Haylie and came back out of her hands much stronger. She put it back in

	you and you felt better. You repeated the process a few more times and you were well.
Darrel	I am not well. But I have no more pain. Did you feel anything during the process?
Rich	I felt a warmth and tingle during the process. And the headache I've had all day is gone. Dad, was that the healing energy you spoke about?
Darrel	Yes. When it is enhanced with the power of Haylie's total trust in me, it has great power.
Denise	You said Haylie scared you and then asked, "How can I keep it from her now?"
Darrel	She did something right in front of us for the first time. You heard what she spoke, but you didn't hear what she said. She spoke, "May I go for the walk with you?" How did she know I was going for a walk? What she said was, "Grandpa, I read your mind and want to go with you." She had not read my mind before. Now, the one thing I have kept from her is not safe and she's not ready for it.
Peggy	Not ready for what?
Darrel	It is time to show you something. (I went to the kitchen, got a knife and returned.) Don't worry, this will not hurt. (I sliced a one inch cut on the back of my forearm. The green blood started to pour out.)
Peggy	Oh, God, what is that?
Darrel	That is what is making me sick. That is what is permeating throughout my body cell by cell. That is what I am dying from. And, that I am dying is what I have kept from Haylie. She could never understand it. It will only get in the way of teaching her all I can with whatever time is left in my life.
Rich	But, Dad, you said a doctor looked at your blood and found nothing wrong.
Darrel	No, Rich. Exactly what I said was that I had my blood tested and that no doctor saw a problem with it. That was because no

	doctor saw it. I did the tests myself at my friend's lab. Please don't be upset, but I tested Haylie's blood also.
Denise	Why would you do that?
Darrel	Haylie and I were changed by the birthday light. You know the one that didn't happen. We both became incredible learning machines. We both could immediately understand each other. We both could sense the other's presence, or else Rich, how could you have just found me? Today I learned we could read each other's mind if we're in close proximity. Then I found I had a predatory organism taking over my body. Haylie had mirrored all the changes in me so far. Was this next?............ So tell me everybody, how does that sudden new fear in your belly and tears in your eyes feel? That is why I tested her. And, thank God, she shows no sign of the organism.
Peggy	How did you know how to perform the tests?
Darrel	Because the first day after the party, I learned everything ever published about the human physiology, medicine and medical equipment. You cannot grasp the learning power I have.
Rich	Did you find out what the organism was?
Darrel	No. But it got worse. The machine printed out an exception to its analysis that read, "Blood sample contains a specimen with no known chemical makeup."
Rich	Dad, how confident are you that Haylie doesn't have it?
Darrel	Very confident. It would have been in her blood stream the same time as mine. And it was not. And I somehow knew it was not contagious. When the birthday light entered me it was at a high intensity level. It definitely changed to a lower intensity before entering Haylie. I think that difference was the organism. It purposely was meant for only me.
Rich	Dad, I know we would all feel better if you got this verified.
Darrel	And you will have to trust me on this one. There is nothing anyone can do for me. My fate is sealed. With Haylie's help, I can get as many comfortable days as possible. I know I need

	every one of them to teach her what she needs to learn for the mission. And no, I will not tell you about that at this time.
Peggy	Honey, will you please reconsider getting another opinion? And do you need a bandage?
Darrel	If you look you'll see I've already healed my arm without you noticing. (I showed them there was no visible wound on my arm-more disbelief came to their faces.) Let's settle my health issue once and for all. I'll make a bet with all of you. I will tell you up front I am going to use your disbelief against you. You will feel 100% confident you will win the bet. I feel 100% confident you will lose. First is the wager. If I lose the bet, then I will immediately go to any doctor or hospital of your choice and allow them to perform whatever tests they desire. I do this knowing I will die before I leave the facility. But if you lose the bet, then you will never again ask, infer or otherwise that I submit to the medical profession. Additionally, Rich and Denise will allow me daily access to Haylie. Do you all agree?
Family	Yes, assuming we agree to the contest.
Darrel	Great. Here is the bet. I believe Haylie is smarter than all of you combined and that she will beat you in any mental game you choose. Games such as scrabble, chess or trivial pursuit are acceptable. The only conditions I impose are for me to be there to read questions if necessary because she cannot read as of yet, and that I be given five minutes alone with her so she can learn the game. We need that time because she's never played any of them. I also promise she will get no help from me during the game. How can you refuse? She is only one-year-old.
Family	It's a bet. We choose trivial pursuit.
Darrel	We'll soon see who wins because our neighbor is bringing her here as we speak. But prepare yourselves for a problem because she's crying. Her arm has been cut.

The door bell rang and the neighbor was in a slight panic. "She fell down and cut her arm on a toy," she said.

"It will be fine," I reassured the neighbor, "and thanks for watching her." Denise unwrapped the bloody cloth and saw the two inch cut below.

Denise	Rich, I think we better take her to the doctor.
Rich	I agree. She may need stitches.
Haylie	(crying hard) Grandpa, will you fix it?
Darrel	(with everybody quiet) Yes, darling, I will. (The healing light was emitted and with one pass over the wound, it was healed. Now disbelief stared at me from all eyes.) Explaining this would only be repeating myself. No more questions. Besides, we have a bet to settle. Haylie, do you want to play a game?
Haylie	Yes, Grandpa. I like games.
Darrel	And I just bet everything that you're going to be good at it. But first Haylie, you need to promise that you will not read my mind unless I specifically ask.
Haylie	I promise Grandpa.
Darrel	Good. Now read my mind. (She put her hands on my face and headed for the computer room.) The rest of you stay here. We'll be back in five minutes.
Rich	I'm starting to believe we will lose the game. (I had to smile.)
Darrel	Let the game begin. Haylie, I think it would be good sportsmanship to let the other team go first.
Haylie	OK, Grandpa.
Darrel	And Haylie, it is very important you do your best. Do not let up because of sympathy. (The family laughed.)
Haylie	OK, Grandpa.
Darrel	First question. What New York Yankee was known as *The Iron Horse?*
Rich	Lou Gehrig.
Haylie	Yah Daddy.

Darrel	How many years are there in a millenium?
All	1,000.
Haylie	Yah.
Darrel	Who was the first Pope to visit Africa? No answer?
	Then I want to pick Haylie up at 9:00 in the morning because you just lost the game.
Denise	Not so fast. I believe she has to answer a few questions.
Darrel	Sure. Haylie, what is the answer to the last question?
Haylie	Pope Paul VI.
Darrel	Correct. What does the beast become in *Beauty and the Beast?*
Haylie	A prince.
Denise	That was too easy, even for a one-year-old.
Darrel	From now on, you can select any question and I'll read it to her. OK, give me one.
	What country was *A Terrible Beauty* to Leon Uris?
Haylie	Ireland.
Darrel	Correct. What's the capital of Bavaria?
Haylie	Munich.
Darrel	Correct. Who wrote The Pirates of Penzance?
Haylie	Gilbert and Sullivan.
Darrel	Correct. By the way family, I will let you concede the game and the bet at any time.

For the next half hour, the family chose the hardest questions they could find and Haylie answered every one of them correctly. Finally, Rich said, "Enough. We concede. How does she know all that?"

Darrel	That is easy to explain and hard to believe. In the five minute time frame, we used the computer to read all the rules, questions and answers in this edition of the game.
Rich	Is that all? I'd like to see that.
Darrel	Not tonight. But what if we agree to show you what Haylie has accomplished every Sunday? Would that make you feel better?
Denise	Yes, it would Dad. Much better. I guess you're picking her up at nine tomorrow.
Rich	Dad, before we go, something you said earlier was haunting me. You said Haylie would never be safer than when she was with you. I think I heard what you really said. You said in the event she got hurt, like cutting her arm, you could fix it.
Darrel	Yes.
Rich	And if she falls off a slide?
Darrel	Yes. If I am close enough to her, then I feel her presence. I felt her falling and instinctively reached out to catch her. Somehow that reaction threw a shield under her although I didn't know how at the time.
Rich	And the dogs?
Darrel	Yes. Although something was very strange about that episode. I put a shield around us and that was when I learned how to do it. Rich, I don't know if you truly heard what I said or merely figured it out with your logical mind. But if anyone in addition to Haylie could begin to hear what I say, the resulting power would be enormous.

That ended one of the strangest days of my life. In many ways it was one of the toughest, but it gave me the access I needed to Haylie. I also saw the trust level of my family members rise to a higher level than they were on the birthday night. Peace had returned. It turned out to be a great day.

Chapter 13
"You Are - The Star"

Promptly at 9:00, Rich dropped Haylie off on his way to work. He wanted to ask some questions but I told him to wait until Sunday. Then I asked him what he thought about pursuing the talent show. He would talk with Denise. They would stop by for a quick chat about it after work. I volunteered that Haylie, grandma and I were going to have a learning day and work on ways to get Haylie to communicate better. Rich left and Peggy asked if I wanted her to leave also. I said, "No babe, no more secrets from you. Haylie will need the power of your trust." That was another offhand remark that would prove critical.

Peggy witnessed first hand the ability of the human learning machines. Now she understood why Haylie was on my shoulders the day she caught us by surprise. She saw the monitor and a seemingly blank computer screen flashing quickly as we had our eyes closed. In one hour we took a break. Peggy asked, "Are you truly learning at the speed of the flashes directly from the computer?"

"Well babe," I replied, "let me put it this way. Haylie and I now know everything about world history and geography that can be learned."

"Amazing," she said.

"Yes," I answered. However, I thought more amazing was her accepting it as fact. That was real progress.

Peggy   What are you going to do now?

Haylie   We are going to have some fun!

Darrel   A one-year-old can only learn for stretches of time. Then she gets to act like she's one. And grandparents deserve some fun too! Where to Haylie?

Haylie   To the playground!

We went out for an hour of play. On the way home, I told Haylie I wanted to get her something if she promised not to tell on me to mommy. That got me the evil eye from grandma. However, she chose to be a part of the process. We got a milkshake - CHOCOLATE! I did share one with Haylie to limit her sugar intake. After that, I could have gotten her to memorize the tax code.

Then we went home for more learning. I told Peggy that she now knew how easy it was to get knowledge into Haylie. Where I was stuck was getting it back out. She knew every word in the dictionary but couldn't spell or write. I told her of the crash course I gave her in the basics of language, but results were painfully slow and therefore boring. Peggy asked, "Was the learning side almost like osmosis?"

I said, "Yes. It basically was bytes of info from the computer being transferred directly into the brain."

She asked, "Was there any visual association with the data such as letters making up the words or visions of their definitions?"

That got me to thinking. "Baby," I said, "you're a genius." Then I explained the method we used to learn music involved vivid pictures of muscle and organ movement. I would try it with speech.

I brought the dictionary back up on the computer and restored the screen function. This time I slowed the process down where the letters were visible for her to associate with the word. It took a lot longer, but she could now see the spelling of the word and its phonics to mesh with the definition. Then we brought up pictures of finger movements needed to write and ingrained them with her ability to feel the specific body actions so she could write. That was the point I realized bringing grandma into the teaching team was a great idea. Haylie needed someone with a lot of patience to practice her new-found love of writing and who could make it all fun. No one was better qualified than Grandma Peggy for that job. The rest of the morning and afternoon, sandwiched around lunch and a nap was a series of encouragement, giggling and laughing. I told Haylie we would wait to show mommy and daddy what we learned during the week until Sunday. However, there was no way to hide the big strides in her verbal skills.

Rich and Denise arrived at our house at the same time. Haylie was so excited by what she had learned she was chattering away. This time she chattered to everyone. She did keep quiet about the writing as she considered that a promise. A welcome relief was on everybody's face.

Rich	Dad, what do you think about the TV show? Won't it take away from the time to teach Haylie what you said she needs to learn?
Darrel	To a degree, yes. But I believe for Haylie to be the key, she has to get notoriety somehow. I think this may be as good a way as any. Additionally, it will peak her interest even higher in some areas.
Denise	What will it involve?
Darrel	Time for sure. Yours and mine at a minimum. But everyone is invited to participate. It will require from one to five trips to New York depending how well we do. The show will pick up the travel and lodging expenses and I will cover the rest. You will be in charge of picking out outfits and I will work the creative side.
Peggy	Do you think we have a chance to do well?
Darrel	I almost guarantee it. You heard her sing. She can compete on talent alone and I will try to stay out of her way. Throw in her age and angelic face and ratings alone will get us through a couple of weeks. I believe I can entice them further with bits and pieces of the story. And maybe, the story is supposed to get out to the public. It sure would be easier to tell if I knew what it was.

The vote was unanimous to try it. I would call the show tomorrow and make arrangements. I called the contact person designated on the letter. She was absolutely bubbly that we were going to try. She indicated they had held one spot open for us. It seemed they could spell "ratings" boys and girls. She apologized for the need to verify age and recording authenticity. I assured her I understood. We were to fly to New York on

Thursday afternoon, stay at the Emerald Palace next door and audition Friday morning. Plane tickets for four arrived that same day.

The "You Are-The Star" format was simple. It started with a two hour beginning with 16 individual or pair acts. Each week, half the acts were cut so it took four weeks in total. The first two weeks, each act had five minutes to perform one song. The host would spend another two minutes interviewing them. Those around for week three had ten minutes for two songs with interviews that followed. The finals in week four had twenty minutes of song and more interviews. At the end of each show the guest judges would select which acts would continue in a dramatic presentation.

All this put us on a very tight schedule. Haylie and I would have to expand our music selection greatly. I had to choose what music we would perform. Denise and Peggy worked on potential outfits. In our spare time I continued to teach Haylie. I figured we were a cinch to get on the show by duplicating the *"You'll Be In My Heart"* song I sent in. If not, why would they go through this much effort? For the first week's show the following Friday, I knew we would feature Haylie's voice and face. That left me in the background where I belonged and playing an instrument that I couldn't play at the moment. Sooooo, we went back to the computer until we learned to read and write music and observed and felt the body movements required. Two hours later Haylie and I were playing the piano. She was limited physically because her small finger size could only hit so many keys. Not to mention she couldn't reach the foot pedals. Still, with the right song I thought we could get to week two.

Wednesday, I took a break from Haylie (and vice versa) to review songs and plan a strategy if we made it through multiple weeks of the show. It started out painstakingly slow. Then I decided to do a merge command of songs on my I-pod list to those with female lead and piano instrumentation. A second merge identified songs that could be sung as a duet. I needed to find seven additional songs. Although I was sure we had the shortest time to prepare, I was confident we needed the least amount of time to practice.

Haylie, Denise, Peggy and I traveled to New York on Thursday. I showed videos to Haylie of past shows that gave her a feel for what to expect. We watched videos on self-confidence, public speaking and self-esteem. Still, there was no sure way to know how she would react in front of an audience. She seemed excited about the coming event. We were met at the airport by a limo service. I was impressed. Arriving at the Emerald Palace Hotel we were met by Rhondell, a member of the concierge staff. He was an impressive young man. He said he was hired by the show to assure our stay would be as smooth and comfortable as possible for as many weeks as we survived on the show. We bypassed check-in and he escorted us to our two suites. Yep, I was impressed. The three girls went window shopping for potential ideas for the show. I enjoyed talking with Rhondell on the values of life. He may have been from the big city, but he was down to earth.

We decided an early night would help our audition chances the next day. We decided against a show on Broadway this trip. I was a little nervous that night. Haylie's reaction in front of an audience was a big unknown.

The host of "You Are-The Star" was Mr. John Franklin. He was employed by Total Television Company (TTC) his entire career. A long-term employee in their national news department, he rose fast within the company and was expected to become their lead anchorman. Then one day he informed the network that he had grown tired of the news division. It seemed his daily duties revolving around the evils of the world had worn him down. He decided to enter a venture where happiness was more of a factor. I liked that about him when I read it. As he was a very popular figure, the network retained his service in their entertainment division and created the current show he hosted.

We met Mr. Franklin at the audition. He was immediately taken with Haylie. She called him Mr. John which he seemed to like, therefore we all addressed him as Mr. John. I found Mr. John to be a sincere and warm man. I was pleased he wasn't one of those celebrities who were so full of themselves. We all knew that kind of celebrity. Those that always had four assistants around to tell them how wonderful they were. Mr. John was nothing like that. He wanted to present a quality product and watch people enjoy themselves. He took the time to talk to us to relieve any fears, told us what was going to happen and sincerely wished us luck. He said he was nervous with having someone as young as Haylie on the show because they were unpredictable. Still, that quality also added a flair which he liked. He told us he was concerned for Haylie's well-being. Therefore, if at any time Denise felt Haylie was being harmed in any manner, she had the total right to pull the plug. Now Denise liked Mr. John.

Mr. John asked me if I thought Haylie was nervous or might balk in front of an audience. I said I had seen only eagerness and suggested we get as many people in the audience as he could find for the audition. He liked that idea. We auditioned to a full house. The time was now.

The music started and Haylie sang like a bird. What we found out about Haylie in front of an audience was-------she was a big ham! She loved it. Everyone there could see it in her face, her movements and her presence. She simply lit up the stage. There was no doubt Haylie put us on the show.

Mr. John was ecstatic. Even a good man could appreciate high ratings. Expectation percolated throughout the studio. Mr. John asked Denise if she was comfortable to continue. Receiving the affirmative, Mr. John brought in personnel to make arrangements and stayed for the meeting. He assured if I wanted Rhondell as our liaison for everything else, then it would be done. When the paperwork was done, Mr. John pulled me aside.

Mr. John	Darrel, I can't help but be excited. Haylie and Grandpa is the best potential act we have ever had. The show is 90% talent and the rest is personal interest stories involving interviews on camera. It doesn't take an old newsman's nose to smell a story here.
Darrel	I know our act is 99% Haylie and grandpa staying out of her way. I'm part of the act because she feels confident with me around. As for the story, you better believe there's a story. But more accurately, you and everyone else will not believe it. My family is just starting to believe it. I ask that you only ask questions about the story to me. Do you agree to that request?
Mr. John	Yes. You have my word. Will you give me a flavor for it?
Darrel	My toughest task will be to condense the story in two minute allotments. Your toughest task will be how much you can really believe of a story involving enormous powers and the reason they were obtained.
Mr. John	Sounds more like science fiction.
Darrel	You cannot imagine how I wish that was the case.

Sure enough, when we left the studio Rhondell and his huge smile awaited. He seemed genuinely as happy as we were about getting on the show. He said he never got a job so easy, paid so well, or had as big of a budget for him to use on our behalf as this one. Someone important in there must have really liked the act. He showed us a little of New York from the limo before taking us to the airport.

We were all ready to be back home. Though the New York experience was exciting, the travel, preparation and logistics were exhausting. Maybe in the future, traveling would be easier. As for now, I needed to think on a wide range of topics. The first show was to be taped Friday morning for the show's primetime slot on Friday night. I needed a plan to bring everything together for the show and the mission. We would not see Haylie again until the family enlightenment session on Sunday.

Between Friday night and Sunday, we discovered way too many well-wishers had heard about our upcoming TV performance. Though well-intentioned, such distractions had to be minimized. Peggy and Rich agreed to be buffers. We all agreed that Haylie would have to be protected from the limelight outside of New York. It would be tough sometimes, but bluntness had its place.

I started the family show-and-tell on Sunday with, "We didn't have as much to show as we hoped because of the TV trip." I told the kids, "Haylie now knows all there is to know in the fields of physics, chemistry, mathematics, physiology, world history and geography. Whew, did I really say there wasn't much to show?" Denise, in particular, tried to test her to no avail. Grandma then took over for the spelling and writing progress. Last on the agenda was to demonstrate our new piano skills. We played and sang the old rock n' roll song, *"Rockin' Robin"*. I told them I thought our second week at the show, if we survived the first, would be an oldies medley of singing, piano playing and dancing. After a good chuckle about grandpa's dancing abilities, the girls started talking about a poodle skirt.

Things were buzzing in the house when I felt Haylie grow quiet. This was the moment I had been waiting for.

Darrel	Quiet everybody. Haylie, stop.(She looked at me.) What is that feeling in your lower belly?
Haylie	I have to go poo poo Grandpa.
Darrel	That's right. The question is do you want to go poo poo in your diaper like a little girl? That would be alright because you are only one. Or you can try to go on the toilet like a big girl. Which do you choose?
Haylie	Like a big girl!
Darrel	Good. Because yesterday grandpa made a new seat for the toilet that just fits your butt size and a step for you to climb up on it. It is on grandpa's bathroom toilet waiting for you. Maybe mommy and grandma will go with you to show you how to clean yourself afterwards. (A new round of surprised faces surfaced as they left for the bathroom.)
Rich	Has she done this before?
Darrel	No. But I can point out to her what she is feeling. She is smart. So why not try?
Rich	Well Dad, we can't accuse the two of you of being unwilling to take chances.

Shortly thereafter, Haylie ran into the living room.

Haylie	Grandpa. Grandpa. I went on the big girl potty!
Darrel	(Denise and Peggy came in.) And I am so proud of you. Maybe next time, you will remember to put your pants back on before you come out. (She was naked as a jaybird.)
Denise	Come on Haylie, lets get a diaper on you.
Darrel	A diaper is OK for you to wear Haylie because you are only one. Or, you can wear these big girl panties I bought for you if you think you're ready to keep using the big girl potty. Which do you choose?
Haylie	Grandpa, I want the big girl panties. But I can't so solemnly promise I won't have an accident. I will try my best.

Darrel	Then big girl panties in grandpa's house it is. Because if you try and fail, then that is alright. If you fail by not trying, then that is not. If you have an accident, grandpa will be happy to clean up the mess.
Denise	Are you sure?
Darrel	Absolutely! I have a lot of experience cleaning up those kind of messes.

The next three days we learned about weather, climate, natural disasters and their relationship with earth. We learned about agriculture, mountains, deserts, oceans, and seas. We learned about inner earth and outer space, even the false conclusions man had made about both. In our spare time, we prepared for Friday's show.

I felt compelled to talk to Rhondell daily because he was important to my family's security in the upcoming weeks. I stressed how important that duty was to me. However, to be honest I really enjoyed talking to him. He impressed me during our first talk. He opened up to me over the phone to parts of his life. He grew up on the streets of New York. His mother refused to let him stay there. She kept the gangs away from him, occasionally at the point of her gun. She died of cancer when he was 18. On her deathbed, she made him promise to make something positive of his life. She made him promise to stay away from the troubles of the street. He promised her that when she looked down, she would be proud of what she was seeing. He swore to me he had tried hard to keep those promises. I told him I wish I had known his mom.

Rhondell said he never knew his father. He regretted that his entire life. He always felt a hole in his life that could never be filled. His mother's strength and passion started him down the road to a better life. He worked these last six years at the hotel; first in the laundry, then bussing tables and finally out front as a concierge. He was challenged constantly by self-important customers. Customers with outlandish needs and greeds. They were those people in the world who delight in putting other people down. Every time the job approached overbearing, he remembered his promises to his mother.

I told Rhondell he would never be put down by me or any other person while I was around. There would be no needs or greeds other than security issues for my family. I wanted and needed him to be close to us. I told him if it were up to me he would get a promotion to a higher position. He was obviously touched by my sincerity. He told me that even if I didn't ask for anything, not to be surprised if a few opportunities showed up.

We flew to New York on Thursday and Rhondell was waiting. More and more, I felt comfortable trusting my family's security with him. Maybe that was because he was the first non-family member to emit a trust glow I could see. He gave us the rehearsal schedule that afternoon and assured all else we needed was at our disposal. He was right. We went right to our two, five-star suites. They were a bit overboard for my tastes, but a heck of a gesture by Mr. John and Rhondell. The girls were certainly pleased.

I asked Rhondell to be with us at all times. He used his new stage pass to accompany us to the rehearsal. All contestants were treated very well. They informed us of the timing we each had on stage. Everyone would be under strict guidelines. The first show was two hours long and all 16 acts would perform. Only eight acts would qualify for the next week. The music performance would stand on the one take opportunity, but if the interview needed some work it would be redone for final showing that night. Everyone was given ten minutes of stage time to assure coordination with the show's musicians went perfectly. They allowed us to go first as a courtesy to Haylie's age. As all I requested was a piano on stage and a bench for Haylie to stand on, we were on stage for only a minute. We toured the dressing rooms and the rest of the family went back to the hotel. Mr. John asked for some of my time. I was positive he wanted to investigate my story. That was fine with me as I planned to investigate his.

Mr. John	Darrel, I feel obligated for the integrity of the show to ask a few questions.
Darrel	Go ahead. I doubt if I haven't heard them before.
Mr. John	Is the story you talked of earlier fit for television?
Darrel	The whole world has to hear it at some point. Don't you really want to know if I'm some sort of a nutcase?
Mr. John	Those are your words not mine. But since you uttered them…..
Darrel	Mr. John, I'll make you a deal. Let's promise from this day forward to talk straight to each other. I am not too good at dancing as I will soon prove.

Mr. John	Fair enough. Are you a nutcase?
Darrel	No. But many will believe I am.
Mr. John	Why?
Darrel	Because it is so difficult to prove something to someone who believes otherwise. And no one will believe what is coming. But that doesn't mean it is not coming.
Mr. John	Can you be more specific?
Darrel	Will you trust me enough to accept my opinion that the story has to have proof shown before acceptance has a chance? I will show you proof. Feats you cannot possibly accept right now.
Mr. John	Yes. As long as you realize I have the right and responsibility to terminate the discussion if I do question your nutcase status down the road.
Darrel	Fair enough. Now let me ask you some questions.
Mr. John	Fire away.
Darrel	We are here because the world needs to see Haylie's talents and powers and hear my story, if you deem it worthy. I chose this particular venue because you walked away from a career most others would die for. You once said you were worn down by the evils of your daily work. I need to know what is in your heart. I need to know more about the man I have selected to participate in a venture so extraordinary that you cannot comprehend it at this point.
Mr. John	I had seen more evil, hatred, blood, guts, injustice and gross intolerance of others than anyone should ever see. One day it hit me that I was a part of it. I was doing nothing to stop it. In fact, I was giving notoriety to it which only inflamed the radicals to do more. That day I realized that nothing could stop the process and that was the day I quit.
Darrel	What if something could stop it?
Mr. John	Then that is the day I sign on to help. What are you saying?

Darrel   I don't know quite yet. But I'm getting close to knowing. You certainly have been battered by the evil of intolerance. What about the evils of greed and polluting the earth?

Mr. John   I admit to having greed in my life. But I stopped chasing the big bucks that were before me. Money is the root of so many evils in this country, particularly in politics. Still, you obviously can sense the potential ratings bonanza Haylie may bring to the show? Is that evil? Have you no greed?

Darrel   Guilty as charged. At least in the past, but never to a level of excess. And certainly no longer.

Mr. John   As for man's curse to the earth of polluting the planet, we should hang our head in shame. We ignore all evidence of what we have done and still are doing. How stupid are we?

Darrel   Mr. John, carefully think before you answer my last question. If you became convinced you could be instrumental in real positive change to earth, what would you do?

Mr. John   (After a long pause) I have lost seven comrades to vicious fanatics. I have lost my wife to a long-running battle with chronic asthma and our polluted environment. I see our choices of political leaders as suicide by stupidity. A little of me dies everyday when I consider my grandkids have a cloudy future at best. The joy and goodness in this world are completely overwhelmed by the evil. The answer to your question is everything I can possibly do. Otherwise, I could never look in the mirror again. If only we had such a chance.

Darrel   Yes. If only we had such a chance.

    That night we all went to see *Guys and Dolls* on Broadway, courtesy of Rhondell's non-requested magic. Haylie was mesmerized by the performers. Peggy and Denise thought it was great. Me, I really enjoyed a night with my brain turned off for the most part.
    Rhondell found we were the last act to perform that next morning so we delayed going until an hour before our time. When we arrived, Haylie watched a couple of the acts. They were really good and Haylie applauded as loud as her little hands would let her. In the dressing room, my first disenchantment was waiting. The girls decided that with the song I chose,

the dress would be formal. There awaiting me was a tuxedo. God, how I hated monkey suits. Golf shirts were much more my style. I got dressed with Peggy's help (who can possibly know what all those garments are for?) and stared in the mirror. "You look great," she said.

I replied, "A tuxedo on me is like a diamond earring on a pig."

She kissed me and said, "Wait until you see Haylie."

She was right about that. If ever I saw an angel, this was it. She wore a beautiful red dress, big girl black shoes, hair puffed up, bracelet on her wrist and a smile that would melt any heart.

Darrel	Darling, you look beautiful.
Haylie	Grandpa, you look handsome.
Darrel	Don't start lying to me now.
Haylie	Grandpa, you know I'd never lie to you.
Darrel	Are you ready to sing really pretty?
Haylie	I can't wait.

If she was nervous, I certainly couldn't tell it and I could sense her every feeling. I, on the other hand was nervous. Having never played the piano in front of an audience was disconcerting. Still, I was confident the learning methods we used couldn't have been better. We were introduced and went on stage.

Mr. John met us on stage and introduced Haylie and Grandpa to the audience. He said Haylie was the youngest contestant in the history of the show by 17 years. He wished us luck and left. We went to the cleanest, prettiest piano I had ever seen. I sat on the bench and Haylie stood on another bench right beside mine, making her the same height as me when seated. She put her hand on my shoulder for balance just as we practiced. I looked dead into the camera and said, "Hello world. You are about to see and hear the first of many unbelievable things." I started to play one of my favorite songs, one requiring a strong female voice. It was the Debbie Boone song, "*You Light up my Life*".

After Haylie sang the first line the audience knew our act was not a publicity stunt by the show. She choreographed her free hand's movement, extended it to the audience and brought it back to her heart as matched the song. She swayed her hand across waves as she sang the lines about the water. She looked me in the eye as she sang "*I love you*" and I whispered, "I love you," back to her. The audience was in the palm of her hand. When she reached the most dramatic part of the song near the end, she absolutely nailed it. After she sang the final words, she put her arms around my neck and kissed me on the cheek as I tried to finish the music. If there was a dry eye in the house, it wasn't mine. She just scored the proverbial ten on the scale. The audience was on their feet and Mr. John was on stage heading for us.

Mr. John   That was awesome. (He put his microphone to Haylie.)

Haylie   Thank you. (Using her little girl's voice.)

Mr. John   How did you learn to sing like that?

Haylie   Grandpa taught me.

Mr. John   Grandpa, you have to be so proud?

Darrel   Proud? My heart burst a few minutes ago.

Mr. John   You told me earlier there was a story behind her singing ability. Would you tell us?

Darrel   A story? It is an incredible story. Maybe "THE" incredible story. But like everything truly incredible, it is hard to believe. Some will say impossible. Our own family could not believe it until they were shown so much proof they could deny it no longer. Haylie and I were changed physically by an event on her birthday.

Mr. John   What event?

Darrel   To answer that before I prove some unbelievable claims would be overwhelming to your trust and logic. Therefore, consider this claim. Music is just one of many incredible talents that Haylie has. She has become a human learning machine. If I tell you she's smart, you probably would believe it.

Mr. John   Yes.

Darrel	But if I tell you she is the second smartest person on earth, you probably would not.
Mr. John	No.
Darrel	Yet your disbelief doesn't make you correct. I can prove her intelligence. Mr. John, you are a Grand Master in chess, are you not?
Mr. John	Yes.
Darrel	If we are back next week, play her a game of chess on rehearsal day. I'll bet anything she beats you.
Mr. John	You're on. What's the bet?
Darrel	A milkshake.
Haylie	CHOCOLATE! (The audience laughed.)
Darrel	And also bring any regular dictionary because the chess game won't be much of a match.
Mr. John	I hope to see you next week. Judges, your selections please.

We advanced to week two. Congratulations, hugs and kisses greeted us backstage. Mr. John came to me, and I asked, "Do we need to touch up the interview?"

He said, "Are you kidding? It's perfect." Then he asked, "Is Haylie good at chess?"

I told him, "I don't know because she has never played." A stunned and disappointed look came across his face. "Oh, don't worry," I told him, "she will be an expert by next week and she will beat you. And remember, we like---CHOCOLATE!" He laughed out loud and wished us a safe week. Rhondell was exuberant and efficient. As soon as we changed clothes, he had us and our luggage headed for the airport. Haylie was home in time to watch her performance with her daddy that night.

On Sunday, the family eagerly got together. We all had been inundated with calls and visits from friends and relations. Everyone was so happy as we reviewed the first week on the show. People kept ringing the doorbell. Grandma had a lot of friends. Finally to her chagrin, I posted a note on the door that said we were practicing and would appreciate being left alone. Yes it certainly was a lack of tact, but as I said before, bluntness had its place.

I told everyone of knowledge learned in weather, climate, agriculture and features of the earth. I asked if anyone wanted to test her, but there were no takers this time. Conversation drifted into next week's show. What were we going to do? We went to the piano and started pounding out the music to *Rockin' Robin* and *Old Time Rock n Roll*. Just for kicks, we followed up with *Moon River*. The family was delighted with her new songs. Then they started ribbing me good naturedly about the selection. "She was 40-years removed from the oldies," they said.

I replied, "That was one great benefit of being her teacher. She only sang good music!"

I said, "Seriously though, I think we have to show more variety. Regardless of her singing talent and the pretty package she makes on stage, we're going to have to show more. Otherwise, we are rolling the dice with the judges' opinions between similar talents. I am thinking about a medley of old rock n' roll songs that include piano playing, old style dancing and a lot of her voice. We have to work on both of our motor skills, but we know a good way to learn them. What do you think?"

We bounced ideas around most of the day and came up with our act. We decided everyone should make the New York trips from now on. We WERE a family!

I called Rhondell and asked for additional accommodations for the next trip. He assured me it would be no problem. Every time I talked to the young man I felt drawn nearer to him. I could feel he was drawing nearer to me too. I found a reason to talk with him several times a day. I told him if his mother was watching, she had to like what she saw. I looked forward to seeing him on Thursday.

We spent the next three days learning and practicing the act. We even managed a little time learning the art of playing chess. The motor skills were coming around fine. I wondered if the world was ready for reintroduction to the hopping, bopping and flailing around of early rock n' roll. Ready or not, here we come.

Amidst all the joy was a downside. I could feel the organism constantly advancing inside me. With Haylie's healing help, I felt no sickness. I also noticed the closer I came to the end, the clearer my understanding came to answering the infuriating whys of the story.

When Rhondell picked us up he was glowing - literally. His trust glow rate was at 81%. Determining the numerical value of the trust glow was one of those things that had become crystal clear. No glow was seen for someone below 50%. I learned the glow could ebb and flow. I saw the individual glows of my family at the birthday party and they were pretty strong. At the depths of despair as the rift developed and then at the family confrontation, they all sank. In fact, Rich and Denise stopped glowing altogether when they became fearful of me around Haylie. With the resurgence of trust, their glows were 91 and 87%. Peggy was at a whopping 98%. Haylie remained the constant 100% and continued to glow 10 times stronger than her grandma.

Rhondell had everything planned and arranged down to the dot. We went straight to our suites and the six of us ate lunch on the terrace. We went to rehearsal that afternoon where I coordinated the music requirements with the show's band. Haylie and Mr. John played their chess match with our family and show personnel as witnesses. That night Rhondell's magic of getting us things we did not request split us up. The girls went back to Broadway to see *Beauty and the Beast* while Rich and I went to Yankee Stadium for a game. Rhondell asked what I wanted him to do with a split venue. I said, "Rhondell, I charge you with the highest responsibility I can at this time in our relationship. I want you to go to the play with the girls and protect their security."

Rhondell fired back a quick, "Yes sir," accompanied with his 83% glow.

I said, "Rhondell, no friend of mine calls me mister or sir, they call me Darrel." He beamed his answer back with his smile and 84% glow.

Rich wondered how Rhondell got us first row seats behind the Yankee dugout. I already stopped doubting Rhondell's talents. I wondered if we would make it out of the stadium alive if everyone knew we were quietly rooting for the Royals.

Meanwhile, the girls had a ball at the play. Haylie was so excited I hoped she would get some sleep that night. Daylight brought an exciting new day.

We were the fourth act on the schedule. Times allotted were the same as the first week as it was a one hour show. Because of the theme of our act, the girls graciously had me in a tee shirt, blue jeans and no shoes. Now, picture a cute one-year-old adorned in a white sweater, poodle skirt, black leotards and saddle shoes. It was time to perform and Mr. John met us on stage.

Mr. John   You all heard the bet made last week. What I didn't know then was Haylie had never played chess before. But I held them to the bet and its time for the winner to collect and----this loser to pay up.

At that point, a beautiful woman came out carrying a tray with a milkshake on it.

Mr. John   CHOCOLATE! (The audience cracked up.) And because I could not believe a one-year-old could defeat a grand master of the game, we played two more games and………

Two more beautiful women came out with milkshakes on a tray.

Mr. John   CHOCOLATE! (Again the audience broke up.) No more chess with you my dear and you will have to wait until the end of the show to enjoy your treasure. Best of luck tonight for the act of "Haylie and Grandpa".

Haylie went to the piano and sat on a booster seat on the bench as I left the stage. Haylie lifted her little hands, smiled really big at the audience and started to play the opening refrains to *Old Time Rock 'N' Roll*. I came running to the stage, sliding like Tom Cruise in *Risky Business* (but with my pants on, of course).

I sang the first four lines of this classic Bob Seger song. I gave my best effort to emulate his strong voice with a condescending tone for others who didn't like what he did. As I finished the lines I slid to the piano and started playing as Haylie hit the floor and started singing.

Haylie nailed the next four lines while she choreographed her dance moves from disco to the bop as matched the lyrics in the song. Then we made a quick musical transition to *"Rockin' Robin."*

I was pounding out the music on the piano and making the bird sounds while Haylie was dancing in a wing flapping movement like a bird.

Haylie started singing the song. She couldn't help herself from adlibbing the word grandpa every time the word robin was supposed to be sung. Her little poodle skirt was flying around as she really got into the song. I would have enjoyed her part even more if I hadn't been scared to death of what I would be doing next.

The show's band took over playing as I joined Haylie in old rock n' roll dancing - swirling her around, picking her up, lifting her over my head, down to my left hip, over my head, down to my right hip, over my head, down between my legs, stepping over her and spinning her on the floor as I slid back to the piano and transitioned into *"Downtown"* in perfect timing with her coming out of the spin and facing the audience.

Haylie sang the first two lines of this classic 60's song without missing a beat. I on the other hand was winded from the dance routine. We transitioned the music and lines to the last verse of the song. As she continued to perform at the highest level, I looked out over the audience. Some were mouthing the words along with her, some looked in shock at what our little dynamo was doing and all had that amazed look on their faces. As she finished the song in style, I thought how lucky our family was that she came into our lives.

From the audience's reaction, I thought my little darling now owned downtown. As for myself, I was glad it was over, glad I didn't drop her in my socked feet and really glad she only weighed 28 pounds. Mr. John came on stage beaming.

Mr. John	Haylie, that was spectacular.
Haylie	Thank you Mr. John.
Mr. John	Tell me the truth, how did you learn to play chess so well? I play competitive chess and I don't think anyone could beat you.
Haylie	I always tell the truth. Grandpa taught me. Grandpa beat me in chess.
Mr. John	Well grandpa, I believe you owe us more of the story.
Darrel	I only beat her once and the rest were draws. Did you bring a dictionary and exactly what edition?
Mr. John	I have The American Heritage Dictionary - Second College Edition.

Darrel	She knows that one. We have faced so much disbelief since her birthday. Therefore Mr. John before we start, I need you to so solemnly swear you don't know what I am going to ask next and that this is not a staged event.
Mr. John	That is easy. I swear.
Darrel	Pick out any word in the book. Pronounce it clearly. Haylie will spell it and give you the definition. Make it hard.
Mr. John	You're on. I know a good one. SLZ' e je.
Haylie	syzygy - either of two points in the orbit of a celestial body where the body is in opposition to or in conjunction with the sun - it's when the earth, sun and moon are aligned in a straight line.
Mr. John	How does she do that?
Darrel	We stopped starting sentences with how. It expresses disbelief and distrust. And trust is going to be so important in the story. Haylie what else can you tell us about that word in the book?
Haylie	It is the last word starting with "S" in the book and it is the 17th word on the right column on page 1,234.
Mr. John	That is correct. I'm speechless.
Darrel	She is a learning machine. Why, is so complicated I still don't know. But how is because of what happened to us on her first birthday. An event changed our physiological components to where our brains became as one. What I know, she can absorb. If I think it, she knows it.
Mr. John	Are you suggesting she can read your mind?
Darrel	I'm telling you she can. If we are here next week, we'll let you test her. You choose whatever format you want. All she needs is to have her hands on my face. Would you like to make a bet on it?
Mr. John	You're on but no bet. Do you know how expensive milkshakes are in New York? (laughter) Darrel, what did happen on her birthday?

Darrel	The truth is everyone needs more proof of unbelievable claims. Otherwise there is no chance they will believe what happened to us.
Mr. John	Ladies and gentlemen - Haylie and Grandpa!

At the end of the show, we were selected as one of the final four acts. We enjoyed the great excitement back stage. Mr. John sought me out for a private conversation.

Darrel	Do we need to redo the interview?
Mr. John	Absolutely not! It was perfect again. You have the world on the edge of their seats. Is the story really that big?
Darrel	I will never lie to you or anybody else Mr. John. It may be the biggest story ever.
Mr. John	I feel compelled to ask for more.
Darrel	You need to trust more to hear more. But I can see you trust pretty well now. (75%)
Mr. John	What does that mean?
Darrel	It too, is part of the story.

As always, it was so good to get back home.

Chapter 14
The Zoo

The family got together on Sunday as usual, after two more crazy days filled with distractions. The newspaper called, 100 other media outlets called, friends called and people were standing around the street corner. We didn't have much for the family show-and-tell. I suggested we talk about the unwanted attention and protecting Haylie from it. We decided no interviews except with Mr. John. I told the family I trusted him much more than the bloodhounds in the press. We decided to make our phone numbers unlisted. I told them of the two songs I planned for the coming show so Denise could plan wardrobe.

I said I wanted to take Haylie and Peggy to the zoo in the morning. I felt we needed to get away from the TV frenzy and plan for the next show later. In other words, we needed a fun day. Haylie was all for it. The zoo was still one of her favorite places. What I didn't say was I had a specific purpose.

I continued to weaken. However, the weaker I got, the clearer the story was getting. I knew all the Whats except the source of the power and the true nature of the organism. I knew all the Hows as everything regarding new powers and abilities were explainable by physics. Granted, it was advanced physics, but physics just as well. The Whys were still the mystery. Why was I chosen for the mission? Why did the mission exist if there were far stronger forces to deal with it than me? Why was I dying before I had a chance to start? Why did I have to choose someone to be the key?

Monday morning was usually the lightest traffic day at the zoo. Still, Haylie and I wore outfits to hide our faces as we certainly didn't want attention. We strolled through the places Haylie enjoyed the most. When we reached the most out of the way corner of the zoo, we sat on a bench.

Darrel I had a purpose for the three of us to be alone.

Peggy Babe, I knew that the instant you suggested we come here.

Darrel You know me very well. I hope you listen very well. I don't know if you will be able to hear what I say today, but if not today, you will have to hear it in the near future. So much depends on it.

Peggy You're scaring me.

Darrel We should all be scared. I have been saying Haylie is the key, although I still don't know for what. I know she is going to need more power than she has. I know the greatest power from good things is in complete trust. 100% trust creates an exponential power to be used. The trouble is only Haylie and I have that level. I am telling both of you that at a specific moment in time, and Haylie will say when that is, she will have to have someone cross a line to help her. It is a line very difficult to cross. It requires that person to lay aside all personal beliefs to allow for acceptance of competing beliefs, and let absolute trust flow up from their belly and out their outstretched fingertips. Do you hear what I say?

Peggy I'm afraid I don't.

Darrel Honey, you are very close to the line. 99% there. When the time comes, throw away everything except what we have meant to each other.

Peggy Now that I understand.

Haylie Grandpa, I have heard most of what you said, but not all. When will I know the rest?

Darrel When I do, darling. When I do.

The next two days we practiced the act for week three. It would be easy as it was mostly singing and predominantly by Haylie. I was in daily touch with Rhondell. He said we hit celebrity status and the logistics would be tougher, but he was up to the task. I told him again how important he was to us. Then the last thing we needed for solitude happened. "Star Magazine" put Haylie on their cover. We never showed it to her.

Chapter 15
Talent Show Semifinals

Telling the story and getting notoriety for Haylie were the two reasons I had for agreeing to do the show. I now knew they were critical to the mission. However, everything else was becoming unwanted and in the way. There were fans and religious freaks out in force at the airport. Rhondell did everything he could to protect us such as slugging one obnoxious fellow. I came close to throwing down a shield. More problems awaited us at the hotel. However, Rhondell hired plenty of big people to keep everyone away. He planned an anonymous path to the show for rehearsal. He was with us the rest of the trip, which included spending the night in the hall outside our suites.

At the studio, Mr. John came up to the entire family with something to say.

Darrel	Mr. John, before you say anything you need to listen. You told Denise that if she had doubts at anytime about concerns for Haylie, then she could pull the plug. Well I now have doubts. You know that winning this show means nothing to me. It never did. This unwanted publicity is causing people to swarm us. That will not happen to our little girl. This is my first and last demand. We need help.
Mr. John	Rhondell, you prepare a list of whatever you deem necessary to assure this family's security, exclusion and comfort. Does your family need anything else, Darrel?

Darrel	No. Thank you. You had something you wanted to say.
Mr. John	I think you should know we have developed a tough scenario for the mind reading challenge. Do you need to prepare for it?
Darrel	Don't say a word. Because you will have to vow again as to its credibility. As long as she is near to me, it doesn't matter the severity of the test.

    I arranged the back up music we needed with the band and we left. We used the underground walkway that connected the two buildings. Rhondell already used his new edict to assure the walkway and hotel lobby were vacated with the elevator doors opened for us when we arrived. Unfortunately, we were now stranded in our suites. Rhondell lightened the burden by bringing spa personnel to the rooms. The girls had a ball with the personal attention. Only Denise objected to room service bringing the milkshakes Rhondell ordered. "CHOCOLATE," he proclaimed loudly with a belly laugh. The night passed so slowly for those of us who got no sleep.

    Each of the remaining four acts were to perform twice, once in each half hour of the show. This allowed Mr. John more interviewing discretion. After introducing all the acts at the same time, he started with our interview. He went straight to the mind reading challenge.

Mr. John	I will start this by having myself and the three judges solemnly swear this test is for real. There has been no pre-warning to anyone as to the format of the test. The judges have each selected one word they alone know as of this moment. I solemnly swear. Judges? (They nodded their agreement.) Darrel, each judge has written their word on a card of which they alone know. They will give me the card face down. Haylie will wear a mask so there is no way she can see, with only her hands on your face as she stands facing you. You will not touch her in any way. You will have your hands kept behind your back and wear a cloth over your mouth. I will flash the words to you and Haylie will guess the words. Do you accept the challenge?
Darrel	Haylie, is it alright for you to wear a mask?

Haylie	Yes, Grandpa.
Darrel	Then I have three things to say. First, Haylie has sworn not to read my mind unless I specifically ask her to. Haylie, read my mind when you are masked. Second, do I hear a bet such as a milkshake?
Haylie	CHOCOLATE!
Darrel	And third, she won't be guessing.
Mr. John	It is worth one more milkshake!

Everything was put in place.

Mr. John	Haylie what is the first word?
Haylie	Celebrity (spoken immediately).
Mr. John	(He looked at the word and showed it to the audience.) Correct. And now the second word?
Haylie	Embellishment!
Mr. John	Correct again. This is getting spooky. What is the third word?
Haylie	Bizarre! (I took off her mask and my muzzle.)
Mr. John	My next word will not be how as I learned that last week. But I can't wait to talk to you two more times tonight. Would one of the staff please go get a milkshake? CHOCOLATE! On with the show.

Because of the initial interview, we were scheduled the fourth and last act. The audience reaction to the mind reading went from applause to amazement to disconcertment. The last was exactly what I had wanted. We waited for the other three acts and corresponding interviews. I felt sorry for them trying to out-do our session. In fact it wasn't fair. It was one of the reasons I knew someone else had to win. Whatever that took. Our act was announced and we went on stage. I went to the piano. Haylie walked to the front of the stage, directly in front of the world. My part was to sing the limited background and play the piano with full symphonic support.

Haylie was about to sing my favorite song, "*I Hope You Dance*" by Lee Ann Womack.

Haylie sang this beautiful song of respecting your true unimportance, giving forth a strong effort, faith, staying true to what was important, love and taking chances. During the short breaks in the song, she danced alone in graceful ballroom moves. Anyone who watched and heard her perform this song had to have the good in their hearts touched. Evil surely had to stand aside for the good in the world for a few minutes. For the first time, I wanted to repeat a song. Yes, grandpa was proud. Yes, for the second time I thought it was impossible to love a child more. For the second time I was terribly wrong with that thought. The audience let her know how much they appreciated her effort. She curtsied to them and flashed the smile they all would love to own.

Mr. John   Haylie, once again that was beautiful.

Haylie   Thank you Mr. John.

Mr. John   Darrel, we used most of your first interview time up earlier. Can you whet our appetite in one minute?

Darrel   You have seen proof of three unbelievable talents that you couldn't imagine a few weeks ago: the incredible singing of a one-year-old, her incredible intelligence, her ability to read my mind. Now, are you ready to go to the twilight zone? Because that is where the story goes from here on!

Mr. John   I can see whetting our appetite was no problem for you. Ladies and gentlemen, a round of applause for Haylie and Grandpa.

At a break in the recording, Mr. John came to my dressing room.

Mr. John   You two are worth your weight in gold. But I'm getting concerned where we're headed. Any hints?

Darrel   We are headed down the path of the truth. Are you sure you want to go?

Mr. John   I'm not sure. But I also don't want to be run out of town by stopping.

Darrel	That's your call. It will not get easier to believe. But you know the story will be told to someone at this point.
Mr. John	That is a fact. But you can trust that I will protect you and your family to the best of my ability.
Darrel	I know I can trust you. I can see significant trust levels. But that is just one more unbelievable claim. Mr. John, I have to ask you to do something for me that you need to think about before answering.
Mr. John	I'm listening.
Darrel	I am assuming we will be back next week. Somehow I know Haylie is going to come to you at the end of that show and ask some specific and strange questions. Will you promise that you will accommodate her requests if you feel you possibly can?
Mr. John	I'm past asking how you know such strange things. Yes, you can count on me.
Darrel	Thank you, it is really important.

Haylie was dressed head to toe in a pristine white outfit for the second song. I was casual. Our selection usually related to a newly married couple. Still, it seemed appropriate between a granddaughter and her grandpa. To be safe, we gave my throat area a shot of healing light. We lessened my part of the duet as much as possible. The symphony joined my piano playing for the Shania Twain song, *"From This Moment On"*.

The song told the story of two people entwined in love. It spoke of promises made to the other. It spoke of commitment, time, deed and sacrifice for the other. It proclaimed the most important thing to each singer was the happiness of the other.

I looked out over the audience who were totally mesmerized by this precious child. They hung on her every word. They watched and listened in amazement and disbelief. I knew they had no chance of believing what I would tell them next. They were not ready for the rest of the story but I'd run out of time. I was back between that rock and hard place.

Time stood at a standstill. I listened as Haylie sang most of the song. I reminisced on the past few weeks. No two people had ever been entwined more than Haylie and me. We gave those promises of total love and trust to each other. There was nothing I would not do for her. I knew I would gladly give my life for her. I was only saddened in knowing I had too little time to give her.

Haylie finished the song beautifully. I survived. Mr. John arrived on stage applauding along with the audience.

Mr. John	Fantastic! Just as the other three acts have been. Our judges have a difficult choice. How do you like your chances to make the finals next week young lady?
Haylie	I don't know. I just sing and dance.
Mr. John	That's a fact. How about you grandpa?
Darrel	I'm sorry, but it is not our priority.
Mr. John	I feel your story is though. Do I dare ask you to take us to the twilight zone?
Darrel	Well, brace yourself because in two minutes you and most of the world will think I'm insane. But I speak only the truth.

The story started a few days before Haylie's first birthday. I had two dreams, at least I thought they were dreams. In those dreams a light surrounded me, overpowered me and lifted me in the air. A voice spoke of a dire situation. It gave me an incredible mission and asked me to make some choices. Impossible choices. I discounted the dreams as just that until another light engulfed Haylie and me at her birthday party just as it had done in my dreams. The light went through me slowly, lessened in intensity and then went through Haylie. That started the amazing chain of events that brought us here today. Mr. John, I can read the questions in your mind-literally. Where did the light come from? I don't know. The Whys are even less clear. I don't know why I was chosen for the mission or why I had to choose a key person for it. I now know all the answers to the Hows through the learning processes I have been through. And I do know what "The Mission" is but will not tell it tonight.

I promise to tell the world all I know next week. I am so close to the answers. I know I'll have them at that time. I have to because I'm about

out of time. (I picked Haylie up and walked off the stage without waiting for a question.)

Mr. John   Well, world, I am speechless. How are you doing? Judges, make your selections please.

All four acts were brought on stage for the judges' selection. Cassandra Johnson was the first selected finalist. She was a good choice as she had a dynamite voice and stage presence. Haylie and Grandpa was named the other finalist. Cheers and tears were shared on stage. Me? I immediately started dreading next week's finale.

Rhondell had outdone himself. He had a helicopter waiting on the hotel building's helipad. We went to a secluded airport to get on our chartered flight to St. Louis. Before boarding I turned to Rhondell, thanked him for not losing trust, shook his hand with unmistaken purpose and gave him the first hug he was to receive. I could tell that he and his 90% trust glow were touched. He emotionally said, "Anything! Anything you need, I will do!" I smiled at him, touched his face and told him I'd be calling him as I got on board.

Flying home, Haylie took a nap and the rest of the family were a buzz of excitement. I was feeling very strange. I could tell the organism was nearing the end of its purpose. That meant something else was coming close too. Yet, my life force was still very strong. I'd already learned the nearer I got to the end, the clearer my thinking became. So it scared me to just now learn the answer to one remaining What and Why. My deadly somber tone burst the family's excitement when I said we needed to talk.

Darrel   Please resist asking too many questions when I'm through. I feel fine. But the organism is nearing the completion of its' task. I now know what that task is. The organism is altering my body, making it change to a system able to accept certain powers I chose in the second dream. Some of those powers you have witnessed. Some you have not or haven't even shown up yet. The problem is the organism was supposed to be removed at the end. The truth is I don't have the power even with Haylie's help to get rid of it. And that explains why I am dying before getting a chance at the mission.

Rich	Just one question Dad. Is there any way to get the power you need to get rid of it?
Darrel	I don't think so. Are any of you ready to intentionally fall off a tall building because you know I will catch you?
Peggy	I don't understand.
Darrel	I know darling. Enough of this. I have to go see my parents tonight. I need to say goodbye. I am going there from the airport and will come home early tomorrow morning.

Haylie gave me a health fix. Rich took everyone home in his car as I started the three hour drive to my parents' house. I arrived in time to watch the show's TV airing that night with them. They were so proud of Haylie. They loved her as much as the rest of us. I felt it was unfortunate they had only seen her a handful of times. Dad said, "That was a whopper of a story you were telling."

Not wanting the night to be about the story, I said, "Yeah, too bad a whopper of a story needed a whopper of an ending." They laughed. Conversation went deep into the night. Somewhere in it, I said goodbye.

Chapter 16
Tragedy

After breakfast I left for home. Waving goodbye to Mom and Dad, I knew it was for the last time in my life. My mind was bombarded as I started the three hour trek home. One-half hour into the ride the most ferocious wave of fear hit me in my heart and belly. I knew something was terribly wrong with Haylie. I was physically too far away from her to know what had happened or to protect her. I was helpless. I was dying of the agony of the unknown.

I started calling all the phone numbers of the family, but I was out in the country and there was no cell signal. I stopped and called from a phone booth. I couldn't get anyone to answer. The car hit 80 miles per hour, then 90 and a hundred. Every mile seemed like ten. In panic I called every minute for the next thirty minutes. The closer I got, the more terrible the feeling in my belly. Finally, Rich's cell phone rang. He picked it up and before saying a word I shouted:

Darrel	What's wrong with Haylie?
Rich	(crying hard) Dad, I can't understand it. I..I..I can't talk.(Peggy took the phone crying.)
Peggy	Oh, honey. It's tragic. Somehow Haylie got out of the house and over the pool fence..and..and..
Darrel	Is she alive?
Peggy	She drowned. (She started to wail.)

Darrel	No! No! No! No! That cannot be. It cannot be! Put Rich back on the phone!
Rich	Dad. I am so sorry. It is not possible that she got into the pool. There is no way …
Darrel	Rich. Stop! It doesn't matter how at this point. It is time for you to trust what I say.
	Do not let anybody touch or poke a hole in her before I get there. I will be there as soon as this car can get me there. Do not let her leave your sight!

The pedal was on the floor. Why wouldn't this car go faster? Get out of my way! I was getting angrier by the second. The black anger light exploded from my hands and burnt a hole through the floor of the car. I was so angry at myself for getting too far away. I knew better! I was angry at fate. I was angry at whatever turned all aspects of our lives upside down. I was angry at God because of all the times religious nuts explained bad things away as simply "God had his reasons". Well, if God did this, then I hated him for it! If somebody spoke those words to me this time, then I would deck them. It took 45 minutes for me to get to the morgue. I could sense where she had been taken. I burst through the doors and the entire family embraced. I was maddened that ten or so other people were there as well as TV trucks in the parking lot.

I told everyone I wanted to see Haylie by myself. I went to the table she was laying on. I couldn't stop the tears from flowing. I wanted to die! I put my head on her chest. I could feel she was dead, but I also felt her life force remained. My mind started racing. I didn't know what to do, but I would do anything! I heard myself screaming inside my head, "TRUST YOURSELF AS YOU WANT OTHERS TO." I went back to the family. I put my hands on the hearts of Rich and Denise, pushed them against the wall and started shouting:

Darrel	THIS IS NOT HOW THIS STORY ENDS!
	IF YOU EVER TRUST ME, DO SO NOW!
	I WANT HER BACK!
	I WANT HER BACK - RIGHT - NOW!

	GET EVERYBODY OUT OF HERE - NOW!
Rich	(feeling sparks coming from me) Everybody get out of here right now! I said now! (He grabbed a bystander by the neck and headed for the door.) Get out of here! (Everyone ran for the door.) Dad, I'll be right outside.

I returned to Haylie. I hit her with all the healing powers I had. Nothing! I knew that was her life force I felt, but it was hiding somewhere inside her. If I could find it, maybe I could heal her. I needed more power! I needed much more power to flood her entire body to find it! Using anger would blow her to pieces. "THINK! WHAT CAN I DO? I HAVE ONE CHANCE," I agonized. A few minutes later, I stumbled through the door and fell on the floor.

Rich	Dad, are you alright?
Darrel	(in a whisper) Listen.

From the other room a faint voice was heard. "Daddy. Mommy." Everyone else ran to Haylie. I smiled at the sounds of their tears of joy, laughter and pure love as I prepared to die.

Haylie	Daddy, Grandpa needs me. Bring him to me and close the door to the others. (Rich dragged me to Haylie who sat on my stomach.) Everybody lift one hand over your head. Get as close as you can to each other and me - but don't touch anybody. (The other three formed an untouched arch over Haylie's head.) Grandpa, I know you're very weak but give me whatever power you can. (I emitted the weakest of light, Haylie absorbed it and drew an additional arc of light from the narrow gap between the others' hands. Then the process was done again and again until I finally had enough strength to rise. We left the morgue to go home.)

We fought our way through the people. Word leaked out that Haylie had been a victim. Therefore every media source in town arrived. They were crowding and firing questions at us. We didn't say a word, got in the cars and went home.

The girls took Haylie to the bedroom and cleaned her up. Rich and I sat in the living room.

Rich	Dad, what happened was impossible.
Darrel	Tell me exactly.
Rich	Denise and I were in the living room touching up some paint. Haylie was in her room singing. She stopped singing and started talking to herself. Then she was quiet so we assumed she was playing with her toys. About five minutes without hearing her, we assumed she was asleep. I went in to cover her up but she wasn't there. We couldn't find her anywhere and we got frantic. Finally, we went to the back door and it was locked. I went outside anyway. I glanced into the pool and saw her at the bottom. Dad, the pool gate was double locked. It was impossible for her to open it. She couldn't come close to reaching the lock. Everything was still locked. Thank God you have special powers. (The girls came into the room. I looked at Haylie who looked away from me, covered her eyes and started humming. She was obviously blocking me.)
Darrel	Haylie, listen to me.
Haylie	Grandpa, you have to promise me something.
Darrel	What?
Haylie	Promise that you won't ask me about the water or read my mind about it. I can't talk about it.
Darrel	(I heard what she said. The key word was can't.) I promise. (The others looked inquisitively at me.) I ask that no one else does either. It is time for us to talk once again.
Rich	Why did Haylie have the rest of us form a pod during your revival Dad?

Darrel	She was using all the power the family could give. She knew trust was the catalyst for the power she needed. I learned that trust was the most powerful positive force in the universe. (I then explained about the relationships of trust. The exponential power yielded by those at 100% trust. The effects of people standing alone was addition as opposed to when entwined with another was multiplication.) She had you standing close to add the sum of your trusts together. Then she entwined with that sum, roughly 2.8 with her stand alone value of 10. The entwinement value was the multiplication of the two or 28. So whatever power I could provide in my weakened state was given back to me 28 times stronger. Usually my power was 10 just like Haylie's, but I could barely give a factor of one at the start. Normally when Haylie and I are entwined we have a power of 10 squared or 100. This was very powerful, but not powerful enough to rid me of the organism. Could you imagine the power of three totally trusting people? It would be 1,000.
Haylie	Grandpa, will you explain how you brought me back? I have to know.
Darrel	When I hovered over you on the table, I could sense you still had your life force. I had to believe that it could be recaptured. I learned that anyone who died of unnatural causes prior to their life force running out still retained it for a period of time. But it was so hard to find as it hid somewhere in your body. It was similar to a duck in the air at night being found by one person with a flashlight on the ground. If one flashlight ray went into the sky it was highly unlikely to find the duck. But if there were billions of flashlights lighting up the entire sky, then the duck would be found. Your life force was hiding like that duck in the dark. I found a way to find your duck by flooding every cell in your body with light. (breaking down) And I found your duck! And once I recaptured your life force I combined it with my healing light to restart your body.
Haylie	I can feel your life force has about run out. Did you use your life force to flood my body to find the duck?
Darrel	**Every last drop I could transfer before I passed out!**

Haylie	But, Grandpa, that means you will…will…
Darrel	Die. And soon. But Haylie, you knew I was dying from the organism anyway. You just never could speak it. Darling, you had to be saved. You were the key.
Haylie	Grandpa, that's just not right.
Darrel	It was the way it had to be.

I spent the next two days regaining strength and preparing for the finale. I also had long talks with Rhondell.

Darrel	Rhondell, I have to ask you to do several large things for me.
Rhondell	What do you want? I will do them.
Darrel	Rhondell, these will test your faith in me.
Rhondell	What do you want? I WILL do them!

Six hours later, the plan was set.

Chapter 17
Finale

Getting to the St. Louis airport was a bad dream. The media vultures were at our doorstep as we left. Then they created a rolling road block all the way to the airport. The private jet awaiting us was in a remote area. Once on board we could breathe. Rhondell had us protected in New York. We went straight from jet to helicopter to helipad to room without seeing a soul.

At the rehearsal, Mr. John came to us with genuine care and concern. He had an accident and was wearing a sling on his arm. Through a forced laugh, I said, "Apparently you didn't have the best of weeks either." We coordinated the four songs we were to perform and headed back to the rooms. That night I gathered the family together for one last conversation. I asked Rhondell to join us.

Darrel   Rhondell is here by my request. I need to hear the words from him just as I do from each of you. This is our last show and I am very glad all of you are here. It is no secret that I am approaching my demise. But I ask that you don't be sad because approaching the end is answering the final questions. And with Haylie's help, I know I will die peaceably when that time comes.

I now know all the answers but two. I know that a man was chosen for a mission he can't possibly achieve without powers granted because it is man's evils that has to be brought down. I know I had to choose a key person to back me up in the event of my failure. I chose Haylie because total trust was required for exponential power generation. Total trust is much more difficult to have than total love. And no adult has the capability yet to achieve total trust in me.

That leaves two unanswered questions:

1. Why was I the one chosen for the mission?

2. Where did the energy light, organism and powers I received come from?

I think I will learn the answers soon.

Rich	You have never told us what the mission is.
Darrel	I will tell you and the world tomorrow during the show.
Rich	What can we do to help?
Darrel	I need all of you to so solemnly swear two things to me. Regardless of how strange they may sound, I need you to trust in their importance and swear without hesitation.

1. When I die, swear to me that you will not let anyone attempt to revive or resuscitate me in any manner. Furthermore, you will not let anyone perform an autopsy or otherwise poke any hole in my body at any time. After the funeral, I ask you have me cremated whenever the family determines the time is proper.

2. Between the time of my death and the end of the song I will ask Haylie to sing at my funeral, you will do everything and anything that Haylie asks you to do.

Everyone so solemnly swore.

Haylie	Grandpa. Will you be giving me more direction than I have now?
Darrel	Much more. The minute I first know it.

The next day brought the finale to more than one thing. The show's finale started with Mr. John on stage.

Mr. John	Before we start the finals, I have a statement to make. I am sure everyone is aware of the near tragedy this week to the Haylie and Grandpa family. The ensuing media frenzy has been downright evil and preposterous, and quite frankly the reason I left that profession. We will not be a part of their evil. Out of our deep respect to the family, there will be no discussion of it on our part.
	And in regard to my arm in this sling, I once again have proven the klutz in me by falling down, breaking my arm and dislocating my shoulder. But, I am a trooper and the show's finale must go on. (He left to a large round of applause.)

Cassandra was to sing the first, third, fifth and seventh songs with us following her. She performed her first song spectacularly. We followed with a new genre. We chose the upbeat and funny country song of Pam Tillis, "*Cleopatra, Queen of Denial*". Haylie had studied and practiced her new country voice. Rich and Rhondell, being fit and fine specimens, were dressed as Egyptian slaves carrying Haylie in on her majesty's fancy table. Of course, the little darling was Egyptian adorned as the queen she was portraying. I actually enjoyed my upbeat piano part. I really enjoyed the other three walking like an Egyptian during their dance moves. It was delightful.

Mr. John	Wonderful. Wonderful. (acting sheepishly) I always wanted to sound like Lawrence Welk. (He came to us.)
Darrel	Haylie, you need to go change for our next song. (I waited for her to leave the stage.) Mr. John, I want to thank you and the show for all the support this past awful week. (choking up) We almost lost our little girl. The world almost lost its best hope.
Mr. John	You are so welcome. Let's move on. You indicated last week that winning this competition is not a priority to you. Why is that?
Darrel	Let me say it this way. We want Cassandra to win this competition. I ask, no, I pray that the judges will vote for her. She is a great performer and therefore worthy. It will mean

so much to her. It means nothing to us. Our purpose of participating is twofold. The first is to let the world know of Haylie and her talents. The second is to tell the story I have been telling. Both are critical to the mission. I am so close to knowing the final answers. I know they will avail themselves to me tonight. They have to.

Mr. John	Ladies and gentlemen, let's hear it for Haylie and Grandpa.

Haylie gave my throat a round of healing prior to our second song. Mr. John greeted us on stage.

Mr. John	Any words before round two?
Darrel	Our next song selection will prove what I said earlier about not wanting to win the competition. Why else would we have Haylie in the background playing piano and me singing a solo? This will be the last solo I ever sing in this life and I want the world to know how I define total love. It is what I have for Peggy. I wrote this song for her to celebrate our 10,000th married day. I hope everyone has felt love in such a special way as I have.

Haylie played the piano and I sang this simple ditty of a song. Yet no one could mistake the genuineness of the words or my feelings.

Mr. John	Beautiful. You indeed are a lucky man. You are down to three more chances to tell your story.
Darrel	After the birthday light, I started getting unique powers. The main power was the ability to learn at a speed beyond comprehension. Another power I received was the ability to see the level of trust another had in me. If that trust level was 50% or higher, I could detect a glow around the person. Mr. John, yours is at 80%, incredibly high for a non-family member. That power can be used by me. Trust is the strongest positive power on earth.
Mr. John	And the strongest being?

Darrel	Hate and anger. In my learning and testing process, I discovered a previously unknown force inside each of us. It is our life force. It is the force that maintains the internal balance necessary for continuation of life. It coordinates the body's healing functions. I found a way to emit, control and use its powers. It gives me tremendous healing powers if the one I am treating has a high enough trust level in me. Someone like you Mr. John. Would you like me to heal your arm and shoulder?
Mr. John	Are you kidding?
Darrel	Just because people don't believe doesn't mean they are not hearing the truth. Take off your sling.
Mr. John	(He carefully had help in removing the sling.) Is this going to hurt?
Darrel	Not at all. But everyone should jack up their disbelief meters for what is about to happen.
	(I emitted the healing light. The audience gasped and Mr. John backed away. Slowly I approached him and used the power to heal his arm and shoulder.)
Mr. John	I…I don't…I don't know…
Darrel	Easy Mr. John. Your arm and shoulder are as good as new (He swung them around pain- free and grinned.) You realize the world is in more disbelief of this than ever before. How does it feel Mr. John to have your personal high level of integrity and honesty but know the world thinks you are helping perpetuate a hoax? I know how that feels. And now, I have only two more short interviews to complete the story. (I walked off.)
Mr. John	We need to take a short break.

I initially refused entry to my dressing room to Mr. John. I felt he needed to sort things out for himself. When he returned, I let him in.

Mr. John	Darrel, what can I say to the audience?

Darrel	I really don't know. I have failed when trying to convince others. Maybe you'll succeed.
Mr. John	My integrity is all I have.
Darrel	It is not all. In fact, you have a great deal to give. I wonder if you will?
Mr. John	I wonder too. And that makes me ashamed.

He was obviously concerned about the perception of fraud as he spoke on stage prior to Cassandra's third song.

Mr. John	I cannot explain what happened earlier. I swear to you, my family and God, that my arm was broken and my shoulder dislocated. And now it is not. I will not ask how. On with the show.

After Cassandra's brilliant song and interview, we took the stage for our third song. I had chosen Vanessa Williams' song, *"Colors of the Wind"*. I loved the music, her strong voice and the powerful lyrics that I hoped everyone would truly hear this time. I played the piano with the symphony joining me to give the song the best sound that it deserved. Haylie was in a beautiful little dress. As animals or objects were named in the song, a video displayed pictures of them on a big screen behind her. As I watched and heard Haylie sing, I could only think, "Earth, wake up and listen!" The song presented a paradoxical question. If a life-form is chopped down before it reaches its potential, then what is that potential?

I know I felt like I was being chopped down. How many more would follow?

Mr. John	Haylie, that was phenomenal.
Haylie	Thank you Mr. John.
Mr. John	Darrel, I can't imagine the sense of pride you have for her.
Darrel	Yes you can Mr. John. Anyone who has truly loved another knows such a pride. She just has more talent and the ethics to use them properly.

Mr. John	Darrel, I don't know after the last interview whether to stand close to you or run.
Darrel	Friends like you Mr. John should stand close. It is people with evil in their hearts who should run. If the majority of people believed my story, what I say next would cause a panic. Because here is the mission! The voice in the second dream said, "Darrel, you have been given the mission of saving Earth from annihilation. Man's evils have made Earth poisonous to the universe." Mr. John, you witnessed the power of trust in healing. The power of hate and anger used against evil is total annihilation. That leaves only two unanswered questions. Why was I chosen for the mission and where did the source of the light and powers come from? I still don't know, but I am so close to the answers I can taste them. The problem with my mission is that I can't do it. I need more power than I currently have to fend off an attack on me. Haylie is the one I chose to be my backup for the mission in the event that I fail. That is why (starting to cry) when Haylie died this week, EVERYTHING - EVERYTHING had to be done to bring her back. (I picked up Haylie and left the stage.)
Mr. John	We will be back shortly. This time I let Mr. John in my room on the first knock.
Mr. John	I doubt if 1% of the people believe this story.
Darrel	I know.
Mr. John	I want you to know, I am in that 1%.
Darrel	I know. I CAN see your trust level keeps rising.
Mr. John	What can I do?
Darrel	You remember what I said last week would happen after the show tonight?
Mr. John	Yes.
Darrel	Keep your word!

As we came on stage for the final time, I was still searching for the final two answers. Mr. John broke the silence.

Mr. John	Haylie, this is your last song. Is it a good one?
Haylie	It is Grandpa's and my favorite, *"You'll Be In My Heart"*. It is the first song Grandpa ever sang to me.
Darrel	Haylie, that's right. But you were only five days old at the time.
Haylie	I remember Grandpa.
Darrel	Mr. John and the world, this is the correct answer when she says or does something beyond your normal realm of belief. I totally believe and trust that you do. And I do!
Mr. John	Darrel, this is your last chance to finish your story.
Darrel	The light that engulfed us was "pure energy". Two things happened immediately. The first was Haylie and I could totally understand the other, feel the other's presence and read each other's mind as you have seen. The second thing was that the energy light made…made
Haylie	Grandpa, the energy light made you very, very sick, didn't it?
Darrel	Yes, Haylie.
Haylie	Grandpa, are you going to …die…tonight?
Darrel	(silence again was deafening) Yes. (Haylie started to cry.) Haylie, you know this has to happen. You know my life force is at its end.
Haylie	Only because of me!
Darrel	You are not to blame! And you have to pay attention during this last song because I know I will learn the last Why and From Where yet tonight. I have to learn it. I am so close. If I can just put the last piece in its place, then …then…

           Oh, God! I know why! I know where from! Why me? What
           have I done to this child? Haylie, come read my mind quickly!
           (She ran and put her hands on my face.)

Haylie   No it will not, Grandpa!

           Yes

           Yes

           Yes

           Yes

           Yes

           I will

           I understand

           Yes

           Do you so solemnly promise, Grandpa?

Darrel   I so solemnly promise!

           Mr. John, you have to start the song -   Now! (The music
           started.)

Darrel   *The first time that I saw your face…the sun began to shine*

Darrel   *The first time that we touched I knew…my life was not just mine*

Haylie   *You'll never have to wonder if… my love will ever end*

Haylie   *I promise that til' my last breath…on me you can depend*

Haylie   *The power of your precious love…you gave me from the start*

Haylie   *The power of your trust has put…a spark into my heart……*

           (I raised one finger, raised that arm into the air, and on "heart"
           I tapped my heart.)

Both   *So whether you're beside me*

Both   *Or whether we're apart*

Haylie	*You'll...Be...In...My...Heart......*
Darrel	*As our love grew and you did too...we walked life hand in hand*
Darrel	*No limit to what you can do...and now I understand*
Haylie	*I will never have to wonder...the times I'm down and out*
Haylie	*You'll always be right there with me...my one thing without doubt*
Haylie	*A day with you, a touch or two...gives power not explained*
Haylie	*The beauty of your love and trust...has opened up my brain......*
	(I raised two fingers, raised that arm into the air, and on "brain" I tapped my forehead.)
Both	*So whether you're beside me*
Both	*Or whether we're apart*
Haylie	*You'll...Be...In...My...Heart......*
Darrel	*And I know I've always wondered...of powers there may be*
Darrel	*That gave us life and challenges...and brought you here to me*
Haylie	*I now believe in miracles...I see one in your face*
Haylie	*An angel who has touched my life...the world's a better place*
Haylie	*No power can exist on earth...to take away your smile*
Haylie	*You give me strength to rise back up...and walk that one last mile......*
	(I raised three fingers and both arms, and on "mile" I thrust both hands at my body.)
Both	*So whether you're beside me*
Both	*Or whether we're apart*
Haylie	*You'll...Be...In...My...Heart......*
	(I picked Haylie up.)

Darrel	*I walk through life in search of truth…and answers are too few*
Darrel	*The one thing I will guarantee…I'd give my life for you*
Haylie	*If I had to unlock the world…then you would be my key*
Haylie	*A walkin' talkin' miracle…but who else would believe*
Haylie	*You heal my wounds with just a touch…and fill my loving cup*
Haylie	*Your precious love lights up my life…and how it lifts me up……*
	(We both raised four fingers and on "up" we raised our arms as far as they could extend.)
Darrel	*Just tap me on my shoulder*
Both	*And we won't be apart*
Haylie	*You'll…Be…In…My…Heart……*
Haylie	*Yes You'll…Be…In…My…Heart…………*
	(I started crying. Haylie wiped my tears away with both hands.)

It was perfect. She was perfect. What kind of a grandpa would burden a child with this?

Mr. John	That could not have been better. Haylie, what do you want to do in the future?
Haylie	(Screaming) Grandma! Daddy! Mommy! Grandpa needs you here NOW!
	Grandma! Daddy! Mommy! Grandpa needs you here NOW!

As they rushed on stage, I put Haylie down and fell to the floor.

Darrel	Remember your promises!

	Denise. You have been my own daughter. (I tapped my heart.)
	Rich. Never can a Dad be so proud!
	Haylie. You have to finish the story. Read my mind. (She put her hands on my face.)
Haylie	Yes. Yes. Yes. Yes. Yes. Yes. I love you so much too, Grandpa.
Darrel	Oh, Peggy *I remember a pretty little girl, just outside the school. Only her face makes my heart race, when she only lets trust… rule…*
	(I commanded my last bit of life force as I allowed the organism to overtake my heart and then darkness.)
Haylie	No, Grandpa, no! I promise I will lead as you asked. I promise I will finish the story.

I can't believe Grandpa is gone. I still need to learn so much from him. I have to do what he asked. I have to or we are all doomed. I need more time to…

Medic 1	Get out of the way! (They ran for Grandpa.)
Haylie	No! You don't touch Grandpa! (I wrapped myself around the first paramedic's leg to slow him down. I sat on his foot and bit his leg. He yelped and tried to get me off, but Mommy knocked him down and sat on him.)
Mommy	You don't touch him!
Medic 2	Move away!
Grandma	(jumping directly in front of him) No! He doesn't want you to touch him! We don't want you to touch him! (He pushed Grandma aside with a great deal of effort.)
Daddy	You WILL stop right there! (Daddy made a fist and reared back his arm.) One more step and I'll knock your lights out!

Rhondell   (jumping on stage and standing by Daddy in the same pose) You heard the man!

Mr. John   You will stop. You will honor the family's request. Or you get hurt! (He assumed Daddy's and Rhondell's stance.)

The paramedics backed down. In five minutes, a doctor that Rhondell had brought pronounced Grandpa dead. We all went back to Grandpa's dressing room. Rhondell brought Grandpa's body with us.

Chapter 18
Preparations

Haylie — You all promised Grandpa to do whatever I asked between now and the end of the song at the funeral. Grandpa told me so much to do. Rhondell, he said you would make arrangements.

Rhondell — They are already made. (Everyone looked quizzically at him.) Your grandpa and I had many conversations over the past weeks. He was so good to me. Like no one ever before. Earlier this week, we talked for six hours making plans. He told me he would die tonight. He chose this plain pine box as the casket he wanted. I long ago stopped doubting him. He told me I was the person he trusted most to handle the chores at this moment. He said he could see I trusted him.

Haylie — 91% is a lot of trust outside the family.

Rhondell — I figured you could see "the glow" as well as him. He hired me to do this job. He paid me $20,000 to take care of you these next three days. I refused to cash this check because I owed him this. (He ripped the check up and threw it away.)

The transportation between here and the St. Louis funeral parlor has been arranged. As he asked, I will stay with the body day and night through the funeral. No one will touch him in any manner he didn't approve. The wake is tomorrow afternoon and the funeral starts at 11:59 the next morning.

Family	Thank you so much. You know he loved you, don't you?
Rhondell	Yes. Like the father I never had. And love was a two-way street.
Haylie	We will leave after Grandma, Daddy and I talk to Mr. John. (We went to his room.)
Mr. John	I am so sorry. But I was expecting you Haylie. Your grandpa told me last week you would be here tonight with some questions. I told your grandpa I would try to say yes.
Haylie	Grandpa said to tell you that I would finish the story. He told me the answers to the last Why and Where From on stage tonight. He trusted you, Mr. John, and offered you and your station the exclusive rights to the end of the story. However, you personally have to come to the funeral in St. Louis. You must bring three cameras to record it and the microphone and sound system I need to be heard talking and singing that last song one more time. Do you agree?
Mr. John	Yes. And I swear to keep the media frenzy at bay to the best of my abilities.
Haylie	Thank you Mr. John. We'll see you in St. Louis tomorrow.

On the flight home, I told Grandma to specifically ask her good friend Marilee to make sure her granddaughter Marci and her mommy were at the funeral. Rhondell was true to his word. He never let Grandpa out of his sight. He hired a flock of large men to keep the media and gawkers away. They were good at their job.

Mr. John showed up before the wake with the equipment requested. I told him to set one camera permanently on the casket and the other two wherever they thought appropriate, but they were to remain in the back of the room. Many people tried to attend the wake, but we strictly limited it to family and known friends of Grandma and Grandpa. I had Daddy take the door off the casket and tilt the coffin up as much as possible. I asked for a step and a bench beside the casket so I could get close to Grandpa. Somehow I felt safer being really close to him even now. I still couldn't believe he was gone.

Chapter 19
Grandma, Cross the Line

I asked Daddy to take us to the funeral parlor early enough for me to make final arrangements. I first organized the chairs and put nametags on the front three rows. I moved Grandma's chair ahead of all others, directly in front of Grandpa's coffin. In the second row to Grandma's right, I put my Oma and Aunt Kristen. To Grandma's left was my chair, then Daddy, Mommy, Mr. John and Rhondell's. Behind Oma was little Marci and her mommy and Grandpa's trusted friends, Roy, Marilee, Tim and Joan. Everyone else could sit as they pleased.

Grandma was happy to have friends and family near. She was especially happy to see Marilee and Roy. She introduced me to them. Marilee was curious as to why the special request for little Marci and her mommy, Gloria, to be here. I told her it was my Grandpa's request. Little Marci was running around wildly when I asked her to come to me. I took her by her hands and looked straight into her eyes.

Me	Marci, this is very important. You are here for an important reason. But you have to sit in your chair and behave like a perfect young lady. If you do, I so solemnly swear that there will be a nice surprise for you later. Do you so solemnly swear to behave here today?
Marci	Yes. (Marci sat in her assigned chair.)

The time neared to start. At 11:57, Daddy rose to address the crowd.

Daddy — Haylie will begin talking precisely at 11:59. Please give her your utmost attention and I ask, no, I demand, you do exactly as she asks.

Me — At this exact moment, two destroyers were launched towards Earth. Grandpa was given the mission to stop the destroyers. Now he is gone and the destroyers are still coming. Grandpa had great powers. I have no powers. I could enhance Grandpa's powers because he used the total trust I had in him. Total trust has a 10 times multiple effect to an existing power. But our combined power of 100 was not strong enough to defeat the organism that eventually killed him.

Grandpa often said that he could show or tell me something in front of others and they would see and hear exactly what he did or said, but only I knew what he meant. It happened so many times. He said I would grow fast, but no one could imagine how fast. He said I would learn fast, but who believed I would learn a billion things more than the norm. He promised I'd be healthy around him and I haven't had a sniffle since. He said I would never be safer than when I was around him. That was proved when he saved me from the attacking dogs, the fall off the slide and…and…and the water. Grandpa showed me what to do today in our last song in front of the world. Did anyone else hear what he said to me?

During that last song, Grandpa raised one finger, lifted his arm and made a specific gesture. Then he did a second, third and fourth. I am going to sing that song once again with a few changes in the words while repeating his gestures. I ask two things from each of you. First, raise your finger and arm along with me. Let the trust flow from deep inside you and out your fingertips. Second, no matter what happens, no one is to leave their seat until the end of the song. Daddy, please tell them.

Daddy — No one will leave his or her seat until the end.

Me — When Grandpa told me to read his mind on stage, he had just learned the final answers to where the energy light came from and why he had been selected for the mission. He told me he was afraid the story would test my faith in him. I told him that it would not and it did not. Grandpa told me the energy light, the poisonous organism and the powers he received had come straight from God. He was chosen for the mission for his specific belief in God, his concern for his fellow man and his willingness to make tough choices. What Grandpa didn't know was those two answers were the only things I knew before he did. For you see, God told me those answers when God came to me and asked me to do something for Grandpa, and I did.

Grandpa told me that God would launch the destroyers today. However, God has given us a second chance to avoid annihilation as God has done for so many other worlds before. In order to survive, we have to eliminate man's evils and greatly enhance his goodness to stop the earth from being destroyed. That was Grandpa's mission.

I have only four more things to address before singing the song. Then everything on earth depends on our success.

4. I repeat, no one is to leave his or her seat until the song is completely over. No matter what happens.

3. To my family, when the song is completely over, so is your promise to Grandpa to do everything I ask.

2. Grandma, everything is arranged today because of you. Grandpa loved you longer and stronger than anything on earth. Now Grandma, you are the most important person on earth. Grandma, do you remember the day at the zoo?

Grandma	Yes, I do. Grandpa said things that scared me. He said if I couldn't hear what he said that day, then I would have to in the near future. But I still can't.
Me	Grandma, you have to hear them now. It is the only chance we have for the mission. Grandpa told you twice about the power of 100% trust. Grandpa and I had it. That was what gave Grandpa so much power. Grandpa and I had a combined power of 100. But it took a power of 1,000 to rid Grandpa of

the organism. It was that organism that changed Grandpa's body to allow for the powers he needed for the mission. We needed a third person of 100% trust to reach the power of 1,000.

Grandma, Grandpa chose me to be the key to the mission as his backup. Grandma, I need power for that task. At the zoo, Grandpa said at a specific moment in time someone would have to cross a line to help me. Grandma, you are that person and that moment is now! The line is the one of 100% trust. It is so difficult for an adult to cross. Grandpa said it required the person to lay aside all personal beliefs which allowed for acceptance of competing beliefs. Achieving that level of trust allowed them to fall off a building without fear because they knew the other would catch them. He said you had to let absolute trust flow from your belly and out your outstretched fingertips. Grandma, can you now hear what Grandpa said?

Grandma	No, I can't! But I remember that grandpa said when this time comes, I need to throw away everything except what we mean to each other!
Me	That's right Grandma. You are almost standing on the line. Do you remember what Grandpa said you lost that first day you heard me sing?
Grandma	When we all doubted you, grandpa said we lost your total trust and it was almost impossible to get back once lost.
Me	Yes, Grandma. Grandma, I so solemnly promise I will give you back my 100% trust if you will give me your 100% trust for the next 10 minutes. But Grandma, if you can't give me 100% trust now, then I will NEVER, EVER trust you 100% again for the rest of my short life!
Grandma	I will give you anything!
Me	Cross the line!
Grandma	How?

Me	You know how! Only you can walk across! I have to have the power!
Daddy	Haylie. I think I know what you need. I can get there darling!
Me	No, Daddy, you can't. You are at 98% but that is so far away from 100%. Grandma is at 99.99%. Only she can take us to a pure power of 100.
Daddy	Mom. Let everything go from your head. Think of only what you and Dad mean to each other. Let it flow out and fall off that building!
Grandma	I want to! I just don't know how!
Me	Grandma? What was the last thing Grandpa said to you?
Grandma	"I remember a pretty little girl just outside the school. Only her face makes my heart race, when she only lets trust rule." The first line was from the song he wrote for me about us. It was the part of the song describing the moment of our first kiss. I didn't recognize the second line.
Me	Those were the words! What did Grandpa say?
Grandma	I don't know!
Me	Remember the zoo. What did he say?
Grandma	You needed power!
Me	GRANDMA! Remember his last words! Remember the zoo!

WHAT DID GRANDPA SAY? |
| Grandma | HE SAID....IF I CAN TOTALLY TRUST HIM AND YOU....THEN HE WOULD COME BACK TO ME! |
| Me | Yes Grandma! If you can hear what he said, then you are standing on the line. All you have to do is fall across. Because the last thing before I sing the song is to tell you the last thing Grandpa told me. Grandpa said if everyone kept their promises, if I did everything he asked and if I got Grandma |

to cross the line to 100%, then he would reach the light we created and increase it to the power of 1,000 - enough to rid the organism. GRANDPA WILL COME BACK TO US DURING THE SONG! Grandma, there are no doors on the coffin because it is not a coffin, it is a bed. And you are right in front of it because the last thing Grandpa saw before he died was your face. And the first thing he wants to see when he reopens his eyes is your face.

Grandma, Grandpa split his remaining life force between his heart and brain and one other place to give me the power of one. Where did he tell us he put the power?

Grandma   I know what he said. I heard what he said! Just tap me on my shoulder.

Me   Yes, Grandma. We need a power of 100 for the heart and 200 for the brain. Daddy, do you hear what I say?

Daddy   Yes, I do.

    I climbed up next to Grandpa and tapped him on his shoulder. The slightest spark was emitted which I increased 10 fold. I nodded at Mr. John and the music started to play. "Grandma, if you love me and ever want to gain my trust back, then cross the line now. Close your mind to everything but what Grandpa means to you. Give me your power!" I screamed. Daddy formed a pod with Mommy and Rhondell.

Haylie   *The first time that I saw your face…the sun began to shine*

*The first time that we touched I knew…my life was not just mine…..*GRANDMA!

Then your heart stopped they think you're dead…but I know you're still strong

*You promised me that you'd come back…I know it won't be long…..*GRANDMA NOW!

(Grandma crossed the line bringing the exponential power I needed.)

The power of a precious love…you taught me from the start

The power of our trust will put…a spark into your heart……

(Grandma and I raised one finger and that arm into the air.)

(The healing light connected between us and raised the power to 100.)

(On "heart" I tapped Grandpa's heart with my other hand.)

(Grandpa's heart and lungs sprung into action as everybody gasped.)

So whether you're beside me…..Thank you Grandma.

Or whether we're apart…..I still need power.

You'll…Be…In…My…Heart……

As our love grew and I did too…we walked life hand in hand

No limit to what you can do…and now I understand

That God looked out and chose Grandpa…and Grandpa then chose me

To show the world without a doubt…The changes that we need

But Grandpa needs our help right now…the duck in him remains

The power of our total trust…will open up his brain……

(Grandma, Daddy's pod and I raised two fingers and that arm into the air.)

(The healing light connected between the three raising the power to 278.)

(On "brain" I tapped Grandpa's head with my other hand.)

(Grandpa's eyes slowly opened, he saw Grandma and smiled.)

So whether you're beside me

Or whether we're apart

You'll…Be…In…My…Heart……

And there's no more need to wonder…of powers there may be

That gave us life and challenges…and make us all to see

Can man survive his evil ways…of punishing our earth

What will it take to realize…it's beyond all our worth

Now the power has been granted…to give the world a jolt

To cleanse us of a lack of love…just like a lightning bolt……

(Everyone raised three fingers and their arms into the air.)

(The healing light connected throughout the room.)

(On "bolt" I thrust both hands towards Grandpa's body.)

(Grandpa's body lurched and he lifted his arms to the top of the coffin sides.)

So whether you're beside me

Or whether we're apart

You'll…Be…In…My…Heart……

We'll walk through life in search of truth…and answers will be new

What will it take to save this earth…we'll give it all for you

With powers they can't understand…a new world will receive

A walkin' talkin' miracle…and all will soon believe

Our wounds will heal with just a touch…and fill our loving cup

And good will soon inherit earth…and it will lift us up……

(Grandpa raised four fingers on both hands.)

(Everyone else raised four fingers and their arms.)

(The healing light connected throughout the room and hovered above Grandpa.)

(Grandpa struggled to reach up to the light.)

(When Grandpa touched the light, he increased the power tenfold.)

So now you're back beside me

I know we'll never part

(Grandpa emitted a strong healing light from both his hands. The lights connected in an arc above his head. He slowly engulfed his body head-to-toe with the light. The increased power destroyed the organism inside him. He sighed in pain-free comfort.)

You'll…Be…In…My…Heart……

Yes You'll…Be…In…My…Heart…………

Me	Grandpa, you came back just like you promised.
Grandpa	I came back because you trusted completely and grandma crossed the line. Thank you darling. The world now has a chance. I love you so much!
Me	I love you Grandpa!
Grandpa	Denise, Rich…help me get out of this …bed…so I can hold your mom.

We enjoyed the hug of all family hugs.

My little darling did it. She was the only person who could get grandma to cross the line. The total love of her granddaughter and the threat of never having Haylie's trust pushed Peggy across the line. Now the family was reunited in each other's arms. A miracle - no. A gift of knowledge from God, physics and the power of trust - yes. Now, the mission began.

Darrel	I know there are a lot of questions. I want to speak to everybody shortly, but first I need to be alone with my family. They have a journey to take and God has promised to restore my life force if Haylie and Peggy made this recapturing of my life happen.

Haylie	Grandpa, I made a promise that I need your help to keep.
Darrel	Oh, yes sweetheart, I can read it in your thoughts. I will need all the power from you and grandma because mine is still very low. (We went to Marci and Gloria.)

Marci, you were promised a nice surprise if you behaved perfectly. Did you behave? |
Marci	Yes.
Darrel	Do you trust me, Marci?
Marci	Yes.
Darrel	I can see you do. Children give their trust so easily. Whereas, adults cannot. Gloria, take Marci's shirt off. (Gloria hesitated with a quizzical look.) Gloria, what else do you need to see to give your trust to me? (She took Marci's shirt off.). For those of you who don't know, Marci has two birth defects. The first is her internal organs are not all completely formed. She is not able to excrete body wastes normally. She is fitted with a tube from her intestines through her side to this external bag. (The bag was removed and I kneeled in front of her.) Because Marci's level of trust is high enough, that all changes now. Haylie and Peggy, touch my shoulders. Marci, put your arms around my neck. I am going to put my hand over the tube. When we are done the tube will be gone, the hole in your side will be healed scar-free and your inside organs will be as normal as any child. (The healing light was emitted and multiplied a hundred-fold by Haylie and Peggy. Seconds later Marci had perfect organs, no tube and perfect skin over the area.)
Gloria	How?
Darrel	How should never start a sentence. It reeks of disbelief and distrust. You must trust that it is. Gloria, take off Marci's shoes and raise her pant legs above her knees. (Gloria didn't hesitate.) Marci's second birth defect is she has only one foot. (The prosthetic foot was taken off.) Marci, do you trust me?
Marci	Yes! Yes!

Darrel	There is nothing I would like better than to give you another foot as pretty as your first. But I need something else first.
Marci	(crying) I will give you everything I have.
Darrel	You have already given me a high level of trust. There is nothing greater you can give. I need something from your mommy.
Gloria	I will give you anything! I will give you my life!
Darrel	Gloria, you have to make a choice. Everyone on earth will have to make the same choice. To save Earth, evil has to be eliminated. It will require hundreds of millions, maybe even billions of people with evil in their hearts to die. That task will be mine alone. I need to raise an army of those who trust in both me and the mission and will help lift up the goodness factor in the world. It is an army that will not fight, as I will fight and win all the battles. It will be an army that will stand solidly with me when the heinous days of vengeance against evil begins. An army that will come running to perform tasks when called by me to clean up the earth. An army that is critical to the success of the mission. Gloria, it is an army made up of all volunteers that have a minimum level of trust in me and our mission to save Earth. You cannot get a foot for Marci by merely giving your life for her. You have to give your trust to me at a level I can see.
Gloria	I swear I will be there when you call. And I am ready to fall off that building.
Darrel	Gloria, I can see your trust level is well in excess of that required for this level of healing. It is time to show the world the power of goodness before it sees the absolute power against evil. Marci, give one hand to mommy and put the other around my neck. Gloria, I am going to emit the healing light and I want you to tell me what you're seeing. (The light was emitted and multiplied as before.)
Gloria	I , I, I can't see anything. Everything has gone fuzzy.
Darrel	Roy, remove Gloria's glasses. I forgot to tell you that eyesight is the easiest thing to heal.

Gloria (without glasses) I can see perfectly. For the first time in my life!

I placed my hands over Marci's knees with the healing lights on. I slowly went down her lower legs and feet area. As it passed over Marci's original foot, a perfect match appeared on the other. I backed a few feet away from Marci.

Darrel Marci, your new foot is the same as the other. You also have the instant knowledge to use it. You can stand, hop, walk and run on it. If you want to thank me, use your new foot to come over here and give me a big hug.

Marci gingerly got off her chair, started hopping up and down and ran to me. That hug left my neck sore. The world saw what it would not believe. It was the first step in raising the army we needed.

Darrel I have things to tell and ask all of you today. We will be back in 30 minutes. When our song plays again we'll return. I'm sure you have plenty to talk about amongst yourselves until then.

My immediate family headed for a secluded back room as Rhondell and Mr. John assured our privacy.

Chapter 20
God's Face

Darrel   My dear family. No man can love, be proud of and trust his family more than I do you. I know you have thousands of questions right now. They will have to wait. Right now, all of you except Haylie are about to take a journey to the past. It is a journey I have been on. It is for the purpose of showing biblical events as they truly happened for you to interpret as you will. In warp speed you will see the creation of Earth, the lives of Noah and Moses and the birth, life, death and resurrection of Christ. You will feel as if you're gone for five years, but in fact you will be gone for five minutes. I do not have the power to do this. God will be here shortly to send you. When you return, God will speak to us all. God is about here.

A floating ball of light appeared. A face developed within the ball.

God   I come to you in a form which you can relate. Three of you will be sent on a journey to see events from earth's past. When you return, we will speak of the future regardless how long that may be.

Instantly the three were gone. Haylie and I played for the five most wonderful minutes a grandpa could enjoy. Five minutes later, the family and God reappeared.

God	You have seen the actual events that have been written about over many ages. You will come to your own conclusion. What you must decide now is your participation in the future. You have only heard the truth. Earth has become poisonous to the universe and therefore to me. Man's evils have created this poison. Earth will be destroyed in a few months if Darrel's mission to save it is not successful. He will need billions of people to help him be successful. Most of all, he needs each of you. With what you have witnessed, you must now decide whether to join the army of goodness. What is your decision?
Family	Yes.
God	What mankind calls the universe is so much larger than he can possibly understand. Millions of planets have gone poisonous in history. Every time that has happened, I have given a second chance to stop total annihilation as I have to Earth. Every planet has failed the second chance to save itself to date. Only four other planets passed the first test that you just succeeded in doing. Failure to choose the proper "Key" person always brings doom. Total trust is nearly nonexistent in adults. (God moved in front of Peggy.) That is why your achieving this level is so impressive. (God moved to Haylie.) That is why your accomplishing this feat is so impressive.
Haylie	Thank you God. It is nice to see you again. (My antennas went up as well as my anger.)
God	Darrel, you are not the only one to feel a presence. It seems you have a question for me.
Darrel	God. Did you make Haylie go into the water?
God	Yes. Do you trust me?
Darrel	Yes, but I admit I am very angry.
God	I know. If you weren't honest, you never would have been chosen as the one for the mission. I recall you were angry with me on that day also.
Darrel	Why?

God	You were failing. You had learned much but was missing the main piece of knowledge you needed. How did you put it? You had to find the duck. How could you find something you didn't know existed? I went to Haylie and told her you were failing. I told her that she was the only one who could make you find the duck. I asked her if she trusted in me. She said yes. I took her to the water and asked her to go in of her own free will to force you to learn. She did and then you did. You see, I trusted you Darrel.
Darrel	And the dogs that attacked?
God	Yes. You asked for the power of defense shields. You already had that power after you learned how to emit power through different emotions. I merely chose the method to force you to find that power.
Darrel	The mission is daunting. It is frightening to learn that no other planet has been successful.
God	You are closer than all but four other planets. They all failed from this point from fear, guilt, weakness and failure to enhance the power of good to the proper level. The mission is daunting. Have I chosen the wrong person?
Darrel	I so solemnly swear that I will give everything in my power to accomplish the mission. (God moved to Rich and Denise. Hands extended from the ball and were placed on their hearts.)
God	A child is the most precious gift. One so special is even more precious. Congratulations. Very Prime.
Rich & Denise	Thank you. (God moved to Haylie.)
God	My dear special child, your grandpa needs your help more than any other. I hope you succeed.
Haylie	God. Grandma always hugs people she cares for when they leave. May I hug you?

God	(obviously touched) Absolutely! (Haylie gave God the long embrace we had come to cherish.) Darrel, you need to be strong!

With that the ball of light shot through my heart and was gone. I instantly felt a huge life force inside me. God restored what I had given away and many times stronger! We all sat in silence for a minute except for Haylie, who was laughing and humming. Looking at my family, I was delighted all their trust glows were incredibly high. Before returning to the parlor, the healing light was used on each of them. Most interesting was their body transformation into remarkably fit people. I came to call it the "Darrel Trust Diet".

Back in the parlor the song that had become our anthem, "You'll Be In My Heart", started to play announcing our arrival. Haylie came in first singing loud. As each person entered they joined in the singing as the audience noticed their new physiques. I entered singing loudly on the last verse, "and how it lifts me up". We urged everyone to join us in finishing the song.

Darrel	I have only a few things to say today as tomorrow, Mr. John and I will host a press conference to inform everyone of what is coming. My dear friends and family, I know you are in a state of shock over what you have seen. Trust me when I say I have been in that state for two and a half months. You will be bombarded with questions, disbeliefs, outrage and other challenges to you and me. Remember, you are very important to the mission and me. We face imminent death if we do not succeed. The status quo of the world is about to be demolished by the New World Order. For that is what we are as of today. We are going to blow up the institutions of status quo. We will not be held hostage to any rules or laws of any land. Friends, God just visited my family in the other room. God just restored my life force. The highest law of any land spoke. I so solemnly swore to God to do everything to eliminate the poison on earth. And that is exactly what I will do. There is so much to do and time is short. That is why we have so much to do tonight. I ask that only my immediate family, Rhondell, Mr. John, Roy, Marilee, Tim and Joan come with

me to our house. Trust is the biggest challenge to saving this planet. Find yours, keep it and let it grow.

That night at the house, our six good friends sat with the family.

Darrel   I need everybody to become a part of the New World Order. If you choose to join, I have a special job for each. You will have to quit your old job. That will not matter because those jobs won't be there long anyway. What you have not seen but will is the incredible powers I have been given to accomplish the mission. The evil in this world will die. Our security to do our jobs will be assured by an impregnable defense shield I will place around each of you. We will make the new rules and each of you will speak for me in your endeavors. I will fight all battles that any of us incur. We will be known as the Inner Circle of the New World Order. We will not allow evil or greed to enter our organization. You know that those of us with 100% trust can see the trust levels of others. We can also see the God blackened-heart of the evil. No one here has a black heart. Death awaits those who cannot lose their black hearts. That is my job. If you choose to join me, I'll give you your new job. And you will handle your new job in totality.

All   I'm in.

Darrel   Mr. John. You will be in charge of the media. Press conferences are for us to inform, not to be interrogated. We will limit the number of questions to a few. No one will speak other than us until you alone select those who may ask a question. Mr. John, you will also join me for the horrible tasks of vengeance ahead. They will be terrible days, but I will need you. Do you remember what you once told me about the opportunity for positive change?

Mr. John   I told you I would do everything I could possibly do. And I will!

Darrel   Rhondell. I recall I promised you a promotion. You will be our minister in charge of all logistics except for transportation. I will handle that for the most part. You speak with my voice. I expect those who house and feed us to do so with willingness. If someone rejects our needs, then I will join you to set them straight. I doubt if there will be any further problems. You will tell people what we need not ask. You will be given additional tasks as necessary. (Rhondell only smiled.)

Haylie. You are a one-year-old and will be given the opportunity to be so. However, you will have major tasks. We will be participating in numerous celebrations to increase our army of the good. I need yours and grandma's powers on most of those days. I charge you with developing a universal language to be distributed in two days. You will also finalize the new energy source we have been working on in the next two weeks. As we go along, we will determine our Minister of Medicine. You will help with discovering a universal cure medicine.

Tim. You will be the Minister of Energy Distribution. When the new energy source is finalized, it will eliminate all sources currently being used. I intend to give it away for next to nothing. It will be manufactured and distributed around the world. You will need to obtain facilities. I will help you persuade the owners of those facilities to donate them to the New World Order.

Roy. You will be the Minister of Finance and Collection. I perceive we will levy a tax on every business and wealthy person. The proceeds will be split among the country they come from and the New World Order. The countries will eliminate all national debts and provide basic services. The New World Order will redirect funds to the other ministers and wherever needed around the world. I will make an example of the first several resisters to the new levy. Collections will be easier thereafter.

Marilee. You are the Minister of Education. Education will be a privilege earned by effort and attitude of the student. It will not be a right. There will be no parental problems tolerated. Violation of the privilege will find the violator out of the classroom, onto the street and praying they don't have a blackened heart.

Peggy and Joan. You will be our joint Ministers of Charity. Once Roy's division is defined and operable, you will have a large budget. Come to think of it all ministers will.

Denise. Your biggest job is raising Haylie. You will determine what is best for her within the confines of her tasks. You will also work with Roy in the finance arena. And you will have one special task.

Denise — What special task?

Darrel — You'll find out in a couple of days.

Rich. You'll be with me most days planning strategy. And, oh yes, you're about to enter politics.

Ministers, start preparing for your tasks. Remember you are the voice of authority. There will be no committees. You will dictate, not request. You will need a staff, but the person's trust is the foremost hiring attribute. We all have huge tasks. Always remind yourself that Earth's survival depends on us.

Did I mention that every minister of the New World Order with a trust level over 80%, such as all of you, are eligible for the Darrel Trust Diet.

Ten minutes later, we had the fittest members in the world.

Chapter 21
The Press and Children In Pain

Day 2. Mr. John announced the press conference would be held at his former employer's St. Louis office. All major networks were invited and informed they would be held to strict guidelines. There would be no intolerance of the rules.

Mr. John   No one will speak unless they are asked to do so. There..

CBS   What gives you....

With that, the black light thrust from my hands, lifted Mr. CBS up, threw him hard against the wall and left him suspended there as if he had been nailed to it. The healing light then emitted, sealed his mouth and left him to breathe through his nostrils. Silence returned.

Mr. John   I will continue. There will be five questions allowed after Darrel's statement. I will choose who asks those questions. Any further breach of these rules will have the violator joining CBS. There is one thing the press will strictly avoid. Under no circumstance will anyone impose questions to Haylie. She is extremely important to success of our mission. But she is only one-year-old and will be given every opportunity to enjoy her youth. Darrel.

Darrel   I will not repeat myself. Mr. CBS is the first to feel vengeance. That is why he has been allowed to live. But from the evil I see in him, I doubt for long. Be warned, virtually all future vengeance will be death. Now if I have your attention, I have a statement.

This all started in what I thought at the time was two dreams. I was engulfed by a light, immobilized and spoke to by a voice. In dream one the voice said, "You will choose one person to be the key to save Earth. This person will be given the power to learn anything that can be taught. The first task for the chosen one will require absolute trust in you. Who do you choose to be the key?" I chose Haylie.

In dream two the voice said, "Darrel, you have been given the mission to save Earth from annihilation. Man's evils have made Earth poisonous to the universe. The evil must be eliminated and goodness enhanced to an abundant level. You will be given ten powers of your choice to accomplish the mission. Choose wisely. What powers do you choose?"

I chose:

1. Identify and measure the trust level of others towards our mission

2. Power to heal equivalent to the trust level of the one being healed

3. Identify those with evil in their hearts

4. Absolute power of vengeance against evil

5. Power to learn at the fastest possible rate

6. Power to move objects

7. Power of instantaneous transport

8. Power to modify weather

9. Power to implant a universal language

10. Power to create impenetrable defense shields and detect anything amiss inside

Of these powers, the first, third, ninth and part of the tenth are God's alone. The three of us who have obtained 100% trust can see and measure a glow around anyone with at least a 50% trust level in our mission. That glow is God's marking of an individual which changes constantly as that individual's trust changes.

The third power is also God's marking of an individual that those at 100% trust can see. This is the marking of an unacceptable level of evil. Make no mistake, everyone on the planet has a degree of evil in them. But those deemed by God at excessive levels are marked with different shades of a black heart that represent the various evils possessed. Vengeance from the black anger light I emit will target the black hearts. When vengeance comes for the individual, there will be no way to hide or escape. There is time for the nearly two billion black hearts on earth to change. All you have to do is lose your greed and intolerances in a very short time period. I am not hopeful that many will do so as evil is deep rooted.

Only God has the ninth power of transplanting a universal language or detecting anything amiss within a perimeter as per the tenth power.

Every other power on the list is within every human. God sent two energy lights through me on Haylie's birthday. The first one seeded only my body with an organism. The purpose of the organism was to unlock the potential of my body. The second light went through Haylie and me. It unlocked the potential of our brains which allowed for the incredible learning abilities we possess. These abilities resulted in the discovery of the life force that lies within all of us. That discovery led to the emission of power to both heal and destroy, move objects, modify weather and create shields. Healing comes from the white light enjoined by my life force. Destruction comes from the black light that is fueled by the powerful emotions of hate and anger. Moving objects and modifying weather is accomplished by emitting the specific atomic formula that matches and attaches to that of the object. Defense shields are invisible emissions that meld elements into a compound impenetrable to any force. The shield will also reflect back any force striking it exactly to where it originated. The shield compound is incredibly complex and the formula will never be made available to others.

All of these powers are explained by physics. The key is the total availability of the brain and body to function. Anyone who reaches this high level of functioning will have these powers available to them.

The organism also had the negative effect of confusing my core body functions on a cellular basis. It had to be ridded from my body after performing its' purpose or it would kill me, as it eventually did. However, there was not enough power to rid the organism from me until the funeral.

I need to address one point right now. Some will call my body coming back to life a resurrection. That is not the case. Resurrection describes a Holy act of bringing the truly dead back to life. The physical body dies when its components stop functioning. If a body dies for a reason other than its' life force dying, the life force remains alive for a short period of time. It lies somewhere in the body. If it can be found, it can be recaptured and whatever physically killed the body can be healed by the laws of physics.

As I approached my body death, I directed my remaining life force to enter my heart and brain. Haylie knew exactly where I put it. Once she gained enough power, she recaptured my life force and recharged my body organs. Adding my power to what she accumulated allowed me to get rid of the organism, but left my body in the advanced state the organism had taken it to. However, my life force was low as I nearly used it up to recapture Haylie's life force when she drowned. Just before my body death, I learned the final answers that last night on stage. It was there that God promised to restore my life force if others could pass the tests of trusting and recapturing. When God visited us after my recapture, God infused a new and large life force into me. Haylie and I returned from physical body deaths. They were not resurrections. They were the result of the power and knowledge of physics. Our life forces, and therefore our lives, were merely recaptured.

You have seen and heard the story from Haylie's birthday party through yesterday's recapturing. What I will tell you now is my conversation with God during my body's death period:

1. Man's evils of polluting the earth, greed and intolerance of others' religion, race and nationality have turned Earth into a poison. All these evils have to be eliminated.

2. The goodness factor on earth has to reach two billion units.

3. Two destroyers were launched at Earth by God at 11:59 AM St. Louis time on July 1. They will hit Earth at the exact same moment on exact opposite sides at 11:59AM, St. Louis time on January 1. They are twice the size of Earth, harder than a diamond, moving 50,000 miles per hour and at impact will not leave a single organism alive. Their exact locations are being distributed to NASA as we speak for verification. Now before the usual disbelief sets in, when verified, how can anyone know of their existence without access to the most powerful telescopes? And even then, what are the odds they would have been spotted? A destroyer of this magnitude has never struck Earth. To all you disbelievers, what are the odds that two would strike simultaneously? Zero is the answer. It is real. It is happening. Nothing man can physically do can stop the destroyers.

4. God has given us a second chance to avoid annihilation by accomplishing items one and two.

5. The greatest powers on earth emits from my hands for both healing and destruction. All of man's arsenal of weapons combined will be defeated if launched.

We have run out of time with the status quo. It changes today. Billions of people are about to die. I have become the First Prime Member of the New World Order. Capable friends and family members have been designated as Ministers of Information, Logistics, Energy Distribution, Finance and Collection, Education, Medicine and Charities per the list in front of you. Together we comprise the Inner Circle of the New World Order. Every government, religious, law, financial, energy, medical, charitable and education institution will be subordinate to the New World Order.

There will be no political correctness in the New World Order as it is merely a way for words to cover the truth. The legal systems of the world will be thrown away. They are merely there for the benefit of lawyers providing for lawyers, dictators continuing to dictate and religious zealots oppressing the people. Every government will be subordinated to the New World Order until January 2, if there is a January 2.

The world is embattled for many reasons. One reason is we can't understand each other. Haylie is finishing a new universal language. It will be known as Earthian. Tomorrow, I will emit Earthian worldwide along with a cleanser to erase all previous languages. Everyone on earth will instantly understand the Earthian language. Everyone on earth will lose his or her knowledge of all previous languages. Every written document will be converted to Earthian. This was the ninth power I requested and is being implemented by God's power. No one will change, add or modify any word of Earthian. Tomorrow, we all will at least understand the words of our fellow man.

Our only priority is to save the world. No one or thing will be allowed to slow down or stop our march to that priority. We will be enlisting billions of people worldwide to join our army. Our army will not fight. I will fight all the battles. Our army will clean up the earth on command and support the New World Order regardless of the huge casualties of evil that must be claimed.

Everything is about to change. I beg the good people of the world to join us. I beg the evil people of the world to lose their evil very quickly. We will take five questions from those selected by Mr. John.

Mr. John	NBC, you are first.
NBC	Aren't you concerned you're starting a panic?
Darrel	The world is being destroyed if we don't change it. I think it's time to panic.
Mr. John	ABC.
ABC	What do you think this will do to the financial markets?
Darrel	I'm sure they're collapsing as I speak. They have to collapse. They are the biggest source of the evil of greed on earth. The world will witness the change from when having lots of money made one powerful into it now made you a target.
Mr. John	FOX.
FOX	This seems to have a religious overtone. Are you declaring yourself a god?
Darrel	That is preposterous. God touched me. I was commanded by God! I am not a god. I do not claim to be, do not want to be and will never be a god. I am a man, albeit, with huge powers.

	When my life force runs out, I die. But you are right about the religious overtone. Every religion has their share of fanatics and intolerance. The greatest number of deaths to come from around the world will be from the evil of religious intolerance. Those deaths will come from all religions and from every country.
Mr. John	CNN.
CNN	Are you saying your organization will not abide by the laws of the United States?
Darrel	Absolutely! Let me be clear. I was born, raised, proud to be and died an American. I came back to life as a member of the New World Order. The United States is no better nor worse than any other nation to us. It just happens to have more evil per capita than most. No country will bind us.
Mr. John	TTC.
TTC	With such an emphatic repudiation of the law of the land, you surely expect retaliation.
Darrel	Yes! AND THEY WILL LOSE!
Mr. John	That is all the questions allowed today. We will have a press conference on the first day of every month and on December 30. We will give advance notice of our schedule. The rest of today will be spent at St. Louis Children's Hospital performing whatever healings the trust levels there will allow. Day three will start the U.S. political change process. Darrel, Rich and I will be visiting the newly elected president and vice-president whether they want us to or not. On day 4, July 4th, we will hold our first celebration here in St. Louis under the Gateway Arch at 11:59 AM. The press is welcome to join us at the hospital, but only two cameras will be allowed. The press here can determine which ones.

Mr. CBS was released, he hit the floor with a thud and his mouth reappeared. Maybe he learned.

Peggy joined us at the hospital for the rest of the day. I needed her additional power. This proved to be the best part of my mission. Helping kids in pain was pure joy. Why couldn't adults trust like the majority of these tykes? Though some of the least fortunate, their trust levels were consistently high. Kids in that group were healed even if their parents had black hearts. Only a handful of kids were denied healings because they didn't trust. Some parents were very vocal in their displeasure with the press conference.

The hospital was accommodating. Though it may had been out of curiosity, they gave us access to whatever kids were authorized by their parents. Some parents came racing in after they heard we were there. We healed burns, bones, cancer and even some attitudes. I asked the healed kids' parents to join our July 4th celebration with the hope they would join our army. Regardless, there were a lot of tears of joy that day at the hospital. Unfortunately, the empty beds would fill too quickly. However, our cause did get a lot of notoriety and press. That would be important as we tried to build our army.

On the way home I considered spending more time doing these great deeds, but I knew they couldn't get us to our goals. Therefore if I spent too much time helping kids, then they all would die on New Year's Day. We used cars to travel today in an attempt to not overwhelm the public beyond the messages of the day. Tomorrow we would use the power of transport. The president issued a statement, unabashedly denying a meeting with us. I knew the secret service guarding the president and vice-president would be on high alert. The first battle and real statement of power happens tomorrow. The stock markets worldwide were down 30% for the day. They had much further to fall.

Chapter 22
U.S. Politics

Haylie downloaded the new Earthian language she had finalized to me before we left. Rich suggested Times Square in New York at the height of morning rush hour would be our launch point. Mr. John had TTC cameras posted everywhere around the square. Our first transport stopped all traffic of all kinds. Our new system of transport used the healing light to molecularly decompose at one location and recompose at another. The people would see a tunnel of light landing on the ground like a windless tornado with everything and everyone transported by it merely walking out of the light.

Without saying a word to the stunned crowd, the strongest emission of light to date was emitted from each hand. This special emission was beyond all previous ones explainable by physics. This one came from a direct empowerment from God. This was a one-time shot per my list of powers requested. My left hand emitted a fine dust-like particle to cleanse all knowledge of existing languages from every source and person. The right hand emitted another fine stream containing the power to infuse Earthian into every person, book, computer and all other forms of the written word. The streams took flight and spread above the earth in a matter of minutes. When they completely encircled Earth, they fell to the ground, through the ground and penetrated all matter which accomplished their intended tasks. Instantly, we understood what everyone was saying around the world. Too bad we still didn't hear what was being said. It was time to go to Washington, D.C.

Evil was easier for me to identify than trust. It incited the extraordinary power of hate and anger in me. Therefore, I knew exactly where to find those I was specifically looking for. I knew Madam Vice-President was being guarded at her residence. Mr. John, Rich and I transported directly into her living room. Defense shields were around us upon arrival. To avoid unnecessary deaths of wholesome secret service agents under orders, the anger light was on and overtook them as previously with Mr. CBS.

Darrel	Madam Vice-President, you have a choice. You order the agents to drop their weapons and leave or you will be responsible for their deaths right now.
V.P.	Please do as he asks. (I knew by their oath they couldn't withdraw, but I wanted to get her response.)
Darrel	Madam V.P., you will be joining us to visit the president. These agents will be freed unharmed as we leave. (The four of us transported to the bunker below the White House. We entered the bunker in the same manner as we did the V.P. residence and found 22 guns aimed at us, but all frozen by the light.)
President	How dare you come here!
Darrel	You have no idea what I dare to do.
President	I order you to… (He assumed the CBS position on the wall with his mouth sealed over.)
Darrel	You will NEVER give another order to me or any member of the New World Order. You will nod yes or no to my questions. If you nod the wrong answer, then you will have your nostrils closed. Good luck breathing out of your ears! (The guns were taken from the agents who were physically thrown out the bunker door. The defense shield was moved to the walls to prevent any re-entry.) Madam V.P., you will sign your resignation to the paper in front of you effective immediately.
V.P.	I can't do that. I am a duly elected…
Darrel	You will sign or die in 10 seconds. Either way, you're out of a job. (She signed.)
	Mr. President, think very carefully what you do next. (The black light emitted, beamed barely over each of his ears and

burnt into the wall behind him.) Are you going to accept this resignation right now? (He nodded yes.) Are you going to nominate my son as your new V.P.? (He nodded yes.) I expect her resignation and your nomination to reach the Senate floor in the next 30 minutes or I'll be back here in 31 minutes in a foul mood. Mr. President, if I come back your death will be the most gruesome in the history of man. Do you understand? (He nodded yes. I slowly lowered him to the floor and restored his mouth.) You should also understand that if any retaliation is attempted on me or our Inner Circle, your door is easy to enter. You cannot hide and no one can protect you.

President   Why are you doing this? You're an American.

Darrel   No, I am not. I am on God's team now. (The three of us transported to the Senate majority leader's office.) Senator, do you know who we are?

Senator   (stunned by the entry) Yes. Did you meet with the President?

Darrel   Yes. The V.P. resigned a few minutes ago. The President is nominating my son as the new V.P. I expect your full and immediate support along with that of your political party. This will take a maximum of two days to ratify.

Senator   Sir, that is incredibly presumptuous on…(My power of persuasion shut him up. He nodded agreement from that point on. He then politely requested other leaders of both parties to join in our conversation. They too were soon properly motivated, except for a fat one who died of a stroke.)

Darrel   Senators, I expect the favorable vote in two days. That vote will identify those who vote against the nomination. I will be particularly interested in that list. (We transported to the office of the Speaker of the House. A similar conversation was had with her and members of rank from both parties.) Representatives, I expect a favorable vote in two days. I'm not a good person to disappoint right now. (The President's new nomination arrived in both Houses of Congress at the 29th minute. The National Press was in overdrive. We were already in St. Louis within the safety of the defense shields.)

I had no desire to eliminate the United States or any other government. They all were needed to complete the mission and hopefully lead the post January 1 world in peace and harmony. My attack on the inept and corrupt political system today was a calculated risk. I knew if I had simply overthrown the government with a military coup, then the entire country and world would be devastated with fear of me and the mission. That would have made it impossible for the mission to succeed. Yet, I knew the mission had no chance for success if the status quo in the strongest country in the world was not destroyed. I concluded that forcing change within the current system was the mission's best chance. It was done as quietly as possible. I knew it was imperative to those in power to also keep it as quiet as possible for the time being. I knew it was impossible to keep these actions quiet forever, but time was my ally. If I could win over the masses prior to their fears blocking the path of successfully completing the mission, then today's events would merely be one of a thousand necessary acts to prevent annihilation.

Mr. John put out a press release inviting all to attend the next day's celebration. It stressed no need to bring an umbrella even though the forecast was for thunderstorms. Per Darrel, the weather would be perfect when the celebration started - trust us.

Chapter 23
St. Louis Celebration

This was our first celebration out of hundreds to come. I didn't know what to expect this soon in our mission, but the 4th of July holiday should swell the crowd. Still, too many people believed we were perpetrating a scam and the bad weather forecast would not help. However, what I did know was to expect some form of military attack. After all, they believed they had so much power and knew exactly where we'd be. It would look like shooting ducks to the supremacists in charge. Rhondell had a slightly elevated stage assembled and Mr. John had his camera crew ready to show the world.

At 11:57, Haylie was transported to the stage and introduced herself in her little girl voice. The crowd proved they needed no introduction as they went wild when she arrived. She pleaded with them to join our army and help save Earth. At 11:59, our anthem music started as did her big voice. As each new line began an Inner Circle member was transported beside her, took her hand and sang with her.

I appeared to sing the last *"and how it lifts me up"*. The light surged from my hands up to the cloudy sky. By altering the moisture content and wind speed, the clouds suddenly disappeared and a bright, mild day greeted us (to the delight of the crowd) just as Haylie finished the song.

Haylie   Grandpa, we need a cloud to shade the sun.

Darrel   What kind of cloud would you like?

Haylie	A duck cloud! (Playing to the nice sized crowd, I rolled my eyes and shook my head in desperation. Then I emitted the light, brought in moisture and formed a perfectly shaped duck.)
Darrel	How's that? (Haylie clapped as the audience oohed and aahed.)

At that point a gunshot was heard from a tall building and again as it hit the shield. The shield reflected the bullet back to the head of the shooter, killing him instantly. The crowd panicked and started to evacuate. I emitted two lightning bolts with instantaneous thunder that shocked everyone, stopping them in their tracks. I calmly implored them to stay which the vast majority did.

Darrel	You have just witnessed the first attack on the New World Order. I'm sure there will be many more until the days of vengeance eliminates them. You also witnessed the feebleness of their weaponry. I so solemnly promise you are perfectly safe at this celebration. Please stay. Let them continue to shoot and die in vain. Let us celebrate the hope we share for a better and long-lived earth. (Cheers)
Haylie	Grandpa, why would they try to hurt you?
Darrel	Darling, what you haven't seen in your life is the true beast in too many humans. Man has been dominated by the wealthy and the ruthless. We have become a threat to their power and therefore we scare them. They should be scared. They depend on the status quo keeping them in dominance. Their dominance through the years has created this poisonous planet. I so solemnly promise to the majority of people, who are the ones with goodness in their hearts and have been dominated all their lives, that it will change. Change has already begun. Every new member in our army lessens their dominance. The days of vengeance against evil starts one week from today. The days of evil's status quo are numbered! (The crowd roared.)

A regiment of 50 soldiers surged from the crowd towards the stage with rifles aimed at me. They ran into the defense shield at the stage, stopping their approach. I engulfed their leader and brought him helplessly inside the shield. His rifle was dissolved in front of all eyes to its molecular dust.

Darrel	What is your name soldier?
Soldier	Captain Dan Reynolds. You are under arrest for high treason.
Darrel	Captain Dan. You and 10 billion others like you will not arrest me for anything. If any of your men shoot, they will die from their own bullet just as the sniper did. We are here in peace today. We are here to heal many people. Captain, you are here because your superiors gave an order. You're here because you gave a vow to follow orders. That doesn't make your orders right. I can see you have no evil in your heart. I therefore have no desire to hurt you or your men who also have no evil. That is why I am merely going to disarm and transport you back to your base. I know I have to find a way around the problem when good people have promised allegiance to evil leaders. Captain, I hope we meet again when you are free to join our army. (All rifles were taken from the soldiers, placed on the stage floor and dissolved molecularly. All the soldiers were transported away unharmed.)

Now, where was I? Thank you again for staying through the interruptions. Thank you for your trust. We need you to join us. The earth's survival needs you to join us.

Did you see the report from NASA today that confirmed the two destroyers were coming at us? Yet, they calculated the odds to be a near miss. Who did this guesswork? I suspect they calculated gravitational force from the sun in their calculations. That would be true except these destroyers are made of a substance that will defy gravitational pull. I am sure NASA will recheck their findings with this variable deleted to find Earth IS the bull's eye. One more thing to those holding hope that the destroyers will miss us. God launched them. Speaking as one of two people God aimed a small funnel of light at from who knows how far away, God's aim is really good.

Haylie	Oh, GRANDPA.
Darrel	Oh, Haylie.
Haylie	The duck cloud is lonely. He needs a giraffe to play with.
Darrel	People, leave it to a child to reset priorities. Sometimes I believe they should be running the earth. I doubt if we'd be facing the mission of our lives if they were. OK Haylie, a giraffe cloud it is. But you have to draw it. Do you know how?
Haylie	Yes, Grandpa. I need to draw a shield in the shape of the giraffe and then bring in the proper moisture, pressure and temperature.
Darrel	That's correct. Hop on my shoulders. (I lifted her up and emitted the shield energy that she absorbed and created the biggest blob of a giraffe imaginable. The crowd went quiet.)
Haylie	Grandpa, how do you like my giraffe?
Darrel	Well Haylie that certainly is something. I am having difficulty finding the proper words to….
Haylie	Grandpa, I know you wouldn't lie to me because you promised.
Darrel	Haylie, darling, that is an awful giraffe. (Her bottom lip started to pout as she was not used to doing anything poorly.) Would you like to learn to do it better?
Haylie	Yes! (Enthusiastically)
Darrel	Remember when grandma taught you how to write and you tried drawing the letters. They weren't too neat either. However, when you felt the muscles you needed to write, then you allowed your hands to be directed by your mind. This is the same thing. Picture the giraffe, close your eyes and let your mind paint the cloud.
Haylie	OK, Grandpa. I'm ready to try again. (She climbed back on my shoulders, closed her eyes and formed a perfect giraffe cloud. The crowd gave her a big cheer.) How do you like that one Grandpa?

Darrel	That is perfect. The lesson to remember is to try. For all our friends out there, maybe you now understand how easy it is to teach her. How about trying her in chess Mr. John?
Mr. John	No thank you.
Darrel	On stage with me are the selected ministers of various important functions to be run by the New World Order. Their names and tasks have been well documented already. I do want to introduce my family members. Rich has received the nomination for V.P. of the U.S. and we await the House and Senate confirmation tomorrow. Peggy is a joint Minister of Charity and the third person to achieve 100% trust. If she had not, no one would be here on January 2. I guess that's about all.
Haylie	Grandpa. You forgot Mommy.
Darrel	I can never forget her. I have told others about my distaste for the in-law tag. Denise is my daughter, will strongly support the Minister of Finance and Collection, is in charge of raising Haylie and has one other important task.
Denise	That is the second time you mentioned a special task. What is it?
Darrel	It is the one God gave you.
Denise	I didn't get one.
Darrel	Sure you did. What did God say to you on Day 1?
Denise	God's hands were on Rich and my hearts. God said a child was the most precious gift. One so special was even more precious. Very Prime. Congratulations. God was being complimentary of Haylie.
Darrel	Well you heard God's words right. But you didn't hear what God said.
Denise	I don't understand.
Darrel	Let's see if those with 100% trust heard what God said. Peggy, did you hear?

Peggy	I think so.
Darrel	Just think it. (I read her mind.) That's right babe.
	Haylie, I know you heard what was said. Tell your mommy. (Haylie walked to Denise and put her hands on Denise's stomach.)
Haylie	Mommy. God said I am going to have a little brother.
Denise	(in tears) Is that true?
Darrel	You know you should never doubt your daughter. It is true. God also suggested his name.
Denise	Prime. He said very Prime though it didn't make much sense at the time. Prime!
Darrel	Know this sweetheart. Your son has great potential. Your pregnancy will be very short and very easy. Prime will be born on December 31. I will be there to assure it. We have so much to do to make sure he sees January 2. (The Inner Circle celebrated along with the crowd.)
Darrel	(to the crowd) The toughest part of our task to save Earth is to reach the goodness level God has demanded. The good people on earth have been beaten down by evil. We must stand up. You must stand up. The purpose of this and many celebrations to come is to raise both the good in the world and the number of kindred spirits who join our army of volunteers. There are four criteria to join our army:

1. You can have no evil that blackens your heart.

2. You have to have a trust level in the mission of at least 50%.

3. You must join of your own free will.

4. When called upon for a task, you must readily step forward to perform it. Only tasks that everyone can perform will be given. No battles will be fought by anyone in the army other than me. The biggest continual task for the army will be to clean up the earth.

A large benefit to joining our army will be the healing you receive equal to your trust level. Those at 50% will receive perfect eyesight and clear skin. Eyes and acne are easy fixes. Those at 60% will lose allergies, asthma and sinus problems. The 70% group will lose non-fatal diseases. The 80% group gives the power to grow missing parts of their bodies and go on the "Darrel Trust Diet". The 90% group, though very rare, will have everything healed.

The healing ability comes from the life force inside each of us. It provides the natural harmony and healing within our bodies. However, the life force has significant more healing power than the body uses. I have learned how to emit my life force, enlarge it with the exponential powers of those who trust at 100%, entwine it with other people's life force and heal those I am entwined with. The healing process comes from knowledge given by God and physics. Granted, it is a high level of physics but physics just the same. That is why I believe anyone who obtains this advanced level of knowledge will have the same power. Albert Einstein's level was at physics to the fourth power. Haylie is at physics to the fifth power already. I am at physics to the seventh. My level is the minimum level required to emit these enormous powers within all of us. I believe Haylie will eventually get to this level.

My life force must stay neutral for any act of outside healing or I start to lose mine. Once lost, it cannot be regained. I can heal without losing my life force by combining the high trust levels from others with my core power. That is why a minimum level of trust is required and joining our army of free will allows me to use it. The greater the healing required, the greater the trust level I need from others to keep my life force neutral. If the combined trust levels of a group enhanced by the power of those at 100% are neutral, then my life force is not reduced. The healing powers are enormous for the participants. That opportunity awaits all of you here today who trust at least 50% and choose to join our army. At the end of the show, I will raise my hands and ask those who want to join our army to do the same. If you trust in us, the healing light will connect me to you, lift you off your feet and heal you to the degree of your trust. I know this as most things you see and hear from me will be met with disbelief. Fight that normal adult response because disbelief walks hand-in-hand with distrust, which will stop you from joining our army. From this moment on, accept these so-called miracles you see merely as it is. That's because those so called miracles are simply physics.

Enough talk. Now we'll show some proof. Haylie has been walking through the crowd with our ministers. She has identified people with obvious physical problems and who have the trust level required to be healed. They are coming onto the stage. I ask each of you to tell of your ailment and the reason for your high trust level.

Frank	My name is Frank. I am 88 years old. I lost my arm in World War II. I have seen more evil than anyone should in a lifetime. You have taken on the duty to fight evil as I did 60 years ago. I will help however I can. The compassion you gave the soldiers who were merely doing their duty makes me trust you. The possibility of my grandchildren living in a world without evil makes me swear to give whatever I have left for the cause.
Darrel	Sir, you have an 82% trust level. Frank, extend your one arm to me. (The healing lights emitted. One light went down his good arm and the other formed a new arm. Frank fell to his knees in homage. I raised him to his feet.) Frank, no member of our army bows to anyone. We are of the same rank. Be there when I call.
Frank	Wherever and whenever. I'll be there!
Darrel	Who is this young lady?
Norma	My name is Norma. I have suffered this hunchback and have been ridiculed my entire life. I saw your compassion with the kids at the hospital. I want to help other kids and you.
Darrel	Norma, give me a hug. Your 75% level will rid you of your burden. (Seconds later, Norma was upright and a strong member of our army.)

The process was repeated for a Vietnam war vet with no legs, a homeless man beaten down by his plight, three autistic kids, a woman with a large growth on her face and a woman left pale and weak from her critical asthma condition. Those watching on TV may have believed it to be hocus pocus, but those in the crowd had to believe their own eyes.

Darrel	The power to heal from my life force is potentially large. The power to destroy is a million times larger. All I need for that power is the hate, anger, ruthlessness and evil that permeates all around us. Those with evil emit so much power. As with trust, I can absorb that power and return it a million fold. There is no power on earth that I cannot defeat. The greater the power used in an effort to destroy me only increases the magnitude of my response. How I wish this power would never have to be used. Utilizing it has grave consequences to all involved. It uses none of my life force, but it has a lasting effect. That is why I alone will fight the battles against evil. I can only plead to those with evil to lose it quickly. Those marked by God as evil will be eliminated by death. There is no joy in this duty. There is only pain. It is a duty I have so solemnly swore to God and to all on earth that I will conquer. But this is a celebration. Peggy and Haylie, can you also feel two incredibly high trust levels in the crowd?
Both	Yes. Amazingly high.
Darrel	We have to bring them on stage. They have so much potential. Over there is one. The lady in the wheel chair in the red dress, please come up here. Ministers please help her. (With a great deal of effort, she rolled on stage.) Madam, tell us your name and how someone I don't know can have a 98% level.
Maggie	My name is Maggie. I am 75-years-old and we met a long time ago. I have loved you for over 30 years.
Darrel	Well congratulations Maggie. Few things stop me in my tracks like that did. I am sorry I don't remember you, but as I know I have been totally faithful to Peggy, I will ask you to explain.
Maggie	Do you remember that terrible snow storm in December 1973?
Darrel	Do I ever. It came the day after we moved to St. Louis. It made me wonder what I was doing here.
Maggie	I was stranded in a snow bank. I had four young kids at home. I was panicking. You stopped to help. You dug me out with a

	shovel. Three times! Then you followed me home because you knew I was scared to death.
Darrel	Maggie, a lot of people would have helped you under the circumstances.
Maggie	No, most people wouldn't help! That's the trouble with people now. It is only me and I with people. I tried to pay you for your help. You would take nothing. You only gave me your first name so I couldn't find and repay you. I asked you to give me some way to repay your kindness. Do you remember what you said?
Darrel	No, I don't.
Maggie	You said to find someone else who needed help and pass it on. I swear to you and God that I have tried to help from that day forward. Then I saw you on the TV show and at the funeral. That is how I know you are whom you say and I pray I can help you save Earth.
Darrel	Thank you Maggie. But I still don't understand how you can trust at 98% from that.
Maggie	Maybe that's because you don't know the result of your kindness. When you left, I walked into my house just after a grease fire started. All the kids were upstairs with no escape as the stairs were on fire. If you had not helped get me home, then all my children would have died. You wonder how I can love you? How can I not! (Maggie started to leave the stage.)
Darrel	Whoa, Maggie, where are you going?
Maggie	You want your army to clean up earth. I am very slow so I am going to start picking up garbage now. (Laughter was everywhere as Maggie started to leave again.)
Darrel	Whoa, Maggie. First, I will but haven't yet asked our army to clean up the trash at the end of this celebration. Second, let me help you.
Maggie	Darrel, I am old. I have four kids, eight grandkids and another three months on the way. I have been in pain for 15 years. Still,

	the only thing I ask of you is to let my family see January 2. I have trash to pick up. (She started leaving again.)
Darrel	Whoa, Maggie. I welcome you with open arms to our army. You are exactly what we need. Maggie, I am exuberant at the possibility of you reaching 100% trust. Do you know what that power would do for our cause?
Maggie	If my math is right, it would increase the power of the other three from 1,000 to 10,000.
Darrel	That is absolutely correct. Let me heal you now and work on that last 2% later.
Maggie	I would welcome relief from the pain. But I am afraid it would be wasted on me as I know my life force is running low.
Darrel	It is running low. I will never tell a lie, Maggie. But your potential is so great for our short-term need. Besides, you deserve the easiest death possible when your life force subsides. (The healing light cured everything physically wrong with Maggie. She got up from her wheelchair and kissed me on the cheek.)
Maggie	Thank you. I never expected to be without pain again. Now I have to get to 100%. (She walked to the edge of the stage and turned around.) This may not be a building but I know you'll catch me. (She fell backwards in peace without so much as flailing her arms. I emitted the shield light beneath her, which caught her before she hit the ground and lifted her back on stage.)
Darrel	Maggie, please quit doing things I don't ask.
Maggie	If you insist. What level am I at now?
Darrel	Over 99%. You will get there soon. Be ready to be with us when you do. And please leave the stage now before you give me a heart attack and Haylie has to help me! (A thunderous ovation from the growing crowd of over 200,000.)

	Friends, I have so much more hope than I did 10 minutes ago. Is it possible there are more Maggie's out there than I believed? If there are, we will be successful in this mission! (Another thunderous applause.)
Darrel	There is another person out there with a high trust level. Another at the 98% level. I know this one. She is my cousin. Marianne, I know you're out there. Please come on stage. (There was no movement.) Marianne, I know you're shy but you either walk up here or you fly up here! (A woman headed for the stage.)
Marianne	You know I don't like getting up in front of people.
Darrel	Shyness is just a slight chemical adjustment away from daring. (I emitted a light and briefly touched her head.)
Marianne	Now I kind of feel like dancing up here.
Darrel	Maybe I adjusted too much. Marianne, we grew up together. We were always close. Tell everyone what I was like and absolutely do not lie. I made a lot of mistakes. But that person died, so we can talk badly about him. How is your trust level so high?
Marianne	Yes, you did make some mistakes. But they were never mistakes from lack of caring. You protected me and others from the bullies. You were always one of the two kids to choose sides for games at school and always picked kids like me who weren't very good at the game. You were a friend to everyone, not just to popular kids. You danced with those who never got asked. You helped my husband and me through some difficult moments. You helped me more when he passed away.
Darrel	OK, here's a twenty-dollar bill for that endorsement. But seriously, 98% is so high.
Marianne	My family never had an easy life. Your kindnesses helped. Maggie's story is not surprising to me at all. I feel happy that her family was saved. You are the type of man who would help other lives be saved if you can. I know you. I know you speak only the truth. And for every person who has been blessed

	with a child, I will do anything to help you stop their pending doom.
Darrel	Thank you Marianne. Do you want to see Haylie again?
Marianne	Yes. I saw her when she was a baby at her introduction party. She was already a grandpa's girl.
Haylie	Hello again Marianne. I remember you at the party.
Marianne	That's amazing, but I watched the TV show and know the correct answer is "I totally believe you do". (Haylie gave her a big hug.)
Haylie	Grandpa. Marianne has no evil and is filled with goodness but has a big sadness in her heart. (Marianne started to cry.)
Darrel	Marianne, I am so sorry. I never meant for this to hurt you.
Marianne	I know. It is all innocent.
Darrel	Haylie, Marianne has sadness because she lost her child in a tragic accident a few days ago. And when a child or grandchild (I start to break up) dies, it is the most pain there is to bear.
Haylie	Can you take away the pain?
Darrel	This is a pain that exists with nothing physically wrong. The healing light has nothing to fix.
Haylie	Will you please try?
Darrel	Yes. (With the combined power of Haylie, Peggy and myself, we hit Marianne with all the power we had.) Marianne, if you look in the mirror you will see you went on the "Darrel Trust Diet". Your lungs are now healthy after smoking for years. The ankle you broke is now perfect. The four diseases you had are gone, as well as all the joint pains you have endured. In fact, your health is now perfect because of your trust level. But I can't take the pain from your heart.
Marianne	I know. But thank you for trying. I will be there when you call.

Haylie	(with a chastising voice) Grandpa. You have such power. Your family and friends trust you so much. So many other people want to trust you. Sometimes the search for knowledge is the hardest thing. We need you to trust yourself!
Darrel	(Now I hung my head in shame.) I am so embarrassed. How can one man be so stupid? I now learn from a one-year-old. Did you hear what she said to me? Or did you only hear her words? Let me tell you what she said so tactfully. She first kicked me hard in the butt. Then she said we are here today because a large part of our mission is to gain trust from people around the world. But the first time a problem surfaces that I don't know the answer to, I have no faith in myself and I give up. Is that right darling?
Haylie	I didn't kick you in the butt Grandpa. (Loud laughter)
Darrel	Yes you did! You just didn't use your foot. And not near hard enough! Haylie, I will make you and the world another promise. This is the last time I fail for not trying. I may fail, but only after the effort is expended. We need all the power we can get. Maggie I need you up here! (Maggie sprinted to the stage.)
Haylie	Grandpa, I want the sadness out of Marianne, but you have to promise not to give away your life force to do it. The mission has to take priority.
Darrel	Agreed. Maggie, I need you to cross the line now! (Maggie turned around and started walking.) Maggie, it won't happen by falling off the stage again.
Maggie	I know. This time I'm going to the top of the Arch to fall.
Darrel	Oh, Maggie stop. Look out at the crowd and tell me what you see.
Maggie	I see…some people…glowing! My kids and grandkids are all glowing very brightly. And you, and Haylie, and Peggy and… me all glow so brightly!
Darrel	Maggie, I am so pleased you have joined the 100% crowd. Marianne, I have to learn something and I need all our power. The four of us will hold hands in a ring around you. We will

	not touch you, but I am going to hit you with all the power we have. I want you to let all your emotions flow. (The light emitted and reached the power of 10,000, then 100,000 and then leapt to 10 million which sent me flying backwards onto the floor.)
Haylie	Grandpa, are you all right! You're weakened. (I emitted the light that the other three 100% enhanced and gave back to me.)
Darrel	I feel great and I have learned some important things. I have learned I cannot take the sadness away from your heart, Marianne.
Marianne	I know, but you all tried so hard.
Darrel	However, I did learn that you Marianne could take your sadness away.
Marianne	How?
Darrel	You have to join me at 100%. You have to let all your negative emotions flow out. You have to believe everything is possible when we connect. And I have to push you to the limit. Are you ready?
Haylie	Grandpa, do you need my help? It weakened you so before.
Darrel	Yes, darling, hold onto my belt. It was the search for knowledge that was exhausting. Now it's up to Marianne. Marianne, are you ready?
Marianne	I don't know.
Darrel	You better know! ARE YOU READY?
Marianne	Yes.
Darrel	Put your arms around my neck. I will put one hand on your heart and one on the side of your face. Answer my questions from your heart not your brain. Don't think! Just answer! Why is there sadness in your heart?
Marianne	(Crying) Because my son Bennett was taken from me.

Darrel	Close your eyes. Picture his face. Do you see it?
Marianne	Yes
Darrel	What is left of him?
Marianne	His son that survived him.
Darrel	WHAT ELSE?
Marianne	My memories.
Darrel	Feel him in your womb as when you were pregnant with him.
Marianne	I can't!
Darrel	DO IT! Feel him grow inside. Smell his breath! Hear his laughter!
Marianne	He had a wonderful laugh.
Darrel	Marianne, there is so much anger in you. Get rid of it!
Marianne	But I am so angry that he was taken!
Darrel	Yes! And it's stopping you from achieving 100%! Get rid of it!
Marianne	HOW?
Darrel	Give it to me! Then give me your trust! You have the answer! Get rid of the sadness!
Marianne	I beg of you. Tell me how?
Darrel	WHAT DOES IT TAKE TO GET RID OF YOUR SADNESS?
Marianne	BRING MY SON BACK!
Darrel	Marianne. I am so proud of you. You have crossed over the line. You have given me everything I need. Your love has totally defined your son. Your anger is gone. His makeup is in your genes. His life force duck is within you. You need to do one more simple thing to lose your sadness.
Marianne	I'll do anything!

Darrel	Open your eyes. (The healing light started creating behind her.) Your gift of love and trust has allowed Bennett to be recaptured as he was. All you have to do to lose your sadness is turn around and give him an overdue hug.

Marianne turned around and fell to the floor in shock, seeing her re-formed son. He fell to the floor to her. The shrieks of joy and love were overwhelming and ongoing. The crowd alternated between disbelief, happiness, awe, more disbelief and elevated levels of trust. I sat with Peggy, Maggie and Haylie taking it all in. I thought back to our family hug three days ago and thoroughly enjoyed a re-creation of that scene before us now. For nearly 20 minutes the tears, hugs, kisses and laughter continued. Finally, from exhaustion, they came and kneeled before us.

Darrel	I am assuming you two will be joining our army. (Loud laughter)
Both	Anything. Anywhere. Anytime.
Darrel	Then I repeat myself from earlier today. Stand up. No member of our army bows before anyone. Marianne, I will need you to join us tomorrow for an incredible day. I will need your power.
Marianne	I will be there. No day can be as incredible as this one. (They were escorted off the stage.)
Darrel	We will test Marianne's last remark.
Haylie	Grandpa, I have some questions.
Darrel	I thought you might.
Haylie	What made the power go from 10,000 to 100,000 to 10 million without using your life force?
Darrel	I learned a way to take my trust from 100% to 101% by boosting the speed around the trust circle. That boost put another exponential factor to our group, taking it to 100,000. What is the most powerful emotion?
Haylie	Trust, but the power went beyond that.

Darrel	Hear what I say. What is the most powerful emotion?
Haylie	Hate and anger, but you had neither of those emotions towards us. And it had to be present to be used.
Darrel	It was present. The anger of Marianne and myself from the day of the accident was enough to take the power two more exponential leaps. That still couldn't totally flood Marianne's body but was enough for me to learn what I needed.
Haylie	What was that Grandpa?
Darrel	Recall the Rothweger theory of living matter. What were the two flaws?
Haylie	He did not allow for the unknown flow of the life force. Therefore, his theory revolved around a constant area for life to move within and we know that is not the case. Therefore, life can be transported between portals. The second flaw was on the genetic level of parental transfer, but he disallowed the parental retainage of the gene. Therefore, the gene can be reconstructed from its last occurrence or from the mother. Grandpa, that is brilliant, but only effective once you find the duck. How did you do that with 10 million of power versus the 10 billion required?
Darrel	And if the polarity of the life force were reversed?
Haylie	GRANDPA! You made a duck magnet!
Darrel	Yes. It is so much easier to find what comes looking for you.
Haylie	Grandpa, that makes restitution day closer.
Darrel	It gets better. What do we now know to be the flaw in Hinesdorff's theory on the difference between living and mineral cells?
Haylie	He incorrectly theorized mineral cells could not be altered by outside forces. But we know your energy power can do just that, to dissolve them molecularly. And Grandpa, if that process is reversed then….reclamation day is possible too.
Darrel	Excellent. Let's test it. (I emitted the red matter transfer light in reverse, directed it towards where the guns had been, and

reassembled them molecularly. Haylie and I both smiled, as we knew a big obstacle for the mission had been removed. The guns were dissolved again.) Tomorrow is the day, Haylie! (I looked around and noticed the stunned crowd, realizing we were so engrossed we had forgotten them.)

Can you believe this all happened because a one-year old pointed out my obvious fault of not trying? And just after I told her of its importance. Haylie, the next time you see me failing, you give grandpa a swift kick in the butt without mincing words.

Haylie	But, Grandpa, I can't get my foot that high. (The crowd cracked up.)
Darrel	Well, then ask me to bend down. (more laughter)
Haylie	OK Grandpa. (The crowd roared.)
Darrel	I apologize to everyone for ignoring you. What you just witnessed was a tremendous learning session. Haylie advanced to physics to the sixth power today. She is merely one level away from emitting power on her own. Near, yet very far away. I just reached physics to the eighth power. Tomorrow the world will see what we learned. Tomorrow is Reclamation and Restitution day. We will be visiting the school tragedy site in Baghdad. I invite all who felt those losses to join us.

Friends, I am exhausted. That proves I am merely mortal. We have had a heck of a day, haven't we? (A roar came from the crowd.) However, you still have the opportunity to join our army if you choose and trust. I am going to walk into the crowd to simply be with you and touch those who trust. There is no need to rush me as everyone will have the opportunity shortly. Three songs will play. The third will be Haylie and our Inner Circle singing our anthem. I will rejoin them on stage and sing the last chorus. At that point, I will raise my arms. If you want to join us, all you have to do is the same. Those with adequate trust levels without evil, blackened-hearts will connect with my healing energy. They will be lifted up and healed to the degree of their trust level. We need billions of people in our worldwide army. St. Louis, lead the way! And new army members, I command you and ask all others to completely clean up these grounds before you leave.

As *"What the World Needs Now is Love"* followed by *"Colors of the Wind"* play, I met the crowd and healed those qualified in the process. Haylie and gang started our anthem. As the last chorus started I was back on stage.

Darrel   You heal my wounds with just a touch …and fill my loving cup

Your precious love lights up my life…and how it lifts me up…….

As the words "lifts me up" were strongly sung, I raised both arms into the air emphatically. Those in the crowd who chose to join our army raised their arms. The healing light connected between me and those who qualified for our army, lifted them off the ground and healed everything the individual's trust level allowed as promised.

As Haylie finished the song, I was saddened that only 40,000 people became new army members. It was a number not near what I'd hoped for nor what we needed at each stop to reach our goal. On the other hand, two more reached the 100% trust level. That was more than I had hoped for during the entire time we had left. That fact, the coverage we received, and the knowledge learned made for an outstanding day. As the song ended, the entire Inner Circle huddled together and transported home.

That night, I went on the offensive again. I made another visit to our illustrious president. After again getting his attention and dealing with the agents, I spoke to him in a manner even he could understand. I told him I'd hold him personally responsible for the next attack on anyone in the New World Order. In fact, I would enjoy making him an example to the world. Then I visited the Speaker of the House and Senate Majority Leader and gently reminded them of tomorrow's deadline for confirmation.

Chapter 24
Restitution and Reclamation Day

This could be the most important day to accomplish our mission. If we pull this off, then the world could never again deny the legitimacy of our mission or power. It started with Mr. John and I transporting into the Al Jazeera television headquarters. We met with the president and managers of the network. We demanded one of their cameras and broadcast crew to accompany us. They would validate the events that were about to happen to the Muslim world.

The president went into a tirade, stating he would never be a pawn to such propaganda. Then he pointed at us, started shouting and burst- literally, when the anger light exploded him all over the walls and the others not surrounded by a shield. We found the second in charge to be most helpful. He suggested we take his best cameraman and anchorman. After talking with those two about honest reporting and the specific questions they were to ask, we deemed them satisfactory. The four of us transported to St. Louis to unite with the entire Inner Circle. Somehow, a small buzzing noise entered my head.

Early yesterday morning, an unbelievable attack claimed many lives in Baghdad. Another suicide bomber unleashed a powerful explosion. This time it was at an elementary school. 173 kids and 23 adults perished in another senseless act of hate. At 8:59 AM, our contingent transported to the hideous site of the school ruins. Tens of thousands of spectators had shown up as well as ten TV crews. We arrived with no pomp and no music.

Immediately, we were attacked by men with rifles and rocket propelled grenades. The shield sent the bullets and grenades back to the senders, killing them instantly. Without acknowledging the attacks, I addressed the crowd.

Darrel   Yesterday, we learned some very important things.

    1. The footprint of all matter stayed at its' last intact place.

    2. We learned inanimate objects could be reconstructed from their footprint in the last position the structures were whole.

    3. We found the way to locate the life force of individuals left behind.

    4. We found if a death was recent enough, one where the life force had not yet perished, then the life-form could be recaptured.

    5. We found two incredible people that crossed the line to 100%. The power of those two combined with the original three raised our base power to 100,000. When Rich, Mr. John and Rhondell formed a pod, our power was nearly 300,000.

    6. We needed 1,000 power units per person to find and recapture the lost life forces at the school.

    Today, we plan to eliminate all doubt as to the power and mission of the New World Order. We plan to recreate the school and recapture the lost life forces. The bomber will also be recaptured and interviewed by the Al Jazeera crew to answer specific questions. Then I will show the world what is coming on vengeance day for all with evil-marked hearts.

The other 100% formed a ring around me. The light was emitted and circled around the schoolyard. The footprints of the school and all those inside were located. The school was reconstructed just as it was before exploding. The healing light emitted and hit the school with one pinpoint ray. The bomber was recaptured, brought out of the school and thrown against a tree. He stayed suspended off the ground. Mr. John escorted the Al Jazeera crew to him for an interview and returned to the pod. The healing light engulfed the school and recaptured the 196 remaining kids and adults. Our Inner Circle helped them out of the school. The emotions that ensued were simply beyond description. Those in the crowd that had come with hope rushed their loved ones. Our army increased by nearly 100% of everyone there. When things finally settled down, all of the Inner Circle were transported to the New York hotel room. I did not want Haylie to see what happened next.

The Al Jazeera interview of the bomber showed the world new insights. He was bewildered that the bomb had not exploded and that all of us had suddenly showed up. He refused to believe what the TV crew told him had transpired, as well as the day's date. In his mind, no time had passed since the point of his dastardly deed. There was no mention of any virgins that had visited him. I ordered everyone to move away from him.

Darrel   Everyone should watch what happens next, regardless of how gruesome it may be. The fate of this evil being will be the fate of all those with evil everywhere in the world. In six days, vengeance of the worst evil begins. There is no hope for those in that group. You can no longer hide or be protected by your power. Vengeance of all others with evil begins on day 48. Those people have time to get rid of their evil before it is too late. Evil, you only understand power. Watch the power God has given me to come after you!

My intent was for the vengeance to be horrific. I believed a gruesome death would persuade millions of others to lose their evil. I knew the truly evil would only respect absolute power. Then I realized that the truly evil could never be converted. Torture would only repulse and turn away the good from our cause. That fact decided a merciful death was best. However, I questioned if my final decision against torture was simply not being strong as God had told me to be. In the end, the anger-enhanced light blew him to oblivion and another buzzing noise began inside my head. I turned to the cameras.

Darrel   Evil ones around the world, I AM COMING FOR YOU! (I transported to the New York hotel.)

The mood was somber within the Inner Circle. All but Haylie had witnessed the public vengeance. Even they were not ready for it. We again talked about the mission and all the death that lay ahead. The Circle was comprised of great people. Vengeance was despicable to good people. I repeated that was why I alone would fight those battles. I alone would pay the price from them. Together we would have to do whatever was necessary to complete the mission, or vengeance would come for every living thing on earth. Their trust in me couldn't waver. They assured me it would not.

I told the Inner Circle I had a House and Senate vote to sit in on. I transported to the Senate floor just as the confirmation hearings were completed. Normally, the vote was taken the next day. I was pleased that my highly noticeable entrance to the Senate balcony coincided with their decision to vote on Rich's confirmation immediately. The vote was 99 to 0 for the nomination. Upon my purely chance meeting with the Speaker of the House, she indicated the hearings were still ongoing. I assured her that was perfectly fine as I had some important business in New York. Fine, that was, as long as I could make an announcement before I was done there. If not, I would change my schedule and return to visit House members one final time.

Mr. John notified the world as to our 2:59 PM celebration scheduled at the former World Trade Center site. The crowd had been gathering for hours and was massive. I called the Inner Circle together to discuss a problem.

Darrel	There is a huge crowd gathering. It is hard to tell how much power we may need at the end. We may have a power shortage with our core 100,000. That leaves three options:
	1. Use the pod power to enhance the core to a maximum of 300,000 and repeat the process many times. I am concerned that using more fractional power to increase the pod will not be stable. And we need all the stability we can get. I am also concerned that any partial healing will appear to be a weakness and actually be detrimental in the long run.
	2. I can again increase my factor to 101%, raising our core to 1,000,000 power units. Adding the pod power to that will be 2.9 million. But my control is challenged when I achieve that level. Therefore, my concerns for stability are again a problem.
	3. We can cancel until a later date when we have more power. This probably makes the most sense, but we will lose

Haylie	Grandpa, if you show me how, I will get to the 101%.
Darrel	Absolutely not. Doing so has a price to pay and you will not pay it.
Rich	Is it possible for a pod at a 29 level to be stable enough?
Darrel	I don't think so. At least not now. I don't know how to best use the pod power at this time. And we can't afford to guess what may happen if we are not stable.
Rich	Dad, come with me. I have something to show you. (He took me to the balcony.) I know I have to be so close to 100%. (Then he stepped onto the ledge and fell off backwards.)
Darrel	(I was caught off guard and instantly panicked. I ran to the ledge and emitted the light that caught and returned him to the balcony. The Circle rushed out.) Son, don't ever do that again! There is no guarantee that act will let you cross the line. And there is no guarantee I can catch you!
Rich	Dad, the guarantee is my faith in you and our mission. Why has everyone started glowing?
Darrel	Oh, Rich. The next Vice-President has just received a higher promotion. You are our sixth at 100% trust. We now have a core power of 1 million. With a stable pod power of 2.9 from Mr. John, Denise and Rhondell, we are ready to go to work.

the opportunity for tremendous gains to our army that we desperately need.

We received word that the House had voted 410 to 25 for Rich's confirmation just before we started. All but Haylie and I were transported to a hastily constructed, elevated stage at 2:58. At 2:59, our anthem began to play as the other 100%'s joined hands in a circle. I transported into the middle of the circle with Haylie on my shoulders. Haylie sang our anthem as I emitted the light over the building construction taking place on the site. All workers and their belongings were gently lifted up and placed on the ground off the Trade Center site. The light was refocused on the new construction, dissolving it molecularly into a fine mist. There was complete silence in the massive crowd. They had no idea what was about to happen.

Darrel	What more does the world need to see to start trusting in our word, our mission and us. If we choose, everyone on earth would be dead in seconds. We have the power to do that. We can do nothing and everyone will be dead on January 1. What the New World Order does not have the power to do is increase the level of goodness on earth. Only the people of earth can increase that level. If we don't accomplish that, then our fate on January 1 is the same annihilation. We need to achieve a two billion goodness factor or we will never see January 2.
	The vengeance of the worst begins six days from today. Our first stop will be back here in the greater New York area. No place on earth has the evil levels of greed, intolerance of other race, religions and nationalities, drugs, gangs and crime bosses as exists here. Millions will die here next week from their evil. They cannot run away and hide elsewhere, as their footprint is here now. The vengeance light will seek them out, regardless where they are next Wednesday. Those with evil here have six days to rid themselves of it. I hope they do.
	The world witnessed the power of our mission today in Baghdad. It saw the recapture of 196 innocent victims. A body that died of unnatural forces left a trace of their life force for a few days. Unfortunately, it was impossible to recapture life forces after that short time period. Otherwise, all victims could be recaptured. However, inanimate objects permanently leave their footprint where they last were whole. After today, the world could never again deny our power or mission.
	The full-powered light was emitted from each hand. The ground began to rumble. As my hands lifted, the Twin Towers started rising as they existed before they fell and before they were struck. Four million people at one place were dead silent. In fifteen minutes the New York skyline was restored.
Darrel	These Twin Towers are now the property of the New World Order. Shields are around both of them that will not allow unauthorized entry. The top fifteen floors of one will be converted to our Inner Circle's New York offices and residences. The remainder will become housing units for our most trusting army members with need.

Does anyone feel like celebrating with us?

The positive response was deafening. The celebration began with extreme enthusiasm. The party made their Times Square New Year's Eve party look tame. There was music, dancing and healings. We invited those who wanted to sing to come on stage. New Yorkers were not shy. One that joined us was outstanding. Her name was Deidra. She starred on Broadway. She hoped some day we would visit her there. I asked if tonight was alright and she beamed her answer. I went into the crowd amongst a group of homeless. I beamed light into a local fast food restaurant and withdrew hundreds of sandwiches, fries and sodas for my new friends to enjoy. Some group started "The Wave" and I thought the whole island started moving.

The celebration went on for three hours. The people weren't ready to stop, but we were exhausted.

Darrel   I want to thank you so much for this magnificent celebration. There will be no joy when I return next week. Only pain and death for the evil await. But today, those with no evil and enough trust in their hearts are about to receive the opportunity to join our army. Haylie will sing our anthem again. When I join her, I will raise my arms. If those qualified choose to join us, then raise your arms with me. The healing light will connect you with me, lift you up and heal you to the level of your trust. If you will not join our army now, God help us all.

The music began and Haylie and our Circle sang. As I joined them for the last chorus, I raised my arms. En masse, the crowd did likewise. We had 3.2 million new army members.

Darrel   Thank you for joining us. We have received word that my son and Inner Circle member, Rich, has been confirmed as the new V.P. of the U.S. (huge ovation). This is the first step to cleaning up the political mess in this country. (More applause) For the next five days, we are going around the world in celebration and to ask for new army members. However, tonight our Inner Circle is going to the theater. I can sense a new army member as of today will entertain us.

This city has long been a pigsty. New army members and everyone else, leave no mess behind today. Then go clean up your neighborhoods. Army, we can be the first planet to ever succeed in God's second chance. It is up to all of us. (We transported back to the hotel amidst thunderous applause.)

The entire Inner Circle was ecstatic with our huge day. We had to add billions to the goodness factor to reach our goal. However, they didn't all have to be in our army. Goodness would count in any form or place. I knew we had made great strides. Untold millions had to be reached with the worldwide coverage. A night at the theater seemed a just reward before our around the world celebration tour began. As with every location we were either at or destined for, a shield was always put in place for our security. That shield also formed the boundary to detect anything amiss inside per God's grant of the tenth power requested. We were nearly ready to transport to the theater boxes that Rhondell had arranged when I felt something amiss at the theater.

Darrel   I know something is wrong at the theater. Stay here until I get back.

I transported into the lobby of the theater, which was unusually empty for ten minutes before show time. I heard a ruckus inside and went in. I asked an usher what was wrong. He said the cast had been practicing a tribute for special guests when the star of the show fell off the stage. She was badly hurt. I walked down the aisle to where paramedics were working feverishly over a young woman.

Darrel   Can I help?

Paramedics (without looking up) Stay back. She is badly hurt.

Deidra   (She spoke through her serious physical and mental pain.) It's you. I was with you today. (Murmurs went through the crowd.)

Darrel   And you joined our army today, didn't you?

Deidra   I couldn't wait to join. I was so excited when you said you were coming here tonight. We were practicing something special for you when I fell.

Darrel	Would you like me to take over for the paramedics?
Deidra	Please.
Darrel	(I took her hand.) Deidra, I will never lie. Your spinal cord has been broken and you are paralyzed from the neck down. It takes so much trust for me to fix something so serious.
Deidra	(crying hysterically) I wanted to sing so much for you, your family, and friends.
Darrel	Oh, Deidra, why do you think you won't? You are at 88% trust and that is enough to heal your injuries. (The healing light performed its task and Deidra was soon on her feet.)
Deidra	I am so thankful. I am so honored. I will do anything you ask of me.
Darrel	Make this a special night for Haylie. She loves the theater. And consider joining us for the upcoming celebrations around the world. (Without waiting for an answer, I transported back to the hotel.)

I told the Circle of the events and that the show was still on. We transported to the empty lobby and walked to our boxes. The audience stood as we sat. To our surprise, the orchestra started playing our anthem. The show's entire cast came on stage with Deidra singing lead in the center. After the first chorus, Deidra pointed at Haylie and waved for her to come to the stage. Haylie's excited look flashed her answer to me and I transported her to the stage. Deidra and Haylie sang the remainder as a duet. At the now known *"And how it lifts me up"* point in the song, the entire audience raised their arms. The entire Inner Circle obliged in kind.

It made only a small addition to our army, but was gratifying that others initiated it. At song's end, the Inner Circle rose as one in ovation. Deidra and Haylie hugged. Deidra had made this a special night for Haylie. Then her performance in *"The Phantom of the Opera"* made it special for all of us. After the final ovations and bows Deidra approached the front of the stage and asked for quiet.

Deidra	Darrel, if you were serious about me joining your team, then this was my final performance here. (I immediately transported her to our boxes.)
Darrel	Don't bother packing. Rhondell will have everything you need in your room tonight. We will be in Chicago at 8:59 tomorrow morning. Welcome! (We transported to the hotel.)

Chapter 25
World Celebrations

The day began with Rich and I transporting to Washington, D.C. for his early morning swearing-in ceremony as Vice-President. Then we immediately transported back to the New York hotel as we had more important duties that awaited us than any political duties that others felt should be his priority.

Before departing for Chicago on day 6, I had strategy meetings with Roy, Marilee, Tim and Joan. Marilee needed to outline the massive changes to education. The overall criteria was to return school systems to teaching and learning and away from dancing around parents, lawyers, funding, status quo and kids and teachers that didn't want to be there. I asked Joan to start prioritizing the charity distributions and to think as large and widespread as she could. Remember, we were on a worldwide basis. I asked Tim to start initiating talks with facilities and personnel of his choice worldwide. We would have a new energy source that would eliminate all others. We needed the capacity to produce it worldwide for greatest efficiency of distribution. He had carte blanche to put a system in place in 30 days. Roy had the toughest task of all. He would dictate what high percentage of funds would be due from every company and every wealthy individual (as he would define) and notify the world of it. On days 19-23, he and I would start collections. Afterwards, they were all transported home to begin their tasks.

Mr. John relayed our schedule to the press. We transported to the steps of Chicago's Sears Tower at precisely 8:59AM with Deidra singing our anthem. The crowd filled the entire area. There was no traffic as all streets were packed with people. I was impressed with the size of the crowd on a Friday morning and highly encouraged that yesterday had been worth all the effort. With Deidra on board, the celebrations were more entertaining. We alternated between songs and serious discussions. The new V.P. gave his vision of changes necessary in the government which rocked the status quo. However, I doubt if his political boss thought highly of his remarks. The crowd was also surprised the V.P. could sing country songs very well. As it turned out, Mr. John was brilliant in choreographing and directing our celebration routine. Then again, nothing was routine when it came to acts of healing.

Peggy noticed Siamese twins with their parents in the crowd. She asked Rhondell to bring them on stage. The mother was a small, meek woman and the father was a hulk of a man. I immediately knew there was a problem coming. Still, I asked Haylie and Peggy to talk to them and evaluate their trust levels. They too could sense the problem once the family was on stage and looked at me in wonder at my request as I went into the crowd. Warily, Haylie approached the two-year-old twins. She took their hands and asked about their trust. She made sure the crowd knew that like most children their level was very high. Peggy asked the mother, Lyndell, about her life and trust in our mission and us. They held hands as Lyndell quietly and warily spoke. Haylie then approached the father, Butch. A few feet from him, she started screaming that he had so much evil in his heart.

Butch	(Threateningly) Why you no good little…(Rich, Rhondell and Mr. John immediately headed to intervene, but I instantly transported one foot from the hulk's face.)
Darrel	You were saying!
Butch	I didn't mean…
Darrel	Yes you did. Bullies always mean what they say until someone punches them in the nose. Let's see what I can guess about you. You are big, strong, mean, loud and love to intimidate those that are weaker. You blame your wife for the Siamese twins, but I assure you their condition came about from your

	genes not hers. I can feel the fear in Lyndell because…you beat her routinely.
Butch	Did that bitch tell you that?
Darrel	That LADY screams for freedom from your sorry self without saying a word. (I emitted a light to the sound system and Martina McBride's *Independence Day* started playing.) Lyndell, I offer you that freedom today.
Butch	You have no right to speak to my wife!
Darrel	Lyndell, if you place your trust in me, he will never hurt you again. If you place enough trust in me, your twins will have a much better life. You don't have to say a word. Just nod yes or no. (She hesitantly nodded yes and moved behind me.)
Butch	You're gonna regret that big time lady. Get the kids cause we're…
Darrel	(The light stopped the music.) Have you heard the words in the song Butch?
Butch	No! And I don't care!
Darrel	You should hear them Butch because they talk about you and every other despicable wife and spouse beater. Bullies, such as you, depend on intimidation and fear to stop anyone from helping those precious innocent people such as Lyndell.
	But Butch, I'm changing the next line in the song to:
	But this time out, one man stands and shouts… I T ' S INDEPENDENCE DAY!

Butch turned his back and then quickly turned to sucker-punch me. His hand broke as he discovered the strength of the shield.

Darrel	You have the evil of greed! You have the evil of intolerance to virtually everyone you have encountered! You have the evil of damaging the earth! In fact, you have the blackest heart we have seen to date. You are everything that God has sent me to destroy! Your only benefit to this earth is to fertilize the

flowers! (The light lifted him high into the sky and the anger light blew him to dust that simply drifted away.)

Lyndell, you may have worries for your survival. You won't have to worry. Our army will be provided for. When our anthem plays again, if you are of strong trust for our cause, you will never worry again. I so solemnly promise.

I went back into the crowd as Deidra and Haylie sang solos. The third song was our anthem which the two sang together. Peggy went to Lyndell and took her hands. Peggy smiled big at Lyndell's trust level and encouraged her to sing the chorus with the other two. She did so reluctantly on the first chorus, but strongly on the second with Peggy's urging. I returned to the stage at the start of the third verse taking Lyndell's hands and smiling my approval of her 83% trust. I took the sweater off the twins, folded it together once and separated it into two small sweaters that I handed to Peggy. I picked the twins up and engulfed us in the healing light. In a few seconds we exited the light, I separated my arms, and the newly separated and perfectly formed twins appeared. I handed one each to Peggy and Lyndell as I joined in singing the song at the key "And how it lifts me up" with my arms in the air. A massive amount of arms in the crowd rose and a large portion were lifted up but none higher than Lyndell. As the song ended, my ribs were temporarily bruised from Lyndell's hug. I smiled as I knew they would heal fast. Rhondell was thrilled to be able to help her start her new life. We transported to the Los Angeles hotel.

The beach at Santa Monica was chosen for our Los Angeles area visit. Our anthem announced our arrival with Haylie and Denise arriving in swimsuits. A very large crowd filled the massive beach and boardwalk area. I could only guess our populist "Save the Earth" theme resounded well in this eco-friendly state. As I greeted the crowd and set the seed for joining our army, Haylie tugged on my hands.

Haylie	Is that ugly haze what they call smog?
Darrel	Yes darling. It is one of many ways that man has poisoned the earth.
Haylie	Grandpa, please make it go away.

Darrel	To make it go away everywhere we have to stop using fossil fuels. That is why we are developing our new source of clean energy. Today, we are announcing a new energy product that will eliminate the use of gasoline, diesel and coal as energy sources. In 12 days, our Minister of Energy will demonstrate our new energy source and plans for production and distribution. Our intent is to provide the product to the world for next to nothing. (Huge cheers.) Did anyone hear the sound of management at Exxon Mobil just fall off their chairs? Or was that the sound of their stock price hitting the floor? Our Minister of Finance and Collections and I will be visiting them before long to discuss those ridiculous profits they have posted from the backs of the people.
Haylie	Grandpa. Can you get rid of that ugly smog today so we can celebrate with our new friends in the sunshine?
Darrel	Yes, but you tell me how.
Haylie	Well, smog is made up of nasty compounds of elements such as carbon dioxide, methane, nitrogen oxides, and volatile organic compounds (VOC) such as benzenes. Nitrous oxides and VOC's form most ground level ozone, or smog. This ozone is harmful versus that in our stratosphere that is critical to protecting earth from the sun's ultraviolet radiation. Some of the compounds are natural in nature while others come mostly from man's doings. Compounds are formed when elements have covalent bonds of common electrons. It takes an energy source such as your energy light to break down the bonds of the compounds into their basic elemental structure. You need to break the compounds down into their carbon, oxygen, hydrogen and nitrogen elements. (A round of applause surged from our ecology friendly crowd.)
Darrel	Congratulations, you have passed chemistry 101 for the millionth time. (The sky was hit with the energy light. As the nasty compounds broke down the smog disappeared, as the individual gaseous elements were invisible. The crowd buzzed in wonderment.) My friends, it is not possible to eliminate smog everywhere by this method. There is too much of it and too little time. The new energy source is that answer. (More applause.)

Haylie	Thanks Grandpa. Mommy and I are going in the water. Is it all right if other kids come play with us?
Darrel	Absolutely! Anyone who wants to join them is welcome. (I started the spiel of the importance of the army when Haylie returned in just a few minutes.)
Haylie	Grandpa, the water is sooooo cold! Will you please heat it up for us?
Darrel	Alright, but we have to be careful not to harm the fish and plant life. (We had everyone get out of a small area of the water. A shield was formed at the water's edge and gently moved away from shore, escorting the fish out of the soon-to-be heated pool.) Haylie, I need a small bit of anger for the anger light to heat things up. What do you suggest?
Haylie	Exxon Mobil! (The crowd laughed.)
Darrel	That's my girl. (The anger light entered the new pool and raised the temperature to 84 degrees.)
Haylie	Thanks Grandpa. (She went off with her many new friends into the water.)
Denise	Uh huh! And who said they would never spoil her? (She walked to the water as the crowd laughed.)
Darrel	At least I didn't turn the water into --- CHOCOLATE! (More laughter)

The show continued with Deidra and Rich entertaining, specific acts of healing, serious conversation and the usual final anthem for army inductees. The new recruits continued to strengthen at each site as a percentage of the total. We were making progress. Then we left for Honolulu. Haylie chose Waikiki Beach as she hadn't got enough of the water. With its expansive area, it also worked well for a large crowd. Besides, the water was already warm enough for Haylie and her new friends. Everything continued to go well as we prepared for our first foreign country celebration the next day. We wondered what our reception would be.

We transported to Tokyo for the night. Our reception at the hotel and at the Kabuki Theater was fantastic. I think Peggy enjoyed the performance even more than Haylie.

The next day we transported to the Peace Park in Hiroshima. This was the site of many international peace rallies and that was exactly what we wanted ourselves considered to be. There was no way to predict the magnitude of the crowd. It was so large that it was very difficult for anyone to move. We were concerned for everyone's safety. It was also a culture more civilized to each other than we were used to. The respect and excitement of the crowd allayed any fears we had. The acts of healing were reacted to with reverence more than surprise. Our newest entourage member from the Kabuki performance, Lin Yang, wowed the crowd with her gracefulness. Our army received 4.1 million new members. Haylie saw the giant pandas before we left for Seoul.

Our 11:59 Seoul celebration was held in Namsan Park. We tried to select a large expanse of open ground, but the crowd again consumed the area. Again, we were received with great respect. The visit was hassle-free and buoyant to our spirits and army count. We managed to go atop the Seoul Tower before heading to our most unknown site -Peking, China.

To make a point, Tiananmen Square was chosen as our site. Mr. John informed the world press that he and I would pre-visit the site at 2:00. We decided that if any problem with the government awaited, they should be ready by then. They were. When we transported into the square, we were surrounded by hundreds of tanks and 100,000 troops. The commander in charge told us to submit to arrest or be destroyed. I emitted the light that sealed the commander's mouth shut to prevent another order being given.

Once again we were faced with the infuriating problem of good people that had sworn to follow orders from evil superiors. I pleaded with the troops to not fire their weapons at us because anyone who did would be killed instantly when the shield deflected the bullets back to their senders. I told them that we wanted them to live and join our army of peace. I asked them to question why we desperately wanted them to live whereas their superiors seemed hell-bent to send them to their deaths in vain.

I emitted the light that unsealed the commander's mouth and pleaded with him not to order the troops to a certain death. He told them to open up their fire. While Mr. John recorded their onslaught on camera for the world to see, every militiaman that fired his weapon was killed by that same bullet which deflected back from the shield. Then every tank that fired was destroyed in a likewise manner. Those that did not fire obliged my request to put their weapon or tank in a pile. The weapons were molecularly dissolved. As the commander had not personally fired upon us, he was still standing. I told him to tell his bosses that we would hold our celebration at 2:59 as planned. If any further militant action was taken against us or any person showing up for the celebration at anytime in the future, then I would personally return and hold the Chinese President responsible for the action.

The celebration took place as scheduled in front of only 50,000 courageous souls. Yet, it was the first time we received 100% of the participants into our army. Additionally, hundreds of millions of the Chinese people would witness the events of the day from one informational source or another. Then to further irritate the Chinese government, we spent the night in Hong Kong, site of the next morning's celebration.

The Hong Kong reception was, well, it was beyond comprehension. I thought it was in expectation of our entourage as well as to thumb their noses at mainland China's autocratic powers. They participated in the songs like it was karaoke. They listened intently to our message. They were deeply interested in the words from the Vice-President about perceived changes in the world political arena. They were so interested in joining the army and its healing effects that they jumped the gun a couple of times in raising their arms. In short, it was a delightful celebration.

Our next celebration was in Lumpini Park in Bangkok. Once again we were in cramped quarters. That couldn't be helped in this city of dense population. The crowd was large and cordial but more reserved. Still, we faced no resistance and the stop was smooth. We visited the Grand Palace and Wat Phra Kaeo Temple before we left the country.

We transported to Nehru Park in Delhi, India for the final celebration of the day. Once again we enjoyed a peaceful celebration in cramped quarters. Again, the people were considerate to each other as well as to us. The show went without a hitch, but we had little audience excitement. Still, we received the exposure we needed in this part of the world. We all rested well from exhaustion before heading to Europe.

The next morning started in Gorky Park in Moscow. We had 300 acres of room and not a clue as to what to expect from the government or the crowd. We were pleasantly surprised. The crowd was fairly large and included a formal welcome from the President's staff. We had no interference even though we continued dead on to our message of upsetting the status quo. The audience was split between the young-adult, semi-western cultured group and the semi-elderly. We had lots of opportunity to demonstrate the healing powers and the younger group got into the music with passion. We briefly visited Red Square before moving on to Budapest.

There we expanded our message to the widening gap between rich and poor, organized crime, filth and graffiti. All were ongoing problems in this historic city. We especially emphasized the evils of greed, crime and denigrating the earth. The message was fondly received by the masses. It was obviously resented by the five armed men who rushed the stage, shooting into the crowd and at us. The two who shot at us in essence shot themselves thanks to the defense shields. The anger light blew two of the others apart immediately and coerced the fifth to name who had sent him before he too exited earth. Organized crime had sent their messengers. I briefly excused myself as the ladies entertained the crowd with song. 30 minutes later, I was back with the crime family boss and three top lieutenants. After forwarding Haylie, Denise and Rhondell to Rome, the Hungarian people witnessed the power of the anger light. They also witnessed the healing powers used on the injured in the crowd. It seemed as if a new day in Hungary had started and our army ranks swelled.

Our Rome celebration was held in the Valley of the Caffarella to allow for the space we anticipated we would need. We enjoyed an exceptional crowd. Particularly cute was the two-year-old Italian girl who shared her spaghetti with Haylie. Making a complete mess of her clothes, Haylie was adored by the crowd. Imagine that! Our army continued to swell and we managed a trip to the Roman Coliseum before departing for Berlin for the night. We arrived in time to tour downtown Berlin by boat. Crowds soon lined the shore with their arms raised. We hailed them back. Somehow those that learned to temporarily fly appeared to be feeling better.

The next morning was day ten of the New World Order. It seemed like we had been going for a month. The celebrations were uplifting for the most part, but the buzz in my head kept increasing and was constant. I was glad tomorrow would be a restful day at home prior to the awful days of vengeance to follow. The Berlin site selected was the Wuhlheide Leisure and Recreation Centre. The show had become routine for us, but the audience hung on every word. The crowd was dressed in a coordinated traditional German alpine style. It represented a time when people were carefree, hardworking and true to the land. I think they were emphasizing the last to us. I was glad they did. Though still mid-morning when we concluded, they asked us to sit and eat traditional food with them. They gave the girls the gift of a traditional dirndl and lederhosen to the men. I promised I would wear it when I returned.

Paris, the City of Lights, was our next stop. Where else but the Eiffel Tower would be appropriate? Of the 10.5 million people in the greater Paris area, half of them must have shown up. After Haylie brought us in with our anthem, she and Denise went to the top of the Tower. Rhondell entered the act with some old rhythm and blues. I told him not to withhold any other talents from us. I decided to turn the stage over to the others as I walked among the crowd. Mr. John and Rich gave the serious talks. I wanted to find strength from our potential new army members I would need for the torturous days ahead. When I returned to the stage, a few needy and trustworthy healings awaited. How happy I'd be if only healings were my sole mission. When the new army members were raised up, they went all the way to the Champs Elysees.

Our last stop before going home was Hyde Park in London. NASA had begrudgingly agreed Earth could be hit if the destroyers were not gravity effected. It had to kill them to give us that boost. I gave the world notice of our upcoming schedule. Tomorrow, day 11 was for rest and catch up with the ministers. Days 12 through 15 would be hell's vengeance of the worst on earth. Mr. John and I were going to the most evil spots on earth to rid it of the deadliest evil-doers. We would go deep into the serpent's lair where greed and intolerance were at its worst. Vengeance would be swift and complete. Full vengeance for every country in the world would start on day 48. I again pleaded with those with evil hearts to find the way to rid themselves of it before it was too late.

The English royalty had secluded box seats built for them near the constructed stage. Armed servicemen guarded them. I told the armed guards they would have to surrender their arms or leave. The royalty left in a tiff. We sure missed them. I explained to the crowd that the status quo was ending. The only royalty in the New World Order was God. Those that demanded pomp and servitude of others were on a short leash. A part of the crowd left with that comment, but they were ones that weren't eligible to join our army anyway. Kingdoms, dynasties and totalitarianism had no place in the New World Order. Besides, more important people got better seats to the celebration.

Deidra, Haylie, Lin Yang and Rich put on a tremendous show. Peggy finally decided to show the world her voice as well. The healings and words of harm and hope were absorbed. At the end, our army did well again with recruits. Our army had already grown to over 30 million and I knew hundreds of millions of others were awaiting their opportunity. At last we went home!

Chapter 26
Vengeance of the Worst

This blessed day of rest was much needed. Only a few items had to be attended to. With my snub of various royalties around the world, the press was killing the New World Order on paper and TV. Some of them decided they had the right to camp outside of the Inner Circle's personal residences. Mr. John informed them at 9AM that they were not to be within one mile of any such residence. They had 15 minutes to withdraw. Somehow CBS did not get the concept of rules. After their truck vanished from creation at 9:15, we were bothered no more. All members of the Circle, their residences and property had constant shields protecting them. Rhondell had our new members from the celebration tour temporarily housed until the New York residences and offices were complete. He would concentrate the next six days on that task. Every available source was at his disposal to expedite that project. The rest of the day I spent playing with Haylie.

Day 12 was the day I had been dreading. There was nothing but pain, suffering and death on the agenda for the next four days. The first stop was Times Square in New York City as promised. With every station in the nation broadcasting to every place in the world, I started crying. What happened next was the saddest day in my life. This city was the worst in the world in harboring the evil of greed. It also had a high level of intolerance for race, creed and nationality. Organized and street crime ran rampant. It was a filthy and polluted place, which disgraced the face of the earth. All those within 30 miles who lived, worked or had left their footprint there from six days ago would feel the vengeance God had requested of me. Millions were about to die. My heart broke.

The anger light came out as black as pitch dark. It formed an umbrella with a 30-mile radius from where I stood. Offshoot rays went darting away for those that had exited the area. The black light fell, penetrating all matter and earth and absorbed into those with blackened hearts. The evil were dissolved molecularly by the black light of death. I went to my knees in sadness. The buzzing grew stronger inside my head. The toll was huge. Of the nearly 18 million people in the area, nearly six million were dead. Wall Street had virtually no executive left. The New York Stock Exchange and Nasdaq Stock Market were now dead as well. 95% of the lawyers, 100% of organized crime, 100% of violent gang members, 97% of those incarcerated and all religious fanatics were gone. The truly evil had left New York City.

I turned and addressed the three cameramen and two reporters who survived. This was the first of 8 stops to rid the worst of evil from earth. It would be followed in the next 142 days with a visit to every country on earth. Evil would be eradicated from our planet. I alone had this duty. I alone would perform this duty to give Earth a chance to survive. I alone would suffer the consequences. Mr. John and I transported to the top of Rocky Mountain National Park to give me time to compose myself for these four days of hell. Mr. John had become a true friend. After an hour he spoke.

Mr. John	Do you remember when you asked me what was inside my heart?
Darrel	Yes. It seems so long ago.
Mr. John	I think I know now. When I was a reporter, I saw so much evil. But evil never cared for their victims. And now I see a man charged with eradicating evil. Yet he grieves about their demise and still he must go on. My heart feels so puny and weak. My heart grieves for your pain. I only wish I could take it from you.
Darrel	You have given me great friendship and so much trust. You have been good to your every word. Yet, when I subject you to this awful duty, your concern is for me. I only wish I was deserving of you.

We stayed another hour overlooking the beautiful mountains. Then begrudgingly we went to the next stop.

The most evil man in the world had been hiding in caves since the 9/11 attacks. His network of Islamic fanatics spread terror and intolerance around the world. Our second and last stop of day 12 was in the mountainous terrain on the border of Afghanistan and Pakistan. We transported directly into the man-made and fortified cave where Mr. Evil was residing. Fierce counterattacks inside the cave were met with death from the shield's return to sender mandate. Mr. Evil was brought outside for all his followers to try and free. Two hours passed to let them amass. A second shield was thrown down around a 50-mile radius to trap all black hearts. No man ever deserved to be tortured to death more than this one. Why couldn't I do it? Was I concerned that a torturous death would cast me into the fold of evil or was I just not being strong as God told me I needed to be? Regardless of the answer, Mr. Evil was blown to pieces with a single ray from the anger light. Then, the black anger light emitted an umbrella over the entire 50-mile radius area, falling to and through the ground, attaching to and destroying every black heart. Nearly a hundred thousand joined the ranks of those departed from earth. I chose to spend the night on a blanket under the stars as Mr. John was sent home for the night. The buzzing continued to grow in my head. I searched for peace all night without success.

Day 13 began early in Iraq. I could not bring myself to target the entire country. When civil war raked a nation, how could anyone not be blackened in the heart? The goodness here deserved a chance. Total vengeance on this nation would wait until stability gave the good a chance to overcome evil. Still, so many hot spots would have to be cleansed.

God alone marked black hearts for any of a multitude of serious evils per my power request. Though all were black, God used different shades to distinguish which evil or evils the heart holder had. Each particular shade could then be targeted individually. Therefore, the only evil targeted would be religious intolerance. The black anger light was used for that specific target over Basra, Najaf, Fallujah, Baghdad, Tikrit, Kirkuk and Mosul. The casualties were massive. Every side of the conflict including some U.S. and British soldiers had victims. Over eight million people died in total. Eight million new buzzes were inside my head. The vengeance was merely at the tip of the iceberg. I didn't want this mission. However, I had so solemnly vowed to do it.

We made a highly visible entry into the heart of Tehran. Again, I wanted to take vengeance on the fewest possible. I wanted to give the oppressed masses the chance and additional time to rid their evil before their total vengeance day. Massive attacks came at us, all repulsed and destroyed. Religious intolerance was the only evil targeted again, claiming one million casualties. The government and clerics were decimated. I knew this opened the door to chaos. Hopefully, those that took over would learn from their predecessors. At least that was the specific message I left.

I spent that night alone again on top of a mountain and under the stars. Looking up, I knew I had become the biggest murderer in the history of earth. Yet, I knew the total was at its infancy. No matter what the mission was, or its importance, total despair set in.

Day 14 was a return to Peking. This was a very difficult task. An incredibly high percentage of the people in this country had no evil. A massive change might upend that fact. I wanted to target as few as possible. Yet, an unstable China with vast powers would be as dangerous as the evils of oppression. Therefore, a highly selected target of those in power with the evil of oppression was called upon. At the same time, all nuclear weapons were targeted to assure some nutcase elsewhere in the country would not retaliate. This was accomplished by sending specific energy to break down plutonium and uranium molecularly. It was also done with no notice to the rest of the world to not upset any perceived power balance. After all, nuclear sources everywhere would soon be a target. The result was but a few thousand highly-positioned casualties and a strong warning to their successors.

The biggest show of force was about to begin. North Korea was the next target. It had become an ever-increasing threat to its neighbors and the world. Their leader was power-crazed and wanted world recognition. He got that today. A shield was placed around the entire country that prevented anyone or thing from entering or leaving. All nuclear elements were again dissolved immediately. We transported to the military parade grounds in the heart of Pyongyang. The country had 1.1 million personnel in its military, enormous artillery and the most oppressive regime of any recognized country. The people lived in fear and had been brainwashed to the need of military force to survive for over 55 years. Still, I held out hope that the people would embrace the goodness so naturally in their culture's hearts, if fear and oppression were removed.

The military might in the heart of the country soon surrounded us. I transported to the President's residence and back to the grounds with the President. The proverbial standoff was at hand. Their President was suspended in the air as anger lights burned all around him while 300,000 troops and artillery were aimed directly at us. Mr. John deserved a lot of credit for staying calm as he addressed the troops.

Mr. John   Your overwhelming number of troops is meaningless.

Your tremendous military power is powerless.

You have seen the strength of our powers demonstrated.

The military might of North Korea will be eliminated today.

Your leaders will be casualties today.

The only question remaining is will you join the casualty list as well from your actions.

We demand you throw down all your weapons for them to be destroyed.

Darrel   We do not wish to destroy the soldiers merely obeying orders. But those orders come from evil leaders. You must decide if you are on the side of evil or good. Your families want you to survive. We want you to survive. Do you? I am going to let the President speak to you shortly. If he has any final courage, he will ask you to lay your weapons down. I suspect he will act like a coward and try to free himself by ordering you to fire upon us. That act will be your certain death! (The President was lowered to the ground 50 yards away from us which gave him confidence of safety from gunfire.)

President   Kill them now! (Military leaders ordered the onslaught. Gunfire started throughout the troops. The shield reflected bullets back to the individual shooters. In seconds 100,000 troops were dead.)

Darrel   Lay down your guns and leave your tanks! (The 200,000 who did not fire obliged. Tank personnel evacuated. All tanks and guns were lifted up and piled in an open area where they were dissolved. The President and military leaders were engulfed and lifted up by the light. In full view of the world, they were blown apart.) Take this message home to your family and friends. Peace has come to this nation. I promise that no outside country will invade or harm this nation. (We transported to the North Korean military headquarters just north of South Korea. All leaders were brought forth. We allowed them to call the massive number of troops to their aid.)

You have all seen the events in Pyongyang. Your leaders there summoned 100,000 of your comrades to their deaths. You have the same choice that they were given. Fire upon us and die. Or lay down your weapons and live in peace. Choose now! Commander, address your troops.

General	Kill them now! (Miraculously, only a few sporadic shots were fired and their shooters were instantly killed. Weapons were thrown to the ground. Tanks were emptied.)
Darrel	Go get your personal effects. Go home. Find and live in peace. I will return to see this peaceful nation and avenge the remaining evil at a later date. First, I have weapons to destroy on both sides of the border. (Every military trademarked item was targeted for destruction with the ex-leaders sitting on top of them. Then we moved to the other side of the border. Generals from both the South Korean and U.S. forces met us.)
US General	Congratulations on your fine work, but those soldiers you freed are still a threat.
Darrel	General, you no longer have an enemy. Go home!
General	You know we can't do that.
Darrel	You will have no weapons to fight with and no one to fight against. Go home!
General	(To his aide) Amass the troops. (To me) Sir, you are under arrest.

The light was emitted and engulfed all of the officers. We moved into the common ground and general assembly was called. Every U.S. and South Korean troop was called to active duty.

Darrel   You have all witnessed what happened twice across the border. It will happen here, right now, if you follow your generals' orders to attack us. No one wants that to happen. Peace has come to this peninsula. The war machines will be disarmed on both sides of a stupid line. You choose to let peace happen, or you choose to die. Lay your weapons down! General, give your next order wisely.

US General   I have to arrest you. (The anger driven light blew the general to pieces.)

Darrel   And now a few words from the South Korean general.

SK General   Lay your weapons down. (The troops obliged. Every military trademarked item within 100 miles was dissolved.)

Darrel   South Korean troops go home to peace. U.S. troops, gather your personal effects. I am sending you back to your U.S. base now. Find peace there. And when you are freed of your vows to the military, please join our army where you can be of real value. (The troops celebrated wildly, got their gear and received instant transport home.)

One more awful day remained. At least this one ended in massive celebration in two countries. The buzzing in my head worsened.

Day 15. Tribal, religious and violent wars had plagued Africa for ages. An example had to be made in the most intolerant area which, hopefully, would foster the riddance of evil elsewhere. We transported to Mogadishu, Somalia. The violence and hatred of the region allowed for no middle ground. War between Somalia and Ethiopia had been nearly constant. Inner Somalia tensions with the Republic of Somaliland and Puntland had led to atrocities that crossed the line into war crimes. There was no possibility of achieving peace with a limited response that targeted only a specific evil. If that was done the other horrific evil groups would quickly dominate and destroy those with goodness. The vast evils of the area left no option but complete vengeance of the black hearts. Somalia was totally shielded. In a scene the world would soon witness in every country, all evil hearts were targeted for elimination. Nearly four million people died, over half of the country. Then a 50-mile radius of Ethiopia bordering Somalia was dealt a similar consequence. A warning was sent to all other countries to allow the remaining citizens to deal with their internal affairs. Stay out!

Thankfully, we had one last stop. Illegal drugs had become one of man's greatest evils. Both those who produced and used them were culprits. Those using were worldwide and would be dealt with accordingly. We decided to take on the producers so we transported to Bogota, Columbia. The President there had tried to deal with the dual problems of drug production and polarization of the wealthy class. Greed from those in power had strapped the country with unemployment and poverty.

A two target cleansing was decided. First, any field, equipment, person or contact involved with the illegal drug industry was targeted for destruction. Second, those with blackened hearts of greed would also be targeted. Notice was given to the Columbian government to convert the assets of the soon-to-be departed into programs of employment for the masses. The black anger light searched and destroyed those defined. The four day vengeance of the worst was concluded.

The New World Order had taken a massive blow from the world media. Hitler to the third power was my new description. All the world markets collapsed after New York. The faith of our army members was being tested. People could be told of the events to come, but the reality still hit hard. We knew to expect retaliation from the U.S. government. To make us easy to find, Mr. John put out a press notice stating we would be at Sea World in Florida tomorrow for rest, healings and additions to our army. I knew there would be little rest.

Chapter 27
Retaliation

I chose Sea World because Haylie loved animals and the park. It also had a few open areas conducive to celebrations. Determined to eliminate any fool-hearted threats, I emitted light as we entered to search out and retrieve any weapons on site. There were a few handguns, knives and one very interesting sniper rifle. They were dissolved and our entourage started enjoying the park. Surprisingly, we received strong positive reaction from the people. We thoroughly enjoyed watching Haylie play in the children's area with hundreds of new friends. During the wonderful Shamu show, I noticed the whales were very active in making noises. At the dolphin encounter, the dolphins flocked to us. I decided to test this phenomenon. I made a circle with my arms and emitted the healing light. When I put my arms in the water, the dolphins swam through my arms carefully without even touching me. Though I couldn't really communicate with them, they felt the unusual presence of the powers. Then they showed off for the crowd doing acrobatics.

We previously announced our celebration would be held at the water-sport lake in front of the grandstand. For grins, I transported the dolphins into the lake. They seemed ecstatic to have a greater volume of water in which to play. Music started the show and the crowd was rocking with the upbeat songs. Then it was time for me to give the first difficult talk about the past four days. I started with a reminder of our dire future if we were not successful in the mission. By now everybody, including NASA, was convinced the destroyers were headed our way. Unfortunately, there were too many articles being published saying man could stop them. I told them many powerful men had already tried to stop me and failed. Did they think if man could not stop my measly powers they would be more successful against God? There was only one way from our pending doom. That was doing everything required with the second chance God had given us. That second chance required heretofore, unimaginable vengeance. As great as the casualties had been to date, they were small versus what was ahead. In tears, I reminded the audience, "If our distaste for necessary vengeance stopped our mission, then that would assure mankind's total vengeance in January."

The crowd was subdued. I told them no person could do what I had been asked to do without having tremendous guilt, sadness and a price to pay. I hoped that trying to save Earth for all those good people on it would allow our army members to keep their trust and support in me and the mission. The ovation was truly appreciated.

What happened next was what I had been expecting. I detected a laser pointed at me. As it was not a threat, I allowed it to penetrate the shield. I moved to the water's edge to get as far away from everyone as I could. Then something unusual happened. A fighter plane buzzed overhead. He made a steep turn and headed back at us. A missile was fired and headed dead at me. I intercepted the missile just before it hit the shield. It was a cruise missile guided by the laser that targeted me. I sat the missile on the ground and addressed the crowd.

Darrel   Don't be alarmed. You are all safe. Except, I would be asking your government if I were you why they would place your lives in peril by this attempt on mine. Normally, such an attack is directed back from where it came. But the order to attack obviously came from superiors of the pilot. I want to know how much higher because vengeance awaits that person.

The fighter plane turned and made another pass without firing. Again this seemed unusual. I latched onto the plane with the energy light and brought it down for a soft landing before us all. Again, I could detect no evil or malice from the pilot so I let him climb down of his own merit. He walked straight for me in an unthreatening manner.

Pilot   Is everybody all right?

Darrel   Yes, but I am amazed you care.

Pilot	Trust me. I care. (His trust glow was at 80%.)
Darrel	I admit I am totally confused. You have a high trust level in the mission and me. Yet, you fired a lethal weapon at us. Why?
Pilot	We fighter pilots are bound by oath to follow orders. This order came down today. Sir, my fellow pilots are good men. I volunteered for the duty to protect them.
Darrel	How so? And what is your name?
Pilot	Major Mike Matthews, sir. I had the greatest faith the mission would fail. I did what I could within my oath to assure its failure. I thought the plane would be destroyed. I didn't want that to happen to my buddies.
Darrel	Major, you did the fly over as a way to warn me, didn't you?
Major	Yes.
Darrel	Major Mike, that was incredibly admirable. Who gave you the mission?
Major Mike	Sir, as much as I would do for you, telling that would break my so solemn oath.
Darrel	I have run into this oath problem often. It is time to fix it. Haylie, come here please.
Haylie	Yes, Grandpa.
Darrel	Tell everyone all the methods for a military person to honorably terminate their oath.
Haylie	1. Formal honorable discharge 2. Presidential grant 3. Death
Darrel	Major Mike, you obviously are not being discharged today and we need to pursue this immediately. I doubt if you get a Presidential grant to talk to us as he may have initiated this attack. That leaves only death.
Major Mike	That is why I took the mission.

Darrel	Oh, but Major Mike, how much do you trust me?
Major Mike	(Smiling) A great deal, sir.
Darrel	Lay down Major. You are about to have the easiest death in mankind's history. (The healing light performed its first non-healing act. Major Mike merely went to sleep and his heart stopped beating. The Park doctor was transported to the site with death certificate in hand. After five quiet minutes, the doctor pronounced the Major dead.) Haylie, I want the Major to wake up to the prettiest face here.
Haylie	Mommy, Grandpa wants you up here. (Laughter)
Darrel	Oh, Deneeeeese? Your daughter obviously wants something from you.
Denise	Oh, Darrrrrrel? I'm not the one who spoils her. (More laughter)
Darrel	Haylie, your mommy is gorgeous, but I think the major would like to see your pretty face. (Haylie and my power easily revived the major as I knew exactly where the duck was placed. He opened his eyes and smiled at Haylie.) Mike, the major died. Like me, you now have no official status in this country. Who ordered you on the mission?
Mike	The General of the Air Force, sir.
Darrel	Three things Mike. My name is Darrel, not sir. I want you in our army. Tomorrow, I will pursue this up the chain of command and punish those responsible.
Mike	Joining your army is a pleasure sir…I mean Darrel.

With that, Deidra and Haylie went right to our anthem. I stayed by the water as the dolphins came to me. They understood what was happening. As the second chorus was sung, the dolphins synchronized their jump, forming the word "TRUST". I froze them in midair in that pose with the energy light for a few seconds. Dumb me had never considered animal help until now. When the crowd and I raised our arms at the familiar timing, the dolphins were out of the water on their tails. Those eligible for our army, human and dolphin, were lifted up and healed as always before. I too was amazed. As always, I ordered the army to leave the place spotless. The dolphins brought the trash in the lake to the boardwalk for disposal. I couldn't read their trust levels, but my bet was 100%.

Chapter 28
New Sheriff in Town

Mr. John and I made an early morning visit to the General of the Air Force on Day 17. Somehow, he was expecting us as armed bodyguards surrounded him in a remote bunker. With the bodyguards helplessly at bay outside the shield, we interrogated the General on camera. He refused to name anyone above him that authorized the air strike. The three of us transported to the Oval Office. It seemed the President wasn't hiding for a change. He had no agents in the room. The shield kept it that way.

President   I have been expecting you.

Darrel   I'll bet you have.

President   I'll make this easy. I gave the order for the air strike and I would again. You are guilty of mass murder in New York and high treason.

Darrel   God says otherwise.

President   God will have you rot in hell.

Darrel   The trouble with you religious zealots is you stopped speaking about God a long time ago. Now you speak for God. The trouble is your intolerance has given you the blackened heart of evil. That is why God has painted you and all like you as a target for vengeance.

President   Now who is talking for God?

Darrel	The difference is God actually told me this. So I am repeating God's words. God never came to you or others who are also speaking for God.
President	So what is your next grandstand play?
Darrel	You die!
President	You wouldn't dare!
Darrel	You die right now! In front of the world! On the steps of the Capitol Building! (We transported to that location. Cameras from all networks rushed to the scene. Every armed official advanced to the shield's edge now knowing if they fired then they died.)
	The world will now know that evil will be extinguished no matter whom, where or when. This man exudes every evil God has instructed me to eliminate. He has greed, intolerance and flagrantly damages earth's ecology. Your death sentence is hereby carried out. (The anger light blew him apart in front of the world. Mr. John and I transported home.)

The nation erupted into chaos. I told Rich earlier that I would be on full alert of any nation doing anything stupid in this transition period. The political powers were forced to elevate the V.P. to President, regardless of the circumstances. Rich took the oath of office that day. He called a press conference immediately.

Rich	These past 17 days have been the most unusual in the history of man. We face imminent destruction from above. We have one chance and that is the one the New World Order is pursuing. I know for a fact that all you have been told by Darrel is the truth. He and the rest of the good people on earth provide our only hope to avoid annihilation. There is an enormous number of people in this country and around the world still to be avenged. Our deceased president was marked by God for vengeance because of his own evils. Our country and the world is naturally upset and fearful of the political upheaval that has occurred. Unfortunately, upheaval will be prevalent until the evil in the world are eliminated. In an effort to assuage fears I make two promises to the people of the United States and

the world. First, our country will become a friend to all other countries. Second, to extinguish all fears that a dictatorial government has been put in place in perpetuity, I promise to resign the presidency as we near January 1. No other member of our immediate family will become president. However, the country and world should know that many changes lie ahead. I ask that all join me to accept these temporary changes that are necessary to increase the survival chances of the planet. If we are successful in our mission, all choices will return to the people on January 2. As repulsive as the many deaths to come will be and the reluctance to accept necessary changes, we must remember the alternative is world apocalypse.

As of this moment, I am issuing a Presidential pardon to Darrel and all others in the New World Order for all acts done or to be done in their pursuit to save this planet. (I transported in.)

Darrel Thank you Mr. President. This world will come together as one or be blown apart as we are. In the next 106 days, we will be visiting all 193 countries. The first act will be to take vengeance on everyone in every country who has been marked by God as having the evils of greed, intolerance or tarnishing the earth. That will be followed by a rebirth of each country. The rebirth will be the New World Order entourage joining the masses who survived the vengeance in music, healing and hope for world survival. Our strongest desire is that the rebirth process will accelerate the goodness factor God has stipulated for our survival. Everyone will lose family and friends during the vengeance. We have to rise above those losses for the sake of mankind.

On day 48 at 12:01AM New York time, an impenetrable shield will wrap every country until all countries have been through their day of vengeance and rebirth. After the last country is through the process on day 153, the shields will come down to a new era of love towards brother nations. There will be no travel between borders during this period. Everyone should return to their own country before day 48 or they will be trapped where they are until day 153. This includes all military personnel and ambassadors. Any weaponry abroad will be tagged as such and dissolved in place as the personnel leave.

Rich	By executive order, I am ordering all military personnel and ambassadors to return home immediately. All citizens are requested to return forthright.
Darrel	Over the next 10 days, new products and guidelines will be issued over a number of areas. They will change how we live. Cooperation is expected and appreciated. Part of that cooperation is for every international transportation company to bend over backwards in the effort to get everyone back to their home country free of charge. For the last time, I plead for those with evil to get rid of it or we will be rid of you.

Chapter 29
Energy

The next morning the world remained in a state of shock. To my delight, no nation took any action to further destabilize the world. It was the perfect timing to announce the first huge improvement to the average person's life. Tim and I addressed the world from our new headquarters in New York. Rhondell had our office and residences completed quickly. He was converting the remaining space to house 4,100 family units at 2,000 square feet each. The cost to the tenants would be nearly free of charge.

I started the conference by introducing the new energy source called hydroline. Though an incredibly complex chemical to make, it was simple to explain its efficiency. It would separate water into its unbonded hydrogen and oxygen components. The hydroline reacted with the hydrogen and formed a low heat emission strong enough to push a piston, heat a house or run a plant. The water was the cooling agent to prevent heat buildup. Emissions were hydrogen and oxygen. A secondary agent in the hydroline allowed the two elements to bond once again into water. For the most part it was a self-contained, closed system. The product was safer than any other source as no combustion was used to create the power. It worked in every engine regardless of size. Therefore, when the supply chain was in production, all other sources of energy would be outlawed. We planned to almost give the product away.

Tim	We have been in contact with the worldwide facilities we require. After this demonstration of hydroline today, those facilities will be worth less than zero as they will need to be cleaned up. We expect the owners to give them to us to

benefit the world. All other oil wells, rigs, tanks, refineries and equipment will be removed and eliminated. We have also developed a product to chemically remove the bonds of oil pollutant compounds in the ground and water, reducing them to their element stage. The companies will be charged for this service as will be addressed tomorrow. We expect worldwide availability of the product in 30 days.

Darrel and I will be visiting the owners of the facilities required after this demonstration to acquire them. Now for the demonstration.

A quick demonstration of hydroline added to pure water to power an engine showed the ease and applicability of the product. Tim and I acquired all the facilities that day. After showing a video of the first negotiating session hitting a snag and the methodology used to convince the owner to relinquish the facility, all other conversations proceeded quickly.

Chapter 30
Finance and Collection

Days 19 through 23 were dedicated to funding everything we needed. Roy and I met with the press. Roy drafted the plan calling for special levies against businesses and wealthy individuals. For any business in the oil industry or in a sin industry (gambling, alcohol, tobacco), the levy would be 90% of available company cash and investments. All other businesses would pay 50%. Any individual with a net worth in excess of 2 million would pay 50% up to 4 million, 75% up to 10 million and 100% over that limit. All funds would be split between the New World Order and the federal government of the company or individual involved. The government would buy back its federal deficit and provide basic services. All salaries and benefits would be limited. Companies were asked to reduce their prices to make only modest profits until January 2. For any individual who was a victim of vengeance, their entire estate would be split as per above.

Roy was working on a separate Finance and Collection Minister for each country. That person would be selected following vengeance and rebirth (V&R) day at each country. Each company or individual would pay the levy to the New World Order prior to their V&R day. The New World Order would remit the appropriate share to the respective government. Any violation would breach the evil of greed and be resolved in that manner.

Roy	Are there any questions from the press?
TTC	Those rates seem unusually high.
Roy	We are in unusual times. A great deal of money will need to be redistributed to create the balance necessary to go beyond

	January 2, if we are successful in seeing that date. Denise and I will determine the % that goes to each minister or infrastructure.
CBS	What gives you the authority to impose such a levy?
Darrel	God.
ABC	What % will the New World Order keep from their portion?
Roy	Next to nothing. We'll keep only that amount necessary to pay fair salaries to our employees. There is no greed within the New World Order.
NBC	Do you think you will face strong resistance from the big companies and wealthy individuals?
Darrel	Not for long.
FOX	Which companies will you start with?
Roy	The oil companies. They are virtually out of business as of yesterday. We will get our levy prior to them distributing any funds elsewhere. Plus, we will be interested in the monster bonuses paid to their executives achieved from the backs of the public. Thank you for coming. We have a lot of work to do.

Roy easily grasped the negotiating skill of telling the other side what to do. We spent the next five days visiting every significant oil company in the world. After the video of the first two sessions was forwarded to all the others, checks were waiting for us when we arrived. Mr. John made a DVD of the process and questions other nations' ministers would follow. For grins, he made a form up for the company or individual to protest. With it came a pre-addressed envelope to me.

Roy then turned his attention to the other sin industries. Occasionally, he requested my attendance to help resolve disputes. He also made videos of those episodes to assure future disputes would be resolved easily. Denise helped make sure all funds were redistributed as quickly as possible. True to our word, the New World Order kept nothing for the Inner Circle as we still had our basic needs provided by those offering their help.

Chapter 31
The New Order of Rules

Each of the next five days brought new announcements to break old molds. Marilee announced the 10 commandments of pre-college education on day 24.

> 1. Education is a privilege, not a right. If you abuse the privilege, you are out. No exceptions. Expelled kids will be transferred to 24/7 supervised work and living communities to perform mandatory work for the government. Each expelled child will be given a second chance to rejoin the school system after three months. No third chances. It will be hard work at no pay until their original class graduates from high school. Any further breach of conduct would be subject to the stiffest penalty.
>
> 2. Teachers will teach for the love of educating the young. If they treat it like it's just a job, then they don't have one. Teachers will have freedom for creativity in their lesson plans. School days will be structured to give teachers the time and venue to collaborate and consult colleagues about reaching individual needs. Every teacher will be given the same realistic budget for incidental classroom expenses.
>
> 3. Parents have no say-so as to discipline, curriculum, grades or complaints. Their three sole purposes in education are making sure their children do not violate number 1 above, assure their child's attendance and to support the school where their child attends.

4. All schools will have equal funding per student and core curriculums of reading, writing and mathematics. Failure to pass these core classes will subject the student to number 1 above. The balance of the child's curriculum of science, social studies, technology and etc. will be a mix of mandatory and elective classes. Advancement to higher curriculum courses will be based solely on performance as determined by teachers and administration.

5. Regional schools for children with learning disabilities will be established. Teachers will determine partial or full movement to regular schools based on the child's progress.

6. Physical education will be a mandatory class with the emphasis on physical. Only those kids with absolute restrictions will be waived from participating.

7. Every child will wear the same outfit as provided by the school.

8. Outstanding classroom performance will allow the child to be sent to a regional school of advanced learning.

9. Verbal or physical abuse to either another student or teacher subjects the child to number 1 above. Self defense is acceptable behavior.

10. Repeat number 1.

Day 25 brought the announcement that all personal use of cell phones, computers and video games were to be limited until January 2. This allowed everyone more time to clean up their street, neighborhood and earth. The secondary purpose was to get people off their ever-growing obese butts and get active. Parents and adults were charged with monitoring this edict while remembering deceit and dishonesty could blacken a heart. There was only one cure for a black heart.

Later that day we visited six schools for the blind around the world. Nearly 100% had trust levels that restored their vision. Would the world see our path to survival? Then we visited six schools for the deaf and restored hearing to 99% of those trusting souls. Would the world hear what was being said?

Day 26 was one of my favorites. That was the day all nuclear power was outlawed. Over the next three days, I visited the leader of every country with nuclear bombs. They were all dissolved. Furthermore, plans to switch nuclear power to hydroline were made and implemented. All nuclear waste would be dissolved molecularly on the day of V&R for the respective country.

Day 27 introduced Eric, our new Minister of the Law. On the V&R day for each country, all laws were voided and replaced with a few pages of simple and moral edicts through January 1. No law could ever be passed again that the average high school student could not interpret for himself or herself. Anyone attempting to pass a law for the purpose of benefiting a profession, themselves, family or friend would be subject to the stiffest penalty. Any disagreement between parties would be handled cordially and submitted to an arbitrator. The arbitrator would issue the decision that day with no appeals. Arbitrators by law would be rotated in and out from all professions. There would be no legal profession going forward.

Day 28 outlawed all illegal drugs and tobacco products. Alcohol remained legal but with strict requirements and personal conduct codes. Those with dependencies had the opportunity to lose them on that country's day of V&R. It only took a 60% trust factor to do it. Anyone caught growing or distributing illegal drugs and tobacco products would be subject to the stiffest penalty. Anyone caught using illegal drugs or tobacco products or of being inebriated while driving or drunk in public would submit themselves to counseling and hard labor for the first offense. They would be given a vaccine that would make those illegal drugs, tobacco products and alcohol taste like a sewer for a second offense.

The strain was showing on all members of the Inner Circle. I felt we needed to recharge our energies with positive reinforcement. That night as a treat for the Inner Circle, we transported to the family-friendly, entertainment town of Branson, Missouri to watch one of our favorite shows. Presley's Country Jubilee was filled with song, music and comedy. We laughed so hard at "Cecil" the hillbilly. Haylie was thrilled to meet him at the intermission. The show brought temporary joy for one night before the ongoing battle for survival resumed in the morning.

Chapter 32
Weather and Climate

Earth became a poison to the universe from the potential to blow itself up and the actual poison man put into the atmosphere. Though contained by the atmosphere to date, the threat of poison escaping, expanding and infesting other systems had to be eliminated. The introduction of hydroline was a vital step. This alone would only help prevent further buildup. Something else had to be done. I spent days 29 through 31 working on this task.

I decided to work from the top down. The stratospheric ozone layer protected Earth from harmful ultraviolet radiation from the sun. At times over Earth's poles, the ozone layer developed holes from many variables coming together at once. The ultimate threat was loss of the ozone layer over other parts or the entire planet. Man's contribution in these holes was the introduction of chlorine and bromine compounds into the atmosphere. In extreme cold, these compounds broke down to their core atomic configuration damaging the fragile ozone compound. The challenge was to remove those harmful atomic configurations from the air. It was challenging because both compounds were found naturally in nature.

As any change to our delicate ecosystem could have adverse results, I decided to err on the side of safety. Therefore I chose a strictly defined target. I created a shield running parallel to the earth encompassing only the stratosphere level. Within that shield, I emitted a light with no heat or absorption properties. I wanted to assure the light itself would not be the energy trigger to a chemical reaction. The light targeted only the atomic numbers for chlorine and bromine atoms, 17 and 35 respectively. All such atoms in the stratosphere attached to the light. The light was withdrawn and the contents were placed in a shielded container. They would be used for safe commercial purposes. I knew this was a temporary fix as compounds, natural and man-made, would continue to find their way into the stratosphere. However, I estimated it would take a few years to reopen ozone holes. I was much more worried about the next January 1.

The troposphere is the atmospheric layer nearest earth. Therefore, it is the one man has screwed up more than any other. The power to modify weather that I have been given is immense. Quite frankly, it scares me to death. Any change here might alter somewhere else. It simply is uncontrollable so caution is my guideline.

There were two areas I wanted to alter cautiously. The first was smog. I told Haylie it couldn't be removed globally by segregating and dissolving the harmful agents as we did in Los Angeles because most agents that produced smog also occurred naturally. My feeble mind could not conclude how to separate the natural from the harmful. Therefore, I concentrated on ground level ozone. Though critical in the stratosphere, it was a health menace in the troposphere. I was frightened by unknown consequences of full removal of the ozone compound. Ozone in the troposphere was formed by an unnatural bonding of three oxygen elements into a compound. I decided to slowly reduce the ozone in the air. After attracting one half of one percent of all ozone near earth, I broke it down to single element units and released the oxygen back into the atmosphere. I took a wait and see the results stance and decided to repeat the test on a weekly basis. Ongoing monitoring would detect any new threats from the tests if they had harmful effects.

The second area I approached very cautiously was global warming. All evidence pointed to man as a critical variable in this long-term problem. Best guesstimates had tragic results to earth in a 50-year time frame if the average temperature continued to rise by three more degrees. Though again I was motivated by January 1, I was concerned about the future of Haylie's children. Two large components to temperature rising on earth were man's pollutants to the atmosphere and ocean temperatures. Two moves on the pollutant front were in process.

Fiddling with the ocean's temperature was also scary at best. The ocean currents forever changed their meanderings. Yet, those currents directly affected climate everywhere on earth. Changing the flow of those currents would invite disaster. Slightly cooling them over time could have a positive effect. The key word here was "slightly". Like the ozone test, I proceeded with great trepidation. If it took centuries to add a degree to our average temperature, I certainly didn't want to cool it off fast. By reversing the polarity of the anger light, great cold could be generated. I targeted all the oceans and large lakes on earth. My intent was to lower the water temperature by .01 of 1 degree. Again I would monitor for any harmful results. If none, I would continue weekly until a reduction was reached of .1 of 1 degree. It was a gamble for sure, but one worth taking.

Another weather change considered was one I felt necessary for economic reasons. The hydroline would strip certain countries of their economies based on oil. With no way to survive in most of those desert climates, two consequences were likely:

> 1. The people would be forced to abandon their homelands and migrate to other countries. This would be perfectly fine as peace WOULD become the norm.
>
> 2. Evil would return. This WOULD not happen.

Agriculture had always been a staple profession for life. Farming would lead the post-evil earth. We would develop new strains of high temperature resistant foods. With just moderate changes to allow sparse rains to the desert climate, plant growth would be possible without changing those climate balances. This would be an ongoing project for Haylie and myself.

Chapter 33
Press Conference # 2

August 1 was Day 32 in our march towards January 1. As promised Mr. John and I went before the press. As everyone would soon be confined to their countries, we chose an international site and media. The conference was held in an outdoor auditorium in Madrid.

Mr. John	As previously stated, no one is to speak until asked. I assume you all understand that. (A nervous laugh came out.) So much has happened in this last month. Darrel will make a statement and then I will select those who will be allowed to ask questions. Darrel.
Darrel	First, I'll address the deaths of millions around the globe so far. For those raised under a doctrine of "You shall not murder", the need for these deaths is painful to accept. However, the supposed author of that doctrine has specifically commanded me to do just that. And the sad truth is the deaths to date are but a few versus what is to come. Still, I pay a great price every minute for every person's passing.

        Some of you have labeled me as Hitler times 1,000. Regardless of Hitler's claims, he was never trying to save Earth, was he? I alone have to live and die with the vengeance of my mission. God will judge me and us on January 1. I hope man can judge me however he chooses on January 2.

        We have made huge gains to our army and the goodness factor on earth. But we have so far to go to get to the 2 billion unit level established by God to save ourselves. And every act of vengeance strains those who would join our side. Quite a paradox we have to solve.

We have begun the detoxification of earth with a new energy source and atmosphere adjustments. We have made temporary changes to cultural life. Shocks to the capitalistic structure that created so much greed are still filtering down. New decrees have been issued to institutions. So much change is still to come.

Mr. John	The man in the back row gets the first question.
Sergio	Darrel, I am Sergio, only a man on the street. You have such power at your disposal. Why don't you simply stop the destroyers?
Darrel	The sheer mass of the destroyers is beyond my power or anything man can oppose it with. Even if I had that much power, do you really think it would stop God from destroying us? We need to accept that the second chance given to us is our only hope. Part of that task is repugnant to those who are good. But those are the terms. And Sergio, I can see you are a good man and there is nothing "only" about you.
Mr. John	Madrid News.
Madrid	The harshness of the decrees appears totalitarian. Yet, you have designated such regimes as oppressive and therefore evil.
Darrel	You are correct on the first, but ours are necessary for changing the status quo. They are also short-term if the people decide to change them. A totalitarian implements rules for their own perpetuity of rule. I assure you I do not want to rule. January 1 marks my last authoritative act. The people hopefully get to decide that next day. You are wrong on the second part; it is God who has designated them as evil.
Mr. John	MSNBC.
MSNBC	There are no longer any financial markets. Personal worth has been largely destroyed. How will the standard of living we enjoyed be restored?

Darrel	By we, you mean the wealthy. Their standard of living will not return. Nor will their power. The markets are just paper assets. Real assets are the quality of life, lack of hunger, housing for all, affordable health, love of friends and family, freedom from fear of evil deeds, meaningful jobs and an earth free of evil and pollution. The standard of living for the good who survive will be far superior than before.
Mr. John	BBC.
BBC	You mentioned the need for two billion units of good. What is that?
Darrel	It is basically the total volume of goodness on earth. Goodness comes from love, trust, respect, kindness and help given to fellow man. A person with 100% goodness traits is equal to one unit. One at 50% is half a unit. That doesn't mean the other 50% of that person is evil. I suspect 50% evil may have God painting the owner with a black heart. It can be a combination of evil, apathy and neutrality. But do you see the number of halves we need to save Earth?
	The total goodness factor comes from everyone on earth, not just those in our army of good. Everyone in our army adds to the factor because they have a 50% minimum trust level. Add their other goodness traits to their trust determines that member's contribution to the goodness factor. The value of being in our army assures a solid addition to the factor and makes that member eligible for healing. God has given me the gift of knowledge as to the total goodness level. I don't question what God has given.
Mr. John	CBS.
CBS	Darrel, what do you want to see this world become?
Darrel	I want to thank our good friends at CBS for a great question.
	1. I want to see non-polluted blue skies above us.
	2. I want fresh, clear water running above and below the ground.

3. I want to see people helping other people with no strings attached.

4. I want to see children playing in their neighborhoods. With their parents free of fear they will be harmed. With neighbors watching out for them. With the kids playing active games instead of being couch potatoes. With the streets clean enough to eat off.

5. (In tears) I want to see all our kids and grandkids see January 2.

Mr. John	Reverend Michaels.
Reverend	You refer to God often, but never as Father as per the Bible.
Darrel	God has come to me five times. Every time, God presented God as either a funnel or ball of light. I don't know if God is male, female, both or neither. I don't plan to ask should I see God again. Therefore, I will never address God by a gender.
Reverend	Do you claim that God chose you because your belief in Him was accurate versus ours?
Darrel	I had some very different perspectives of God than most religions. God chose me for a variety of reasons. My belief of God's true existence and my personal attributes were why I was selected for this mission. But that doesn't mean I was totally right in my original beliefs. In fact, one of my beliefs was proven wrong.
	You see I believed God could not possibly be interested in the individual man or possibly man at all. I believed God simply had bigger things to worry about. But God proved that wrong to me. God chose one man, me, out of all for this mission. God painted both trust glows and blackened hearts on individuals which proved God was knowledgeable of every person. God gave us a second chance which proved he was concerned about all of us.
	I now have less disbelief in impossible feats as told from the past. I disbelieved the story of Noah because building such

a large ark and collecting all species seemed impossible to me. Yet, how many so called impossible things have I now witnessed. And who is now out building a large army and counting all the goodness in the world that seemed impossible before the mission?

I disbelieved the story of Moses of both his powers and returning alone with the Ten Commandments from the mountaintop. Yet, who today has told a story of powers received straight from God or learned knowledge given by God? And who coincidently was given ten powers and the commandments to eradicate evil and enhance goodness on earth?

Who is to really say what beliefs are accurate?

Reverend	I find it blasphemous that you label our strong religious beliefs, ones that we know are the real truths of God and His Son, as intolerance to others. If ours are the correct beliefs, how can that be intolerance?
Darrel	That is just plain warped. Every religion professes that theirs is the true belief. Therefore, it can only be other religions that are intolerant. That supremacy of view has made the perfect recipe for hatred and war throughout earth's history. I have not, nor will not ask any person of any faith to give up their faith. I am simply saying when those with faith poison this earth with intolerance of others, God has targeted them as evil.
Reverend	I am appalled by your references to God and inferences of inaccuracies within the Bible. I am prepared to die for my beliefs.
Darrel	Reverend, has God ever come to you and spoke?
Reverend	I speak to God daily! He speaks to me in other ways.
Darrel	Reverend, God speaks directly when God chooses to do so. I know that as a fact. And God is so tired of people like you speaking for God, instead of God. My family and I were sent on a journey by God to witness events spoken of in the Bible. Not everything man writes is true. As for being prepared to

die for your beliefs, that's good, because you alone will make that decision.

Reverend   I believe you are the Anti-Christ. I call for all those of my faith to oppose you from this day forward.

Darrel   The Anti-Christ? Reverend, you are so far…..

God is coming! Reverend, God will answer for God.

Total darkness surrounded Earth. Not a sound was heard nor a movement made. A ball of light appeared high over the auditorium and floated down to us. A face appeared within the light.

God   I am God. I come to you in a form which you can relate. (The light came directly in front of me.) Those that I have spoken to speak the truth. (The light went directly in front of the Reverend.) Those that I have not spoken to need to listen more and talk less, if at all.

The ball of light vanished and daylight returned to earth.

Mr. John   I believe that ends this press conference.

Chapter 34
Clean the World

During vengeance of the worst, a German manufacturer, Hans, requested a meeting to discuss a machine he had in production with the New World Order. Basically, it was a highly mobile burner of waste products. I had Haylie meet with him for possibilities. The machine was very efficient. It used the combination of heat, compression and air flow cycles to reduce the time of disposal and residuals. With Haylie's help, the machine was modified to run off hydroline at high internal temperatures, while cool and clean on the outside. A new chemical was added to the process to enhance waste matter decomposition. The machine was exactly what we needed for world clean up.

Hans was at the Berlin celebration and a member of our army. He wanted to help our cause however possible. He ramped up production of the machine. The New World Order funded the production of units to be shipped around the world. Hans would accept only his cost as payment. Hans was also rewarded with great health.

Cleaning up the earth would be a continual task. The first effort would be massive. I issued a call for all army members, future army members and the rest of earth's population to spend the next ten days picking up trash, planting trees, cleaning neighborhoods, fixing blighted facilities and spreading the word of cleanup importance. I requested all employers to not only allow their employees to participate, but to also encourage them to help.

Everyone in the Inner Circle was highly visible in these manual tasks. Worldwide participation was estimated over one billion. Trash was put in biodegradable containers supplied by manufacturers. The containers were piled in designated spots where the new Hansburner (as we called it) had arrived or would be soon. Millions of neighborhoods received a face-lift. The world had actually come together to a degree in the effort. It may have had limited benefit as compared to the total task necessary to clean the earth, but the message and effort were huge. The Inner Circle was tired and sore. I told them it proved we needed to do more exercises and besides, in one quick healing session the soreness was gone.

Chapter 35
Calm Before the Storm

The first round of total vengeance was only days away. How I dreaded it! Days 43 and 44 were used to meet with the ministers on progress and plans. We decided to treat ourselves by meeting on the island of Barbados. The press was not eager to follow as a huge hurricane was bearing down on the island. We, on the other hand, looked at it as the opportunity to learn and experiment.

Haylie suggested we counter the storm with a significant force in the opposite direction. Hurricanes developed from warm tropical temperatures and airflows, coupled with low barometric pressures. As the storm approached, I brought in cold air from high altitudes and a high barometric pressure zone. The new front was whipped into a wind opposite of the hurricane flow and rammed into it. A violent merging of the two masses created lightning and thunder beyond belief. Then, it just petered away to nothing. Very interesting! It made for a beautiful day in Barbados! Haylie and mommy went to the beach.

Each minister had made great progress. Tim reported every facility was at or nearing hydroline production capability. The ones already producing were distributing product throughout the areas they were to provide. Tim had taken the bull by the horns and sent notice to every oil producer and refiner that told them to be closed two days after that area's hydroline production was up and running. He requested my initial help for compliance.

Roy and Denise had already raised 350 billion dollars. He said the surface had just been scratched. The international network was coming together better than hoped, as qualified potential ministers had started volunteering for our cause. Transfer of funds was awaiting the other ministers' requests.

Marilee and Eric said their programs were ready, but probably should wait until after each country's V&R for easiest implementation for the survivors. Peggy and Joan had concentrated on food and shelter for all. Worldwide volunteerism was gathering steam, the same as finance and collection had seen. They too expected greater reception after V&R. The President of the United States said he was as ready as possible for the country's V&R. It would be devastating for the nation, but change would be easier afterwards.

I told everybody that truly testing days were ahead. The massive amount of deaths coming was staggering. We would need to meet it with a strong positive message. Haylie asked if I was all right as she noticed my life force ebbing somewhat. I told her our task was large. I needed all the 100% with me during the rebirths for power to offset the healings. However, I only wanted them there after the vengeance was complete. Mr. John and I would handle that task alone.

We did enjoy our free time on the island. That was until I felt a great pain inside our army.

Chapter 36
Maggie

That night and the next morning I was by Maggie's side. Her life force was running out and I was losing a great friend, person and power. She was in no pain. I made sure of that. She talked of the hope she had as she was dying. She thanked me for all she said I'd done for her. I told her that she'd repaid that debt a thousand fold.

I talked to each of her kids and grandchildren. That first day on stage she said she'd tried to help others as I'd requested long ago. Her family told me of her never-ending attempts to do so. In addition to her full- time job, she worked tirelessly for the benefit of the homeless. She gave generously of her time and resources even when they were scarce. For the last twenty years she convinced her family at Christmas to buy one small gift for the others. Then whatever would have been spent was given to unknown people on the street in need. She had been approached by the media for a personal interest story and refused. She told them to talk to the ones they were trying to help. She had always told her family that anonymous giving was the best. Someone in her past had taught her that lesson.

Hearing the glorious person Maggie had been through her life made me feel small. Remembering all the petty envies, greeds, self-centered acts and apathies that were strewn through my life made me ashamed. Yet with one small act of kindness, I unknowingly helped shape a truly awesome person. How many other awesome people may have been in the world today if I or another had been generous in our small acts of kindness?

Maggie's children were outstanding individuals. If a person was judged by those that survived them, then Maggie had a front row seat of honor. As she neared her death, she challenged each one of them to get to the 100%

trust level. She said it was unlikely to be obtained, but failure for not trying was unacceptable in her family.

I asked Maggie if there was anything I could do as her last wish. She looked me squarely in the eye and said, "Let my kids and grandkids see January second." Then the great lady died. I asked the world to mourn our loss. Rich ordered flags at half-staff. I looked for a way to fill the huge hole in my heart. Some things were just not possible.

The next day I spoke at her funeral. I told the world of her last words. Once again, I so solemnly promised to do everything I could to save the world. I begged for everyone's help.

Chapter 37
United Nations Speech

I asked to address the United Nations the day before V&R was to commence. They graciously accepted.

Darrel   Throughout my lifetime, including today, this organization has effectively been the non- United Nations. It has been an organization of bickering, power-brokering and little accomplishment. There is so much death coming. And I am so sad before you today. There simply is no choice. The world should prepare for the following events.

One second after midnight tonight, a shield will surround every country on earth. They will remain in place until all countries are subjected to vengeance. No one or thing will be let in or out. The 30-day "Get home" period is over at midnight. All members of the United Nations and their staff will be transported to their home countries immediately following this session.

I will visit every one of the 193 countries and their territories over the next 106 days. Then the shields will all come down. In the next 15 days, all the North American and Caribbean countries will be targeted. The first step will be the black anger light searching out and destroying all those with blackened hearts of evil. (Booing came from the members. I merely raised my hand in a stop sign.) For those people of good hearts remaining, a rebirth of their nation will be held. That may be an oxymoron to some at this point. But if only good survives, joy can come to their hearts. Those are who we want and need as members in our army.

No one on earth wants this. Certainly not me. I have begged numerous times for those with evil to lose it. I am ashamed at how few have done so. It shows why man's evils have made our planet poisonous to the universe. Still, it doesn't make the job easier. God has demanded this or vengeance comes to everyone.

I will appear before this body again on December 29. What will the world be like on that day? The destroyers will be in sight to the naked eye and storming in on us. Will they stop? I don't know. Not achieving the levels dictated by God between now and then will guarantee they will not stop. I ask that you join me in the total effort required to let our kids see January 2.

Chapter 38
Hell Comes to Earth

At 12:01 AM on day 48, shields went around all countries. The buzzing in my head continued and I wondered how loud it would become. I cried all night hoping daylight would not come. God said I needed to be strong. How? How could one be so calloused to not feel agony? How could one be so burdened?

The first country for vengeance was the United States of America and its territories. As the black anger light spread over the country I pleaded for it to claim me, but there was no such luck. How could I feel so evil if I was not? I waited for the casualty count and knew it would be high in this land of greed and intolerance. My greatest fears were realized as 25% were gone. There was no rebirth planned as so many celebrations had already been held here. I sat alone on top of Mount Washington and cried for three hours before going to Canada.

Canada fared better than the U.S., but that was little consolation when 12% of the people were claimed. The performers tried to put on a good rebirth show in Toronto, but it lacked compassion. Our army grew but lightly. Nighttime brought loud buzzing and no sleep.

Two to three countries a day were visited in the next 14 days. Though the casualties in Latin America were in the 10% range, the body count was high. I was starting to weaken by the day in body and spirit. Tomorrow was a scheduled press day. I never thought I would look forward to one, but one day away from this destruction was a blessing.

The press conference started with Mr. John making an announcement.

Mr. John	There is no joy to report. To your individual credit, I am glad some in the media have survived. Albeit, with a large turnover. To blame anyone for the mounting casualties would be blaming God. And God has only acted out of kindness in giving us the chance to right man's mistakes. Darrel has no statement. The first question is from FOX.
FOX	Did you expect the heavy toll being taken?
Darrel	Yes. I knew the number of blackened hearts. And I knew few had rid themselves of it.
Mr. John	CBS.
CBS	Is there still time for others to lose their evil.
Darrel	Yes. Beg them to.
Mr. John	NBC.
NBC	This all seems like a gross disaster to mankind. Is there no other way?
Darrel	It is. And, no.
Mr. John	CNN.
CNN	As atrocious as it sounds, wouldn't it be easier to do a worldwide vengeance rather than one country at a time. Waiting for it to come over months has to be torturous for those still ahead.
Darrel	I only wish I could get this nightmare over faster. But the truth is I don't have the power to do that much targeted vengeance at one time. If I try to go beyond my controllable power, then instability occurs. That may lead to vengeance taken on good people by mistake. That I cannot live with. And I do hold out hope that those with evil in countries not yet visited can somehow get rid of it.
Mr. John	ABC.
ABC	Darrel, I personally believe in you and the mission. I assume that's why I'm still here. You are obviously disturbed by your unenviable task. But I feel you are suffering additionally. Are you?

Darrel	I am devastated by the task. And yes, I have two growing problems. The first problem is for every death from vengeance there is a corresponding buzz that enters my head. I have tried, but I cannot get it out. The second isn't worth discussing. The next 29 days will cover all of Africa and the Australian continent.

The next 29 days were hell. Still, Mr. John, Rhondell, Haylie, Peggy, Deidra and Lin Yang managed to put more passion into the rebirths. We reached the point where the shock of what was happening was gone. The death toll could never leave. Even after the first trip to Somalia, hatred between tribes and nations flourished. That all ended during this trip. We still had three continents and 97 countries to go. Would it ever end?

On day 93, we were home for the next press conference. Surprisingly, Peggy and Haylie demanded to be there.

Mr. John	Haylie. (To my surprise.)
Haylie	Grandpa, why is your life force dwindling?
Darrel	You know there are a lot of factors involved…
Haylie	Grandpa, why is your life force dwindling?
Darrel	I don't think that question…
Haylie	You are avoiding me Grandpa. I know you would never lie, so please directly answer these next two questions. You said taking vengeance comes from anger and has no effect on your life force. Is that correct?
Darrel	Yes.
Haylie	You said when trust levels of a group are neutral in celebrations then your life force is not reduced. Is that correct?
Darrel	That is not what I said. (She thought back to what was said at the St. Louis celebration.)
Haylie	Oh, no, Grandpa! You said "if" it is neutral. No wonder the math hasn't worked for the large rebirths. And we no longer

	have Maggie. And Daddy hasn't been with us. Grandpa, these rebirths are killing you! Why would you do…
Darrel	THAT IS ENOUGH! There will be no more questions from you today young lady. (It was the first time I had ever spoken to her with an angry voice. She buried her face in her hands and cried uncontrollably.)
Peggy	I HAVE A QUESTION! Answer her last one. Why would you do that? Whether you answer here tonight, tomorrow or whenever, you owe me the answer.
Darrel	How could I not? The planet was at risk. I didn't choose this! I was chosen! I had to!
Peggy	You will stop. We will find another way. Our numbers have to be getting close. There is no reason you have…
Darrel	Honey, stop. If I stop, then I only represent a lie. What promise would you have me break? I promised Haylie I would never again fail for not trying. Is that the promise you would have me break?
Peggy	This isn't trying; it's suicide! She will release you from that vow.
Darrel	I promised Maggie I would do everything to save her children and grandchildren. Is that the promise I should break?
Peggy	She and her kids would not want you to do this.
Darrel	So you're saying it's all right to try to barely cross the line, hoping we don't go backwards. You're saying that giving 80% effort ought to be good enough. Over a billion people will die of vengeance to save Earth! How can anyone suggest my life is worth more than the mission? I promised every good person in the world that I will do everything to complete the mission, not 80%. Is my promise to every soul on earth the one you would have me break?
Peggy	But…but…
Darrel	How about the promise I made to God to do everything? Is that the promise I should break?

Peggy	No.
Darrel	I love you two more than any man should love anything. But this is what's going to happen with no more discussion today, tomorrow or ever again. I am going to time the balance of my life force to the last rebirth I can manage. On December 31, I will extract the final vengeance worldwide. On January 1, I pray the destroyers will be stopped. If they are stopped that day, then I will transfer my remaining small life force to Haylie. I will do this because I cannot get the buzzing out of my head. It is so strong, I cannot rest. It is driving me insane. The voices call on me to join them in their fate. And in my heart, I know that I should. (Haylie walked up to me and took my hand, being careful not to ask a question.)
Haylie	Grandpa, we should go to a park for the rest of the day. Just you, Grandma and me.
Darrel	Where should we go? (She put my hand to her face and thought.) Good choice.

The three of us transported to the top of the pass of the Beartooth Scenic Highway near Yellowstone National Park. Not a word was spoken for an hour.

Haylie	Grandpa, I think we should have another celebration in St. Louis. It would lift your spirits.
Peggy	That is a great idea.
Darrel	Somehow I doubt our reception would be very good.
Haylie	You may be surprised. Besides, we need to find out what the after effect of vengeance day is at some point. Grandma and I will make all the arrangements.
Darrel	Alright. We have 11 days to do South American and island nations. That puts us back in St. Louis a week from Saturday. We'll do it then. I could sure use a lift about now.
Haylie	Yah. It will be fun. We....Grandpa I feel something strange.

Darrel	Don't worry darling. What you're feeling is God coming to talk to us. (The ball of light appeared.)
God	Darrel, do not despair. You were chosen for many reasons. One of those was for the goodness in your heart. But those with goodness cannot bear the guilt of the dead. It is the paradox that no one before you has beaten.
Darrel	God, if I can just get rid of the voices.
God	That is unlikely. Your guilt is too strong. It is the reason the others failed. It is why you too are failing.
Darrel	God. Please don't give up on me or us now.
God	I haven't. But, have you? (And God was gone.)

We sat in silence until sunset and then went home. In the morning we transported to the country where a saber rattling president resided, pretending to help the common man but really only helping himself.

Rhondell requested to join Mr. John and me for the vengeance going forward. I told him I wanted no one else to suffer. He said he couldn't suffer more than by doing nothing to help me with the burden. He promised somehow or some way he could find small ways to help. I reluctantly agreed. Eleven grueling days later we went home. 42 more days and 84 more countries remained. However, for one day I would enjoy being home regardless of the reception.

.

Chapter 39
The Second St. Louis Celebration

The celebration was scheduled for 11:59 in Forest Park. It seemed strange when I was asked to be ready by 9:30. Then Haylie told me we were going by car because we hadn't for so long. I asked no questions. When our immediate family members left the house, our neighbors and friends were lining the street throughout the subdivision. A white limousine with two sunroofs awaited. It was a beautiful day so we stood through the sunroofs as we drove. I was touched that the neighbors yelled and waved their support to us. As we left the subdivision, the feeder road to the highway was also lined with well-wishers. As we passed, the people raised their arms and we responded in kind. The way people were lifted up as we slowly drove by looked like the wave done at ballparks. There was no other traffic on the roads. People lined the next road and the next all the way to the interstate. The further we went, the more people there were and the more vocal they were in their support. People lined the shoulder and median of the interstate. It was an unbelievable turnout that gained many new army members.

We suddenly turned off into a retail area again packed with a crowd. We pulled into a favorite restaurant of mine at 10:30. They served great burgers, breads and dairy products. Haylie grabbed me by the hand and hurried me inside. People applauded and stepped aside to let us go to the front of the line.

Haylie Grandpa, Mommy says we can order milkshakes - CHOCOLATE!

Large milkshakes were ordered and consumed. It was hard to remember a meal I enjoyed more. Then we went back to the limo and rode to the park. The crowd continued to be everywhere in huge numbers. The entire 12 miles to the park were lined with supporters, well-wishers and new army members. It was hard to imagine such an outpouring. Once inside the park the numbers swelled substantially. We drove to the top of Art Hill that overlooked a huge expanse of the park and surrounding area. There was no vacant spot as far as the eye could see. I was totally overwhelmed. Then everyone stood in unison while cheering and applauding. I broke down and sat on the steps with my hands covering my face. Family arms were around me for support. The entire Inner Circle was at my side. Our anthem started playing and the crowd sang it to us. After several attempts to gain composure, I addressed the crowd.

Darrel	Several days ago, I had doubts I could finish the mission. God came to Haylie, Peggy and I on a high mountain in Montana. God told us that I was failing the mission just as others had failed because of the unbearable guilt from the vengeance demanded. I asked God to not give up on me and us. God said I was the only one who could give up on me. I have had a lack of strength since V&R days began. However, I so solemnly swear that you have given me back the strength today to complete this mission. (Loud cheers.) WE WILL BE THE FIRST EVER TO SUCCEED IN GOD'S SECOND CHANCE!

The crowd went wild. The music started and our performers were better than ever. The crowd participated in every song. They saluted the President's speech. Star entertainers still alive joined the entourage. The celebration lasted for hours. I spent most of it walking through the crowd and hugging people. Captain Dan from the first St. Louis celebration was near the stage. We embraced. He said he was so happy to be free of any oath. I told him how happy I was to see him and his 92% trust. Also, from that 4th of July celebration were Frank who hugged me with both arms and Norma who straightened my back with her embrace. I was very proud of both of their stories of things accomplished in helping others since we last saw each other.

Before the finale, I could feel Maggie's kids and grandchildren near the stage. I called them all up in tribute to the great lady. I went to her pregnant daughter, Annie, and rubbed her protruding belly.

Darrel	Annie, you are having a girl.
Annie	That's correct and I will not ask how you know.
Darrel	Thank you for that. I am so happy to see your entire family at sky-high trust levels. I have a suggestion for your new daughter's name.
Annie	I hope it's Maggie because that's what we want to name her.
Darrel	I won't ask how you know either. (lots of laughter) Here are a couple things you don't know. Little Maggie will be born on December 31 the same day as our little Prime. I want you at the same hospital as Denise. I will be there. You will have a smooth and easy delivery. Little Maggie has great potential. I can feel that. And to my great friend Maggie, (looking upward) little Maggie WILL see January 2.
Rich	I want to announce to the world today my nomination for Vice-President. I am choosing the man I have the most faith in to lead the people. The man who has been there for our mission whenever asked. He is the man I now call my brother. My nomination is Rhondell! (A large and long ovation followed.)
Rhondell	I am overwhelmed. I accept the nomination and so solemnly swear to do my best.
Darrel	There can be no better choice. I feel like I have two sons. No father can be more proud. (The three of us embraced.)

Our anthem started playing with Deidra leading. At the proper time, all arms went up and so did almost everybody in the park. I couldn't understand why my life force wasn't drained. However, the fact was I lost none that day. I felt goodness overflowing the park and surmised its' abundance provided the balance needed. The crowd was larger than the greater St. Louis population. People had to come from hundreds of miles around. I could not look forward to tomorrow, but I was ready for the duration after today.

Chapter 40
To The End

The next 18 days completed V&R in Asia. There were so many deaths, agonies and new voices in my head. Amidst the tragic despair we noticed a small blip to the upside. There was a positive carry-over effect from the St. Louis celebration broadcast worldwide. Countries seemed resolved to their vengeance cleansing at this time. Therefore, the rebirths became much larger and compassionate. People were starting to step up and share the burden. Step up and be counted on the positive side. We were making great strides towards our goodness goals. The Inner Circle constantly reminded ourselves of that fact as we trudged through the vengeance abyss.

As the day of vengeance came to a new country, we frequently encountered armed resistance that was easily quashed. That was understandable when those in power were threatened. It was also understandable because politicians were casualties over 90% of the time. We learned that following the vengeance we needed to set the seed for the next government during the rebirth. We gave these few guidelines:

1. No one would stay in a position of power for more than one year.
2. Those elected must place the welfare of the people above everything else.
3. Those elected must pledge themselves and their country to friendship and cooperation with all other countries for the betterment of earth.
4. Those elected must pledge to protect earth from all poisons.

I thought the single most encouraging sign was the stature of those elected after the vengeance, who seemed to embrace the guidelines. I felt if Earth did see January 2, then these new world leaders would embrace peace and brotherhood far beyond.

Rhondell and Mr. John walked every step with me. When I fell they picked me up. When I needed an arm around me, I had two. They worked tirelessly and took charge of the rebirths. Mr. John made a CD of peaceful sounds for me to listen to at nights to try and block out the voices. After Rhondell joined us, a chocolate milkshake was waiting for me at the end of each day.

Mercifully, 18 days and Asia's vengeance passed and only Europe remained. That left us with 45 more countries in 24 days. I had to break away for a while. My life force was dwindling fast. The power from the other 100%s could refresh me physically on a daily basis. Nothing could stem my life force loss or mental torture. We had a press conference scheduled tomorrow and then another world clean up the following five days. I had six days respite from the last vengeance push.

Mr. John	This November 1 press conference marks Day 124. There are 61 days of opportunity remaining for our mission. All the necessary vengeance completed and yet to come is bringing us closer to the elimination of evil. We are amassing huge gains towards the goodness factor. We must keep the faith. We must stay vigilant. We must rise individually and take a heavier share of the burden than we have been asked to do previously. While it is true that some powers so critical to the mission are fading, the power of the masses is rising exponentially. TTC you have the first question.
TTC	Darrel, the world is concerned about your growing weariness that is quite evident. How much life force do you have remaining?
Darrel	Enough to finish the job.
Mr. John	New York Times.
NY Times	Europe is the last continent for V&R. Are we close to achieving the goodness factor?

Darrel	We have approximately 1.5 billion units. We need two billion. I want to reach four billion to help sway God by our total collective efforts.
Mr. John	Chicago Tribune.
Tribune	What can those of us already adding to the factor do?
Darrel	If you're personal goodness factor is at 50%, get to 51%. If it is at 92%, get to 93%.
Mr. John	People Magazine.
People	How far along are the different ministers in their tasks?
Darrel	Tim has energy totally running. A few new facilities may be started where distribution takes a little longer than we'd like. But the world is now 100% hydroline. The earth is getting cleaner because of this. And the people love the cost, or rather the lack of it. Roy and Denise have collected twelve trillion dollars and much more is still to come. We are distributing it back as fast as needs are identified. No government 30 days past V&R has any debt. The new education standards are in place 30 days after V&R. Marilee has them working smoothly. Privilege is once again understood. Kids are becoming active outdoors and enjoy playing games with each other. No one seems to miss drugs and tobacco. The legal system is operating very smoothly because there are no lawyers getting in the way. The explosion of volunteers joining our Charity Ministers is dynamic. We have hopes of closing this division in the near future as peace, goodwill to others and pride in one's own efforts may actually eliminate those in need. What a sweet world that will be to live in!
Mr. John	NBC.
NBC	Is Haylie ready to take over for you?
Darrel	I think the people are ready to take over. If they decide they need her for any reason, I have total trust in my granddaughter. Her job is to grow up happy.

The next five days is another around-the-world clean up. Army members, show the world our pride in earth. If you will excuse me I need some rest. I have trash to pick up the next five days.

The world came out as one to clean up. I was particularly impressed with Europe just days before their coming vengeance. The pictures of little Haylie on her knees fishing trash out from under a bush had to encourage maximum effort. If not, seeing her very pregnant mommy beside her had to embarrass even the biggest freeloaders. The Hansburners got a serious workout for days following the cleanup. I asked and received permission from the trainers at Sea World for an experiment. I asked for the dolphins and most of the whales to be released into the waters around the world. I tried my best to communicate with them prior to their freedom.

Then we entered the 24 final days of hell. It was a seemingly endless trudge. I received the tiniest satisfaction that Europe's vengeance numbers were lower than they originally were to be. Why did it take so long in this horrible process until evil was eliminated by many? I hung my head in shame that I had not been able to convince many others to do so. The rebirths became stronger. The entourage carried them for me. My job was only at the end when arms were raised. Every last bit of power from our clan and the crowd was squeezed together to help the task. I was appreciative of Europe's compassion. I was quickly approaching uselessness.

I collapsed after the final country's vengeance was taken. I was so relieved it was over. There was so much agony in all our hearts and so many voices in my head.

Mr. John	The world owes you gratitude it cannot possibly give.
Rhondell	I owe you everything important in my life.
Darrel	I subjected the two of you to the worst duty in the history of man. I forever apologize for that. Still, you refused to quit or to allow me to quit. The world will forever owe you. Yet, through these horrors I received two incredible gifts. For you see, I have a new brother. And I have a new son. Who wants to go home?
Mr. John	Brother, let's go home!
Rhondell	Dad, let's go home!

Both   Why are we all glowing so brightly?

Major Mike who was now in our army, attended the December 1 press conference with Mr. John and me.

Maj. Mike   As you all know, 90% of all former military personnel around the world are now civilians. The rest of us known as protectors are dedicated to serving the needs of the people and being available for special projects. The next 20 days are designated for our final push to clean up the world. It is much cleaner than before, but if you look you'll find a way to take it to the next level. One major venture is being attempted. 24 days ago the dolphins and whales from Sea World that attached themselves to our mission were released into the oceans of the world. Prior to release, Darrel tried to communicate our clean up plans starting tomorrow. He attempted to get them to spread that word throughout the oceans. Our hopes, not necessarily our expectations, are for them to bring trash from the ocean into harbors for disposal. I ask all protectors around the world to report to the listed harbors to remove the trash we hope shows up for proper disposal. I further ask no boat activity inside those harbors to assure the continued health and safety of our water friends.

Mr. John   Greenpeace.

Greenpeace   Do you think that will happen?

Darrel   We will soon see. How many miracles do we need to see before we believe?

Mr. John   BBC.

BBC   The death toll was huge in Europe as elsewhere. Is vengeance done?

Darrel   There will be one last sweep of earth on December 31. There will be some people that have found evil since their country's V&R. Thankfully the number as of now is small. What you do after January 1, if you are here, is someone else's question.

Mr. John	Al Jazeera.
Al Jazeera	You previously mentioned the hope of creating a desert crop to replace lost oil revenues. Is that still on schedule?
Darrel	We anticipate two major announcements on Day175. One deals with desert crops and the other with medical cures.
Mr. John	Final question is from the Tokyo Times.
Tokyo	We have no question. Only gratitude. (Bows are exchanged.)

The next day brought a new era of clean up. I had witnessed many amazing things in my life, particularly in the last seven months. Nothing! Absolutely nothing had been more amazing than what happened that day. At dawn, trash started appearing in 100 designated harbors around the world. Drove after drove of creatures brought everything in their world deemed not to belong. It was a scene from Dr. Seuss. There were big fish, little fish, blue fish, red fish, fast fish, slow fish, young fish and nearly dead fish. Who above the water guessed the species below the water had some way to communicate in this magnitude. The protectors were totally overwhelmed. Calls for huge reinforcements were made. Every available rake or other source of retriever was brought in. Multiple Hansburners were immediately shipped to the sites.

Man had a few slick slogans to accompany water environmental campaigns such as "Save the Waves" and "Save the Whales". This was the marine-life counter slogan of "Humans, take back your trash". It was particularly funny to see some of their "trash" was once our treasure. There were precious coins, bars of gold and silver, paintings and other treasures from boat wrecks. As greed was nearly nonexistent, these formerly considered riches were housed in a traveling museum to be taken around the world. It was a museum where sea creatures showed mankind how warped their historical sense of value had been.

The land part of the clean up went spectacularly. Countless leaders around the world rose up to lead their country's pride for excellence. Though it was not a contest, no country wanted to appear as trailing. I hazard a guess that earth had never been as spotless in 10,000 years. Earth clean up ended on that 20th day. So much trash continued to be brought from the ocean, those operations were extended five more days.

Chapter 41
Cures, Crops and World Joy

Day 175 began with Haylie hosting an announcement at our world headquarters.

Haylie   Grandpa and I had been working on a health drug for some time. We were hoping for a universal cure for all aches and diseases. We knew long ago we could make a drug that would recognize an individual's chromosome makeup. Therefore, we could make it attack anything foreign to the footprint. However, the problem was our bodies are dependent on certain bacteria to function, such as in our intestines and stomach. They too would be attacked with a blanket mission. Therefore, we had to place certain restrictions on the capabilities of the drug.

This new drug, named Healright, will cure 90% of known ailments. We will continue to search for the cure for all others. Dr. Ghandi from India will lead the worldwide production and distribution of the product. We anticipate the cost to the user will be $5.00 per year.

The second announcement is two new desert food crops. The first is the Destatoe and the second is the Desabean. As their names indicate, the first will grow two feet below the surface and the second in a pod off the vine. Both plants have been genetically altered to achieve 99% water retainage. Unless their stalk is broken, water virtually is trapped inside to provide all nourishment necessary for production. The Destatoe has an abundance of starches for hundreds of uses and the Desabean has an equally high vegetable content. Grandpa has given instructions for creating the slightest amount of rainfall over the areas for the crops to flourish, but not alter the desert climate necessary for earth's ecological balance. In short, these crops will allow the deserts to feed many people. Food production will be the main job profession. No one will be hungry again.

As the world knows, my Grandpa's strength is waning. He will rarely perform any healings going forward. Still, it is important to celebrate our new world. The next four days will be world celebrations. Grandpa will designate the itinerary of the final five days. Celebrate with us. Celebrate on your own. Our goodness numbers have passed the two billion threshold. Grandpa has never been satisfied with just reaching the numbers required. He has pledged to give everything. (Crying) And he has! Will you do the same these last nine days?

For the next four days our entourage transported from one big celebration to another. We joined 40 celebrations for short time periods. We were in all six habitable continents including areas of all major religions. Celebrations were large all over the planet. The gloom and doom had passed. Past problems seemed insignificant because the destroyers were within ten million miles.

We thoroughly enjoyed the celebrations. Our reception in Germany wearing the traditional clothes they gave us was totally raucous. Our stop in Pyongyang was received with complete warmth. Imagine a culture held hostage by fear and intimidation their entire lives that was freed to celebrate without limit. Yes, that was what we saw. My heart swelled with pride when I saw the black and white man in Cape Town celebrate hand in hand. Partying in Rio de Janeiro as only they could, without interference from gangs or hoodlums was priceless. We watched our Moscow friends sing with all their heart and soul in the middle of Red Square. One would have thought hate and distrust had never existed. The celebrations raged worldwide, whether we were there or not. Why did humans only learn to live when faced with imminent death?

Chapter 42
United Nations II Day

The 181st day was December 28. I rested and prepared for my second trip to the United Nations in the morning. The remaining plans were announced to the world. Day 183 would be Haylie's first press conference. Day 184 was New Year's Eve. That day the black anger light would be unleashed for the final time. It would go worldwide and take vengeance on newly-formed black hearts. That would eliminate the evil on earth that God had marked. That day would also see the arrival of Prime and little Maggie at the same hospital. I would hold two babies that had great potential for earth. I was saddened by the fact that I would only hold them for a short time.

The final day was Day 185, January 1. The entire Inner Circle and their families would be at the Gateway Arch in St. Louis. That was one destroyer's impact point with the other's being exactly opposite in the Indian Ocean. We would await God's answer together.

The weather around the planet was virtually perfect and forecasted to stay that way through the 1st. 65 degrees in St. Louis for a stretch of days this time of year was highly unusual. It made me wonder if it was a fluke or being controlled. I spent the day in slow motion as that was my only speed at this point. My life force was on empty and the voices in my head were in overdrive. I was ready for the end if it brought internal peace. I walked most of the day in thought and observed the wonderful sights I passed. Had we done enough, I asked myself for the millionth time?

I walked into the United Nations assisted by the President of the United States. Rich announced to the nation his intent to resign January 2, to be a full time daddy. We were received with a warm, warm welcome.

When they finally settled down I went to the podium. I then applauded all the members.

Darrel   This is the first time in the history of this organization that we are truly "United" nations. (We all gave a rousing ovation to all on earth.) I have the deepest regret to report nearly 1.7 billion people lost their lives to the vengeance. And I have 1.7 billion voices inside my head every day. My life is about through. I welcome the end if it silences the voices. I have done everything I can, as I so solemnly promised, to accomplish the mission. Hopefully, five billion people will see January 2.

It is my honor to report the goodness factor on earth is over 3.6 billion versus the two billion God specified as a minimum. It is my honor to say earth has been cleaned up better than ever before. Have we done enough to stop the destroyers? I don't know. Only God knows. We will receive God's answer in three days. But I'm hopeful because we've put forth our best effort.

Yesterday I walked, rested and thought about what I'd say today. I made a list of things we have accomplished and would like to share some of them with you:

1. There are no walls around any nation, real or perceived.

2. Love and trust are facts around the world instead of in poets' dreams.

3. Religions practice in peace with respect and tolerance of other religions.

4. The clean-up we have done to this planet, land and waters is astounding.

5. There are more worldwide leaders doing the right thing now than combined in the history of man.

6. We have a new, clean, renewable and affordable energy source.

7. We have new medical cures.

8. We have new crops and new acreage to grow them.

9. We have an education system in place to bring forth quality adults.

I know there's great fear on earth of the approaching destroyers. They are within 3.6 million miles. They are visible to the naked eye at night. I have a different perspective. I say to welcome the destroyers. If we have not been successful in our mission, God is sending us to a merciful, quick, and painless death. If we are successful, the destroyers will be stopped and we inherit a wonderful planet. Those are the only two choices and they are both acceptable.

A while back at a press conference someone asked me, "What is it you want to see?" Yesterday while walking, this is what I saw:

1. I saw the non-polluted blue sky above.

2. I saw fresh, clear water running in the stream and into the ground.

3. I saw people helping other people.

4. I saw children playing in their neighborhoods and on playgrounds. They were playing active games without parental supervision. I saw all the adults casually watching over all of the children.

5. And I hope I saw what our kids and grandkids will see on January 2.

Take care of this world when I am gone.

Chapter 43
Haylie's Press Conference

I sat in the back of the room as an interested spectator. I knew a plan was being drafted that had to be killed. That had to happen today.

Mr. John	The rules of past press conferences are over. Haylie will point at raised hands to ask their questions.
ABC	What do you perceive to be your job going forward?
Haylie	Unemployed. I plan to be a child turning two in April.
BBC	Do you feel you're ready to fill your grandpa's shoes?
Haylie	No. But who could? Besides, my feet are smaller. (Laughter) Seriously though, Grandpa's job and therefore mine too, ends on January 1. The individual countries and world organizations will dictate all rules going forward.
Al Jazeera	Will you interfere with politics on an individual country basis?
Haylie	No. As just another citizen of the world, I hope they follow the guidelines that Grandpa issued for world leaders. After all we've been through, the people of the world should demand that of them.
Paris Times	Are you suggesting that neither you nor the New World Order will wield any power after January 1?
Haylie	That is correct. That is what we promised.

Tokyo	Do you anticipate further vengeance being necessary?
Haylie	I hope not, but it's foolish to expect it won't be necessary. Man's history leads to evil. We have to constantly be aware of those that walk the evil path. If evil surfaces, the world leaders will have to do whatever is necessary for the benefit of all. I certainly will not take vengeance and risk the voices that haunt Grandpa.
Fox	Are you suggesting you have the ability to emit power.
Haylie	Yes. (She looked straight at me. It was something I already knew.)
NBC	Will you use it to heal as your grandfather has done?
Haylie	Only when there is no negative draw on my life force or a specified exception. Otherwise, I have solemnly sworn not to. Mr. John, do you really have a question?
Mr. John	Yes I do. (As we had planned at the correct moment.) Have you accepted the fact that your grandpa's life force is about to end?
Haylie	No! Grandpa, do you really have a question?
Darrel	Yes I do. Why haven't you accepted it?
Haylie	Grandpa, I can't lose you. Not when there's another way.
Darrel	Haylie, you so solemnly swore.
Haylie	I know Grandpa. But this has to be that exception. I know I can transfer a small piece of my life force.
Darrel	And can you take away the voices in my head that persecute me every day? I want no part of a continued life if they stay with me.
Haylie	No I can't Grandpa, but…
Darrel	Listen carefully Haylie because I'm going to make this crystal clear. Do you think your newfound powers are stronger than what I have left? Or faster?
Haylie	Of course not.

Darrel	Then know this Haylie. The instant I sense you attempting to transfer life force to me, I will take vengeance on myself before you do. And Haylie, I WILL kill my duck!
Haylie	(crying) Grandpa please!
Darrel	Haylie, I don't know if there is an eternal afterlife or not. If there is then my eternal last thought of you, the one that I have loved so much, (starting to cry) will be that you broke a promise so solemnly sworn to me. Is that the eternal memory you want me to have of you?
Haylie	No, Grandpa! I promise I won't! (She ran to my arms.) I just can't bear the thought of going on without you.
Darrel	Then go on knowing that you have been my Special Angel.

Chapter 44
Prime and Little Maggie

Barely a thousand people were taken in the final vengeance. It was a relatively low number, but a thousand more voices in my head. A degree of relief came with the knowledge I would never take another life. Further relief came by knowing the joy that two precious babies about to enter the world would bring.

Denise and Annie were in the same room. I made sure they were completely comfortable and that their deliveries were perfect and pain free. At exactly 11:59 AM, Prime and Maggie were born. I had so much joy in my heart. Our family and Inner Circle felt so much joy. The world celebrated with us. Denise and Annie were on their feet immediately. Denise came to me with an incredible glow.

Denise   Dad. Prime glows just like all of us in this room. I am so sorry I didn't get to this level early enough to help more.

Darrel   There will be no more "sorry" in this family. You have been the perfect daughter. You have blessed me so many times. Here comes Prime and Maggie.

I held my grandson and what felt like my granddaughter. They were both perfect. I sang them a special song I had heard 500 times in the last seven months. Still, it seemed as appropriate as ever. I hoped they would remember it as Haylie did. I loved and I cried. Then I loved and I cried some more. I felt blessed to see and hold them and angered that it wouldn't be for very long. Still, if they saw January 2, then my life was a success.

Haylie was in 7th heaven. She was allowed to hold Prime. She too sang a special song to him. She would be a great sister and teacher. Sometimes I had to remember she was less than two-years-old. The world may never know that she was the one responsible in the event we were successful in the mission.

I gave the president and new daddy a big hug. What more could he have done? He conquered his disbeliefs. He had been the best president the country had seen and he had the grace to walk away.

Mr. John asked to be sent to his family for this special night before --- whatever we would name the next day . I told him I would send him anywhere he wanted, do anything I could for him and would be forever grateful for his entry into my family's life.

I told everybody that Peggy and I were going someplace special so I could see one last beautiful sunset. Rhondell was standing alone. He lit up when I added, "And I want my other son to go with us." We transported to a rock ledge on Kilimanjaro Mountain overlooking Serengeti National Park in Africa. It was a beautiful clear day. When we looked up we saw the snow-capped mountaintop. We could see a herd of wildebeest below. I sat between the absolute love of my life and my newly found son. I was at peace even with the voices.

Rhondell	I feel so selfish.
Darrel	Why is that?
Rhondell	Because you are the one dying and I feel bad for me. I have wanted a father all my life. Just as I get a great one, I will lose him.
Peggy	Son, you have gained an entire family that loves you in addition to a father.
Rhondell	I know. I love you all so much too. But it's just not fair to lose Dad. He gave his all and received so little back in return.
Darrel	Son, I want you to look at it from a different perspective. It is the one I truly have. I have received more back than anyone. First of all, I welcome my death as I am confident the voices will stop. That will be a true blessing. Before all of this began, I had only known three great men. Now, I can add everyone in our Inner Circle to that list and hundreds more around the

	world. I learned great people seldom come to you. You have to go find them and that I have done. I received six more months with this wonderful woman that I have shared a life with. I got six more months of being grandpa to the most wonderful child in the history of man. I saw my son totally believe in me and make a great President. My daughter gave me such blessings. I saw this world come together for the first time ever. I got a new brother. And I got an incredible new son who will make another great President. Tell me what other man got more?
Rhondell	How can anyone argue with you? The greatest thing that has ever happened in my life is you coming into it and then taking me into your family. Never have I had so many great things in my life than at this moment. Still, for the second time in my life, I am saddened beyond words.
Darrel	Then put this joy into your heart. I believe I will meet your mother's spirit shortly. The two of us WILL look down and we WILL be incredibly proud of what we see!
Rhondell	I so solemnly swear you will be.
Darrel	Son, I want to tell you something that I hope you can hear better than I did when I first heard these words.
Peggy	I know you are thinking about my Dad. (I nodded yes.) Please listen carefully Rhondell.
Darrel	Son, I am so proud of what you have done in your career. I am so proud of how you took care of your mom and us. (I put my hand on his arm with affection.) I am so proud of the man you have become.
Rhondell	Dad, I hear what you are saying. Rich and I WILL take care of our family!

I put my hands on his face and kissed his forehead.

Chapter 45
God's Blessing Day-Finale

I decided to call this last day, "God's Blessing Day". Even if it didn't turn out to be, we would never know it. We went to the Arch at 9:59 AM, two hours before impact. With the clear blue sky overhead, we saw shadows of the destroyer a mere 100,000 miles from Earth. It was another peculiarly warm winter day. The crowd was already gathering in tremendous numbers. Our entourage decided to make it a formal celebration. Our theme was forgetting fear and celebrating life. Celebrate they did.

I was holding Prime and Maggie on my lap. They were perfectly content to sleep amidst all the noise. I kept asking myself what more could we have done? I found peace by not having any answers to the question. The nearer the destroyer came, the louder the crowd got. At 11:30, the destroyer was only 25,000 miles away and in clear view. It had gone from a dot to a mass. The crowd lost some of their passion but pushed on. At 11:45 it was 12,000 miles away, closing fast and growing huge to the naked eye. I rose to address the crowd.

Darrel	I don't know what's going to happen, but I know I've found peace on earth. I now know that what I once thought important has no value at all. The only real value in our lives is our importance to each other. Therefore I tell every person on earth, you have so much value to me. I embrace these next few minutes. God is about to speak to us in one way or another. This time we will all hear what is said.

We are going to play our anthem one more time. The song is four minutes, eighteen seconds long. We will start the song exactly four minutes, twenty seconds before impact. At the song's end, we will have the answer to our efforts' worthiness. I ask St. Louis and the world to sing with us. Sing loud. Sing clear. There will be no healing, but at that usual moment we will reach towards the destroyer because it is God. We will see if God lifts us up.

The music started at the precise moment. Haylie and Deidra alternated in leading the singing. Virtually everyone on earth was singing with them. At the last "And how it lifts me up", we all raised our arms. The destroyer entered earth's atmosphere without a spark. As the music finished, the destroyer was approaching the top of the arch with all of us still reaching for it. In that last second of life, the destroyer stopped instantly - and then vanished.

Words couldn't describe the wild celebration that followed. There had never been more love for brother man than at that moment in time. I closed my eyes and the questions that haunted me my entire life popped into my head. When I look into my soul, what do I see? Do I like who I am? Do I respect the person I see in the mirror? Do I question if I am doing my part to better this world? Do I realize how insignificant I really am?

That day, everyone on earth passed the test to those questions. After the celebrations died down from exhaustion, Haylie looked at me. She just felt what I did. I addressed the crowd.

Darrel	Friends, please be quiet and sit down or kneel. God is coming! (A hush fell over the massive crowd. A bright tornado-like light came from above. It landed on the stage where our Inner Circle was standing. God appeared in the ball-shaped light as we had witnessed before.)
God	Earthlings, I am the one you know as God. I come to you in a form of which you can relate. You have done what no other life-form has accomplished in all history. You have made good on your second chance. You have earned the right to live. There will never be a third chance granted. Make sure all generations who follow you will remember these words.
Haylie	God?

Darrel	Haylie, please be quiet.
God	Let her speak. She has EARNED that right.
Haylie	Thank you God. We have all worked so hard. But Grandpa has given his life force away for all of us.
God	That is true. What are you asking?
Haylie	I'm asking you to give Grandpa a life force so he can stay with us where he is loved. He deserves that.
God	(God moved to me.) She is very good, isn't she?
Darrel	Yes God. And very stubborn too.
God	Haylie, doesn't he deserve to be with me? I have a new mission for him.
Haylie	No one deserves to be with you more than Grandpa. God isn't it true that the rest of Grandpa's normal life, if he had his life force back would be a blip in time for you?
God	Yes. Why does that matter?
Haylie	Because that blip in time for you is an eternity for us. You still would have Grandpa after that blip in time.
God	(God again moved in front of me.) Oh, she is good.
Darrel	That is a fact, but this brashness shows she still has a lot to learn.
Haylie	That is true Grandpa. God, I need Grandpa so much to teach me?
God	You understand that when a life force is through, it is that person's time also?
Haylie	Yes.
God	And what if your grandpa's time was just one more day?
Haylie	Then we would have one more precious day with him. And if that is his normal life force time, I would accept that.
God	(again to me) I'm glad it was your task to teach her.

Darrel   So am I.

God   Haylie, I am going to sing a song to you and all on earth. During the song I will decide if your grandpa leaves with me or stays here. I will lift him up, give him back a life force and remove the voices from his head. If he leaves with me, then that is my decision. If he is lowered to the ground, he stays here as his home. (God came and whispered to me where only I could hear.) Will you accept a new mission that will take you across the universe?

Darrel   Yes. Anything you desire. (God moved to Haylie.)

God   Haylie? Is there anything else you desire?

Haylie   Yes. If you're leaving, then I need a hug. (God once again embraced Haylie. And I am sure once again was touched by her genuine love.)

God   If ever I see you again and I am quite certain I will, you will owe me something special.

Haylie   What?

God   A MILKSHAKE - CHOCOLATE! (Everyone laughed as the music to our anthem began to play mysteriously. Then nature joined in as a symphony. Wind blew between the legs of the Arch that sounded like a flute. It bounced off the tall buildings that made the sounds of a harp. The river started rolling aggressively providing the bass. The birds started singing as a backup choir. God sang in the strongest voice imaginable.)

The first time that I saw your face…I asked the sun to shine

The first time that we touched I knew…this life-form could be fine

You'll never have to wonder if… my love will ever end

I promise that til' your last breath…on me you can depend

The power of your precious love…you gave me from the start

The power of your trust has put…a spark into my heart……

So whether you're beside me

Or whether we're apart

You'll…Be…In…My…Heart……

Now love is new it's up to you…give out a helping hand

No limit to those who are true…do you now understand

You will never have to wonder…the times you're down and out

I'll always be right there with you…go walk life without doubt

A day with you, a touch or two…gives powers not explained

The beauty of man's love and trust…has opened up his brain……

So whether you're beside me

Or whether we're apart

You'll…Be…In…My…Heart……

(God lifted me into the air and hit me with a bolt of lightning. A large life force surged inside me and the voices left. God told me the decision telepathically and I nodded my acceptance and obedience.)

And I know I'd always wondered…if man could ever be

The one who rose up from the dust…and belonged here with me

You've cast aside the evil ways…now always protect Earth

You surely now must realize…it's beyond all your worth

With the powers that were granted…it gave the world a jolt

It brought you trust and love shot out…just like a lightning bolt……

So whether you're beside me

Or whether we're apart

You'll…Be…In…My…Heart……

(I emitted an incredibly, strong light from both my hands. I cloud-printed in bold letters.)

HEART! LOVE! TRUST! THANK YOU GOD!

Now walk through life in search of truth…with answers that are new

The one thing I will guarantee…I've given life to you

Third chances will not come your way…and this you should believe

A walkin' talkin' miracle…has earned this last reprieve

Your wounds will heal with just a touch…as no one is corrupt

Your precious love lights up my life…and how it lifts us up……

So whether you're beside me

Or whether we're apart

You'll…Be…In…My…Heart……

Yes You'll…Be…In…My…Heart…………

God lowered me to the ground. Haylie and the rest of my family rushed to me. Haylie leapt into my arms.

Haylie	GRANDPA! God has given you back a life force!
Darrel	Yes. God has given me a large life force and taken away the voices in my head. Haylie, God has given me a mission that will take me far away from Earth. (Sadness streaked across her face.)
	Oh, but Haylie, God told me to tell you something. God said that no one should work all the time. Everyone needs to rest somewhere. God thinks Earth is a great place now for me to call home.

Haylie   (Haylie's face burst with happiness as only hers could. I lifted her over my head, she looked up, extended her open arms to God and shouted at the top of her voice.)

THANK YOU GOD!   I OWE YOU A MILKSHAKE!   I LOVE YOU, GOD!

God's response was a huge, belly laugh that reverberated across the landscape like thunder. God blew hard one time and cloud-printed words below those of mine.

YOU ARE WELCOME!
YOU'LL BE IN MY HEART!

About the Author

Darrel Huisinga was raised on a Midwestern farm where he learned the virtues of hard work and ethics. The same virtues he later took into the business world from lowest accountant to Corporate President and CEO.

Exposure to greed and unethical practices in business, politics and the world has led to this first book. The question the book asks is the same one Mr. Huisinga has asked of himself. "If I had the power to positively change the world, would I have the courage to do so?"

Mr. Huisinga currently resides in St. Louis. His greatest accomplishments are his family and becoming "Grandpa".